Please Excuse Our Confusion

Jasmine Cartwright

Dream Writer Publishing

ISBN: 979-8-9891877-0-6 (Paperback)
ISBN: 979-8-9891877-1-3 (Ebook - EPUB)

Book Cover by Canvaish and Jasmine Cartwright
Edited by Tamala Floyd and Dream Writer Publishing

First edition 2023

To Granny.

"There is nowhere you could go that I won't be with you."
— Gramma Tala, *Moana*

"The more you like yourself, the less you are like anyone else, which makes you unique."

– Walt Disney

Contents

Chapter One

The truth is—everybody has a secret. Everyone has something about themselves that they hope to never have to divulge to anybody. Something they hope to take to their graves. While most people might be interested in why somebody is keeping their secrets, I find it more enthralling the lengths they take to keep their skeletons in the closet.

No pun intended.

"Get out of your head and listen to me, Bo!"

"I am listening." I kick my feet out and splash Manny from the side of the pool. He's lounging on the pizza-shaped float that Geoff bought for a pool party last summer.

"I think this would be a perfect year for us to finally do the *do,*" Manny presses after he's avoided my splash attack.

"No." I deadpan. "I already told you I'm not crossing that line."

"Aww, C'mon, Bo!" he pleads, floating towards me with his head resting on the crust of the pepperoni slice. He's not the tallest guy, about five foot six, so he fits on the oversized pizza float perfectly.

I shake my head and push the float backward with my bare foot. "Nope, not happening."

He grins at me and attempts to splash me from afar, failing miserably. "Such a prude."

My best friend, Christina Harris, is sitting next to me on the edge of the pool. She gives Manny her evilest eye as the water falls short of hitting us. If I were to ask her why she's dressed in a bikini just to dip her feet in my pool, instead of actually swimming, she'd respond with, "Girl, I'm not getting my hair wet! Not all of us can be born with easy mixed-girl hair!" She'd be joking, but I would still die a little on the inside. Of course, I'd smile and play it off for their sake.

"Watch it, Manny. You know I can't get my hair wet!" See? Told you!

I laugh under my breath and slink down into the pool, bobbing my small body towards Manny and the pizza float to flip him over without drowning. I'm only five-three, and Manny is floating toward the deep end.

"Speaking of which," Manny draws out. "You should let your hair grow this year. You'll look a lot more feminine with long hair."

His words cause me to lose my step and accidentally dip under the water. I recover quickly and roll my eyes at him.

"Really, Manny?" Christina sucks her teeth at him. "You're such an asshole."

"What?" Manny shrugs his shoulders defensively. "It was just a suggestion."

"You basically just told her she looks like a man," Christina yells at him. "Which, in that case, I don't see the prob—"

"Christina, no," I scold her. I turn back to Manny and flip him the bird. "I like my short hair."

"Okay, okay! *lo siento*!" He put his hands in the air defensively. I take my chance at that moment to swim over and flip the pizza slice, sending him flailing in six feet of pool water.

Christina and I laugh, and Manny swims to the opposite side of the pool and hoists himself out.

"I need to go home and help my dad fix his truck," he tells us as he dries his slick, black hair with one of my beach towels. His usual pompadour style has fallen loosely around his handsome face.

Manny Herrera. My best friend.

If anyone knows a thing or two about secrets, it's him. The extremes he'll go to keep those secrets buried are what they make Hallmark movies of.

"Mind giving me a ride somewhere?" Christina asks him, standing up from the side of the pool and slipping on her flip-flops. She knows he'll say yes, asking is just a courtesy.

Manny rolls his eyes. "Sure, since I'm such an asshole..."

"I mean, you are an asshole." Christina shrugs. "We just love you despite that. I don't know why, but we do."

I walk them through the house and to the front door. Geoff has been on a cleaning spree again. Our contemporary modern-style home is rarely dirty. Geoff is a neat freak and insists on cleaning and dusting every chance he gets, though. I think it stops him from fussing over us so much.

"Smells like lavender," Manny comments as we walk through the living room. The entire house has gray wooden floors and crisp white walls, to contrast the black and steel appliances in the kitchen and décor in the living rooms.

"Geoff's new floor cleaner." It's better than the vanilla kick he was on last month. I hate vanilla.

"What are you going to do for an entire month without us?" Christina pouts and wraps her arms around my shoulders.

"I'll be telling preteens they're worthy of self-love." I smile at her and embrace her back.

"You're such an angel," she mocks me sweetly.

"I can't believe you're spending the last month of summer at fat camp," Manny huffs. "We should be out on the scene!"

Christina rolls her eyes and throws him a cynical look. "The scene?"

"It's not fat camp," I shoot back defensively. "It's a self-esteem camp, Emmanuel!"

"Whatever. Have fun and don't get bitten by a rattlesnake. I need you for at least another year." He's somewhat joking, I think.

I hug him tight and then close the door behind them. I love my friends. We're an inseparable, trio for sure. Still, sometimes I welcome the peace and quiet, and I'm really looking forward to my summer job.

Every summer I spend the last few weeks before school starts, working at a youth camp in the Arbuckle Wilderness, counseling kids with esteem issues. Pretty ironic considering my own secrets.

"Manny and Christina gone?" Geoff asks me as he saunters down the stairs towards the kitchen. He's wearing these silly rubber utility gloves. Probably just finished cleaning the bathrooms upstairs.

"Yeah, Manny had to help his dad with something. I think Christina had a date." I hop up on one of the stainless-steel barstools next to the island, while Geoff puts the rubber gloves under the sink and washes his hands.

"Would be nice to see you go out on a date for once." He smirks, but doesn't look at me. He walks over to the refrigerator and pulls out the chicken breast he's been marinating for dinner.

I roll my eyes at him. "Very funny."

"I'm only slightly joking," he tells me as he loads the chicken pieces into a glass pan and places it in the oven. "Do you *really* want to go off to college next year with *zero* dating experience?" Geoff's got an amazing talent for emphasis. He adds it to at least two words in every sentence.

"You know, it's not that simple," I sigh.

"It's not?" Geoff raises an eyebrow. He's feeling extra cheeky today. I'm not ready for it.

"Besides, dating isn't really my... thing," I respond. There's a random streak on the black granite countertop that I trace over. Geoff must have missed a spot.

"It's not your *thing*? What does that even *mean*, Bowie?" He sucks his teeth and whips his head around to me.

"I don't know. I just don't care about dating right now. Life's hectic enough," I reply in an exasperated tone. I'm over this topic.

"Well, you know how I feel about *that*. It's not healthy for either of you." Geoff returns to the carrots he's now chopping and starts shaking his head at me. This man's attitude is one for the record books.

"Well, I'm going to go make sure I'm packed for camp, and then take a shower," I say after a few moments of silence and slide off the barstool.

"You do that," Geoff huffs at me. "Your dad should be home soon, and dinner will be ready shortly."

I skip over to him and stand on my tip-toes to kiss his cheek. "You know you're my shining star."

"I'm fading out. You see these grays?" he replies with a scrunched face, motioning toward his spiked blonde hair. He always keeps a similar pompadour style like Manny's, not a hair out of place.

"It comes with the territory." I shrug. "You're still Hot Stuff."

I retreat to my room, but instead of rechecking my packed bags, flop down on my bed and stare at the ceiling. I do this a lot. Lay here and stare at the ceiling, and think.

I think about my parents, my friends, and school. But mostly I think about the secrets, both Manny's and my own. Geoff says it's dangerous to live in your own head too much, but most of the time it's the only place I can retreat to.

I had a diary once, but Geoff found it one day while he was on a cleaning spree. I snatched it out of his hands, ran downstairs, and tossed it in the fireplace. Geoff went ballistic. Apparently, burning books in the open hearth, which sits in the middle of the second living room, isn't good for the atmosphere of the house. I just couldn't risk letting them find out the truth about me. About what I think about every day.

So now I keep it all stored inside my mental diary. I just bottle it all up and keep it inside. It sucks, but it's all I can do.

I'm descending the stairs after my shower, just as Mark is walking in through the front door, handsome as ever in his uniform. He's tall, with a broader build, rugged features, and dark brown hair. Christina swears he looks like Henry Cavill.

"Hey, Sweet Pea." He smiles wearily and walks over to kiss my forehead.

"Hey, Dad." I smile. "Just a warning, he's in extreme mode."

Mark chuckles, just as we hear Geoff yelling from the kitchen.

"I can hear you, you know!" he snaps, and Mark and I laugh. We join him in the kitchen just as he is taking the chicken out of the oven. I take my seat on the barstool again, and Mark places his car keys and cell phone on the island counter.

"You were supposed to be here half an hour ago. Go shower so we can have dinner. I want to get a movie night in before Bowie leaves," Geoff tells Mark.

"Sorry, flight was delayed," Mark murmurs. He's taller than Geoff by a few inches, so he has to lean down a bit to kiss him quickly on the lips.

"You fly the plane. How can you let it get delayed?" Geoff gripes.

I laugh, and Mark walks out of the kitchen, ruffling my cropped hair on his way out to shower.

"You two are always ganging up on me," Geoff whines, handing me a stack of plates. "Set the table, Junior." He calls me Junior whenever he feels like I'm allied against him. It's short for Mark Jr.

"I love you, Dad!" I sing out as I skip to the table with the glass plates. Geoff only replies with a 'hmph' sound. Geoff always dominates the conversation at dinner. Mark and I are more similar. We're quiet and occasionally sarcastic. Geoff's outgoing and very vocal. We're the perfect mesh.

"I can't believe they're releasing that baby back to its mother tomorrow. Twelve weeks in NICU, and I've already given them the reports. Drugs in the system, but they're handing him right over? Because the *mother* passed a drug screening?" He puts air-quotations around the word *mother*. "It's disgusting."

"That's really sad," I reply, pushing my peas around my plate. The chicken was amazing, but I'll never be able to force myself to eat peas. Give it up Geoff!

"It's terrible!" His voice just raised three octaves. Mark doesn't engage in conversation much. He just nods his head until he feels like speaking.

"Anyway," Geoff huffs. He literally stuffs a spoonful of peas in his mouth and eats them. Gross! "Are you ready for camp tomorrow?" he asks, switching subjects.

I nod and swallow my last bite of chicken. "I'm leading the nature walks this year."

"Just don't get bitten by a rattlesnake." Geoff furrows his brows.

"What's with everyone saying that?" I frown.

Mark laughs. "Then it's on to senior year?"

I nod and reply with a simple, "Yep."

"I told her she needs to start dating," Geoff chimes in, pointing his spoon at me. I see a speck of pea-juice drip off and resist vomiting.

"Woah!" Mark frowns. Where Geoff plays the role of the fun parent, Mark balances us out by attempting to bring some authority into the house. He typically fails.

"Oh please, she's wasting her time being Manny's puppet." Geoff rolls his blue eyes and stands to gather our plates.

"Hey!" I retort defensively.

"No offense, Sweetie. I'm just saying. You're seventeen years old. You should be out dating and enjoying life."

"I don't think being seventeen warrants dating," Mark quips.

"And I am enjoying life," I added, crossing my arms as he takes my plate. I see him frown at the untouched peas and smile to myself triumphantly.

"There you go again, ganging up on me!" Geoff whines again. Mark holds in his laugh and I shake my head. "Just for that, I'm picking the movie tonight." He saunters off into the kitchen with our dishes and Mark looks over at me and winks. Geoff decides on some stupid rom-com. He snuggles against Mark's right side, so I stretch out on the left with my feet in Mark's lap, just to pester Geoff.

"What are you two going to do for an entire month without me?" I feign concern.

"You don't wanna know, kid," Geoff says, knocking my feet away from his face and off Mark's lap.

"Gross!" I scrunch my face and place my foot back on my father's lap, wiggling my toes to piss off my other dad some more. Again, Mark only chuckles.

The movie plays and Geoff is the only one really invested in it. Mark is probably tired from flying all day, but these moments mean everything to Geoff, so they mean just as much to him. I sit there and watch my parents cuddle on the couch, a full display of their unconditional love in a big pristine home, and I think about how lucky I am to have them.

And then my mind wanders back to everything I'm missing.

Everything I don't have.

All the things I don't know.

Chapter Two

Here's the story.

It was December 2nd, a freezing Sunday night outside of Integris Baptist Medical Center. There had been an ice storm the night before, and the city was quiet. Ezra Brown, a patient transfer worker for the hospital, was outside having a smoke break in the bitter cold. He had huddled close to a dumpster so that he could avoid the icy winds and light his cigarette. That's when he heard it—small labored breathing. Upon further investigation, he found her. A little baby girl, wrapped in a thin receiving blanket and stuffed between the dumpster and the brick siding of the building.

The baby girl, (Spoiler Alert: She's me!) was suffering from extreme hypothermia and had to be rushed upstairs to the ninth-floor NICU ward. Dr. Geoffrey Denton placed her under his expert care and nursed her back to perfect health.

Geoff says that he knew from the moment that he saw me in the hospital incubator that he loved me. It took him two weeks to convince Mark that they had to adopt me. It was Mark who named me Bowie, after his favorite musician ever. David Bowie.

Bowie Phoenix Monroe, estimated date of birth: December 1st. Race: Unknown.

Geoff also says that he gave me Mark's last name so that Mark couldn't back out on adopting me. Mark maintains that would have never happened. They weren't married yet. It wasn't legal in the Bible Belt back then.

I grew up happy, always smiling and wanted for nothing. Geoff was the disciplinarian, while Mark took to the doting daddy role. It was only when I met Christina in elementary school that I realized my idea of normalcy wasn't universally accepted. Christina had a different set of parents than I did.

She had a mom.

She invited me to her seventh birthday party. While Geoff was somewhere else socializing with other parents, Christina and I were overseeing the passing out of birthday cake with her mom.

"Momma? How come Bowie has two daddies?" she asked her mother, Ms. Shonda.

"Because that's who God blessed her with, baby." Ms. Shonda smiled as she sliced another piece of the chocolate cake and handed it to one of Christina's cousins.

"I want two daddies." Christina smacked her lips and folded her arms across her chest. Her braided hair was pulled up into two pigtails. Alternating pink and white beads covered the ends that clanked together as she cocked her head to the side.

"Girl, hush your mouth and pass out these plates!" Ms. Shonda scolded her with a laugh.

All the while, I stood there, confused. I didn't know there was an option to have a mom. I knew what it meant to be adopted, but it never occurred to me I was supposed to have a mother.

That night when we were eating dinner, I asked my parents about it. Mark was home, which is rare since he is an airline pilot and works a lot.

"Which one of you is my daddy?" I asked them. We were eating meatloaf and mashed potatoes that night. Mark and I both ate ours with extra ketchup. My parents both furrowed their brows and looked at each other.

"We both are, Sweet Pea," Mark responded finally.

"Then which one of you is my mommy?" I frowned. "Like Ms. Shonda?"

I remember hearing Geoff groan, and Mark wiping his mouth on his napkin. They were trying to come up with the perfect way to explain this to me; that our family was unique. Again, Mark spoke up first.

"Neither one of us, Bowie. You have two daddies."

I frowned, thought about it, and then shrugged. We continued dinner as usual.

Neither Mark nor Geoff's parents are supportive of their relationship, so I never grew up with grandparents. It was just the three of us, and that was enough. Still, in hindsight, I wonder if more explanation was necessary. If love was enough to raise an abandoned little girl to be a confident young woman?

Chapter Three

The first few days of camp are always the most hectic. The counselors are trying to figure out what we're supposed to be doing, and the campers are always freaking out. I mean, can you blame them? One, they're away from home for a month in the middle of nowhere; and Two, they're preteens who are here because they suffer from some kind of self-esteem issue.

It's not a weight-loss camp like Manny joked about. Some kids are bullied for their weight, while others stutter, but most are just shy because they view themselves as inadequate. My job is to pull them out of their shell. Help them realize just how great they are. The irony kills me every year.

Rhonda, the camp leader, tells me I have my first nature walk on Saturday. Twelve kids, so I'll need an assistant. She assigned one of the other senior counselors to assist me. Travis, who I'm convinced is more freaked out than the kids.

"I hate nature walks," he complains to me on Friday during lunch. "What if we get bitten by a rattlesnake?"

He continues past the table where I'm seated, and I roll my eyes and stare off at the lake. I wonder what my friends are doing. Knowing Christina, she's probably hanging out with her latest summer fling or working. Manny's probably at work too, but he's most likely mapping out our senior year together, making sure everything goes as smoothly as possible. We've had this agreement going on for four years now. It's finally almost over. I miss them both, but I've convinced myself that coming here every summer and working is good for me. It helps me clear my head.

My thoughts are interrupted when a lanky boy, with a head full of dark curls and a Colgate smile, flops down on the bench across from me. I've seen him around a few times this week. He's a new counselor who's been running the sports. It's easy to notice a new face here, especially since there are very few of us who aren't white.

"Hi." He's grinning at me.

"Hi." I raise a brow back and give him a suspicious smile.

"I'm Jonah. Jonah Taylor."

"Okay?" I look around to see if anyone is watching us. Is this some type of prank?

"Wow." He grins wider. "Most people respond with their name."

I eye him. His dark hair is piled on top of his head in ringlets and shiny curls that fall across his forehead and frame his ears. My eyes momentarily lock onto the identical dimples on both of his cheeks.

"I'm Bowie. Bowie Monroe, but everyone calls me Bo," I tell him. As if it's even possible, his grin widens some more.

"Nice to meet you, Bo Monroe," he replies coolly. "Hey! That rhymes."

I raise my brows at him and give a tight smile. "Yes, it does."

We have an awkward silence, where he grins at me, and I wonder if he's got some kind of mental disorder.

"This food sucks. No wonder these kids are depressed," he says after a while, and even though it's in poor taste, I can't help but laugh. He claps his hands together once in triumph. "Finally, an actual smile!"

"If you wanted me to smile, you could have just asked," I tell him, replacing my smile with a smirk. "You didn't have to insult an entire camp of twelve-year-olds."

"I'm sorry. I was getting desperate." He shrugs. "But about that gross lunch." He pauses and motions to my plate. There's a small pile of what is supposed to be goulash and a piece of garlic bread. He's right; it's bland and seasonless. I'm only eating it to set an example for the campers.

"What about it?" I ask him, putting the fork down.

"It sucks, right?" he asks. His grin has transformed into a smirk to match mine.

"Not really." I have to fight to maintain my smirk.

"Okay, then I guess you wouldn't be interested in sneaking off to find food that's actually edible?" He raises an eyebrow.

"Nope. Not at all." This time, I give my sweetest fake smile.

"Ouch." He feigns a shot through the heart, and for the first time since he's sat down, I realize what's happening.

He's hitting on me!

Full panic floods in, and I lose all the fun in this conversation. Luckily, Travis slams down next to him, also in full panic mode.

"Bowie. Please tell me you've packed *Benadryl* for the hike tomorrow! There's no way I can do this, Bowie. I hate nature walks! I'm allergic to insect bites. Did you know that?"

Then why do you work at a wilderness summer camp? I think it, but I won't say it out loud.

"I'll make sure to pack extra *Benadryl*, Travis," I assure him. "Everything will be alright."

The bugle sounds, signaling the end of lunch. "Well, I'd better round up my group." I stand to leave with my tray. Travis is still mumbling something pessimistic about tomorrow's hike, and Jonah is still smirking at me.

I'll make a mental note to avoid him at all costs this summer. Being hit on by cute guys doesn't fit into *the plan*.

Chapter Four

The next morning, I round up my group and wait at the bottom of the trail for Travis. It's six o'clock in the morning, and the sun is just barely peeking over the mountains. It's so beautiful out here. When people think about Oklahoma, they think of flat plains and farmlands. They'd be surprised by the beauty of the Arbuckle Mountains and Turner Falls. Families come here for vacations, camping, and the ride-along safari. Mark took me a few times when I was a kid. Geoff hated it, so it was usually just the two of us.

At 6:05 a.m., the tall, long-limbed form that is Jonah Taylor comes into view before us.

"What are you doing here?" I eye him suspiciously.

He shrugs and (you guessed it) grins. "Travis begged me to trade activities with him today."

I cock my head to the side and frown, giving him a look that screams *'bullshit.'*

"Okay, okay. I offered to switch activities with him, but he was more than willing to switch, trust me. He wasn't looking forward to this nature hike thing. Refereeing basketball games for kids who probably won't feel confident enough to shoot the ball is perfect for him."

I roll my eyes. "Whatever. Where is your backpack?"

"I came prepared!" He turns and shows me a Nike drawstring backpack on his back.

"Alright, let's get started," I say, turning away from him. "Everyone has their maps?"

The kids all nod sleepily and wave their trail maps in the air. Attached to the maps is a scavenger hunt with a list of native animals we're supposed to find.

We head down the trail that leads into the wooded mountain area. I notice Jonah walking next to me. He has a bounce in his step that slightly causes his curls to dance across his forehead. I can't tell if this is his natural gait or if he's excited.

"So, are you a nature-lover, or did Rhonda just volunteer you for this job, too?" he asks.

"You know you're supposed to be bringing up the rear, right?" I respond instead of telling him I love it out here.

"Huh?" He furrows his brows in confusion.

"A mountain lion could snatch the kids in the back. Your job is to make sure that doesn't happen, by being *back there*." I point to the back of the line.

Jonah chuckles and pulls out his map. "Funny, I don't see mountain lions on the list?" He's being sarcastic, making fun of Rhonda's scavenger hunt, which consists mostly of plants, random bugs, and birds. He's got a sense of humor. I like it, even though I'm not supposed to. Cute boys with a great sense of humor who hit on you aren't part of the plan.

"Back of the line, Jonah," I sing out in fake niceness.

He grins harder and falls back, and I swear I hear him mumble something, but I can't make it out.

An hour into our hike, we found a few plants from the list, a hawk, and a field mouse I allow the campers to mark as an Eastern chipmunk, because we were getting bored. I'm beginning to think that half of these creatures aren't really out here, but Jonah insists they are.

Ethan Walher, who is single-handedly the reason everyone thinks that this is a fat camp, starts complaining about eating lunch. It's barely ten o'clock, and Jonah has already passed out snacks twice.

"Okay, we'll head over to that giant rock and stop for lunch," I tell the group, and Ethan groans and wheezes.

"Camp Counselor Bo? What's the point of this nature hike?" A sassy, eighth-grader named Paisley asks me, stopping to pose with her hands on her nonexistent hips with much attitude.

To encourage you to find interest in something other than boys, Paisley. That way, you're not pregnant by your sophomore year, I want to say. I'm much bolder in my head. On the outside, I'm a pushover, especially with my friends and family.

"It's getting you to try new things. I bet you didn't even notice the sunrise?" Jonah pipes up as he walks past the preteen. She melts when he passes her, and I want to roll my eyes.

"Thank you, Camp Counselor Jonah. I couldn't have said it better myself." I muster up my sweetest smile and fight the urge to melt like Paisley when he winks in return.

It takes us another fifteen minutes of walking to reach the giant rock formations and set up lunch. I pass Ethan a sandwich and water bottle, and he grunts in what I can only assume is delight. I perch myself against the giant, dusty rock and gulp my water. Paisley and a few of the other girl campers have circled around

Jonah, who is eating his sandwich and staring off into the sky obliviously.

He's really handsome. Tall, with long arms and legs, and a chestnut-brown complexion. Long, thick eyelashes border his dark brown eyes, and he's got full lips wrapped around a beautiful set of teeth. He's hiking in a pair of mesh basketball shorts, a plain black t-shirt, and expensive-looking Nike sneakers, which tells me he wasn't really prepared for today's activity.

"Look up there. A Scissortail!" He points out into the distance, and the campers scramble to get their binoculars out and scribble their check marks on the scavenger hunt. Scissor-tailed flycatcher is at the top of Rhonda's list. It's the state bird.

I temporarily glance at the bird before returning my gaze to Jonah. He's standing now, with his right hand creating a makeshift visor to shield the sun. I'm admiring the deep dimples that have formed on his cheeks when I feel a quick, intense pinch and then a burning sensation on my ankle.

Something just bit me!

I scream and jump off the rock. "Oh my gosh, I just got bit! Rattlesnake! It's a rattlesnake!" While I shriek, I silently curse all the people who predicted this terrible moment. *"Don't get bitten by a rattlesnake."*

Some campers freak out; others grab their scavenger hunts and rejoice.

"Is it a Western Diamondback?" Ethan huffs. "Western Diamondback is on the list!"

"I don't know, *Ethan*, but I'm probably going to die!" I'm completely freaking out, and all these little bastards can think about is that stupid scavenger hunt? And why the hell would Rhonda put poisonous snakes on a summer camp scavenger hunt led by a seventeen-year-old girl?

"It's not a rattlesnake, and you won't die," Jonah speaks up from behind me. I turn to find him holding up a big black snake, grinning as usual. "It's just a rat snake."

"Eww! Put it down!" I screech at him. The pain pulsates through my ankle, and I cry out again. Jonah drops the snake and walks over to me. It slithers away, and I glare at it with disgust on my face. God, I hate snakes.

I give a small yelp when he swiftly picks me up by the waist and sits me on the rock. He does it rather effortlessly since I'm significantly shorter than him.

"What are you do—" I try to ask as he takes my ankle in his hands, but he cuts me off.

"Lesson time, kids!" he announces, and all the campers gather around. He keeps a firm grip on my ankle, even though there are little streams of blood trickling down it from the tiny scrape marks.

"Now say that was indeed a rattlesnake, or copperhead, or something poisonous." He's speaking in a mocking tone like he's a professor of science or a wildlife show host. "Anybody know the proper first aid to administer?"

"Call 911!" one of Paisley's cohorts answers with an eye roll.

Jonah chuckles and shakes his head. "Consider the fact that you're in the wilderness and only have a few minutes to act."

"Motrin!" Ethan calls out proudly.

"Uh... no..." Jonah's teetering on the edge of bursting with laughter at this point. I'm not sure what he was expecting out of this camp, but he's learning quickly that these kids are rough.

"Funny story, though." He waves his finger at Ethan. With his other hand, he rolls my ankle in slow circles. The pulsating pain hasn't subsided yet. "I went to the Rattlesnake Derby with my friends once. And we came across this guy who had been bitten by a rattlesnake, and his arm was like, three times bigger than normal. He said he was just going to treat it with some ibuprofen." The kids all stare at him expectantly as he pauses and laughs. He turns to me and shakes his head. "Never saw that guy again."

"How enlightening," I say, snatching my foot from his grasp. I wince at the sudden jolt of pain.

"The proper way is to rinse the site, and wrap it up tight, so the poison doesn't reach the heart." He's smirking at me. He suggestively adds, "If you have a buddy, they could suck the poison out too."

I return his smirk with a challenge in my eyes. *Holy crap! Am I flirting back?*

"I think it's more of a pressure bite. That's why it hurts so much," he tells me. "I think this hike is over."

Nodding in agreement, I flex my ankle again—another sharp pain.

"I don't think I can put any weight on it," I absently reply. What a great way to spend my last summer as a counselor.

"Alright..." Jonah murmurs and looks around like he's formulating a plan. He grabs my backpack and hands it to Shelby, an extremely timid and insecure camper with a face riddled with acne. She's the sweetest kid in the entire camp.

"You carry this one," he tells her. He shrugs off his backpack and hands it to Ethan. "And you take mine." Ethan opens his mouth to complain, but Jonah wags his index finger at him.

"No complaining. This just turned into a survival lesson!" Jonah is animated as he addresses the group. "Our freckle-faced scout leader, with the rhyming name, has just been bit by a diamondback rattlesnake. We've got to get her back to safety so she can sue the organization over their sketchy scavenger hunt." The kids gasp and start scrambling to collect their packs.

"Nice jokes from the guy with the *Chad Danforth* hair." I was supposed to say that in my head, but I didn't. Jonah laughs and shakes his head, causing those damn curls to bounce around. He takes my water bottle and pours it over my ankle, rinsing away the blood. I wince at the slight sting as the water flushes the wound. Next, he takes a roll of gauze tape from my pack that Shelby is holding and wraps my ankle.

"C'mon, let's get you back to camp." He turns his back to me and positions his body between my legs. He wants me to get on his back.

"You're seriously going to carry me all the way back?" I ask, raising a brow. We've been walking for four hours. Without stopping, we'd make it back to camp within an hour, but that's a lot of walking, especially when you're carrying someone!

Damn that Rhonda and her stupid cell phone rules. What kind of responsible adult sends a teenager out in the middle of the wilderness with twelve eighth-graders and no form of communication? Geoff was right; this camp is a sham.

"Hop on, Bo," Jonah urges. "I'll be fine."

I hesitate for a moment and then consider my options. I have none. So, I wrap my arms around Jonah's neck, and he reaches around to hoist my body up. My polyester shorts start riding up my thighs, and I pray my ass doesn't fall out of the bottom of them.

Jonah is mindful to keep his hands on my thighs as we take off down the trail.

"Alright, campers, lead the way," he instructs the kids. "Use your maps to help save Freckles."

"Will you stop calling me that?" I nudge the side of his head playfully. "I'm sensitive about my freckles." Actually, I love the mask of brown freckles that span from cheek to cheek across the bridge of my nose.

"You shouldn't be. I think they're cute," Jonah says casually, but in a low voice so that the campers can't hear us.

"Thanks... I guess." My face heats with embarrassment.

"Aren't you happy that Travis *practically begged* me to switch activities today?" he asks me in a dramatic tone.

I can't help but laugh. "Oh God, I can only imagine it! He'd be freaking out worse than me!"

We share a laugh at Travis' expense and continue down the trail behind the campers. I slide down a bit, and Jonah does a little hopping movement to hoist me back up. I absently nuzzle my face against his hair as another jolt of pain shoots through my ankle. His hair smells earthy, in a good way. Like it has captured the essence of everything the wind has carried through it.

"So, do you have a boyfriend?" We're walking downhill now, and I can feel my butt bouncing with his hard steps. This entire situation is downright humiliating.

I scoff at his question. "You're not seriously asking me that *now*!"

He laughs, and from his side profile, I can see the dimple again. "*You're* the one sniffing my hair!"

"It was an accident. My leg is throbbing really badly!"

He reaches down and massages my ankle again. "So, is that a no?"

I can't help but smile, even with the sick feeling rising in my stomach. What's the best response to that question? The truth? Or maybe lie?

The lines are blurred on which one is which, actually.

"No," I finally respond. "I don't have a boyfriend."

"Good." He smiles and adjusts my body up against his back again as I slip.

"Maybe you should take a break," I suggest to him. We're about a mile away from camp, and even though I'm short, I'm sure I'm getting heavy.

"You're light as a feather," he tells me, taking a moment to jog in place to prove his point.

"Yeah, whatever," I snort, reaching back, attempting to pull my shorts down further over my butt.

"Please don't tell me you're one of those self-conscious girls who think they're fat when they aren't."

"No, I'm not. I'm just acknowledging that I'm probably getting heavy," I shoot back.

"If I carry you the whole way, you have to let me take you to my favorite diner and treat you to some delicious chicken-fried steak," he proposes. I can hear the excitement in his voice, and it brings back the butterflies. He's asking me out on a date. It hasn't even been a full day!

"We're not allowed to leave camp," I remind him.

"We'll sneak out after lights-out." He shrugs. "Where's your sense of adventure?"

"I traded it in for a sense of responsibility."

He chuckles and continues to trek on. "Your loss. It's way better than that shitty mess-hall food."

He's probably right, but I have a code to uphold. I'm probably the most responsible person in the world. I never cheat, steal, sneak around, or lie.

Okay, maybe I lie. But that's a different story.

Chapter Five

"Just so we're clear, it *was not* a rattlesnake?" Geoff asks for the hundredth time.

"No, it was just a rat snake, apparently. It still hurt, though." I reach down and massage my ankle, which is now wrapped in medical gauze from the medic cabin.

Jonah stayed true to his word and carried me all the way back to camp without stopping. He even pointed out some plants and animals from the scavenger hunt we missed on our way up. When we reached the medic cabin, he set me down and reminded me, I owe him a *"chicken-fried date."*

"Well, I'm glad you're okay. I bet that Travis-kid wasn't much help," he huffs into the phone. "That kid sounds like he needs to be in a white room."

I laugh at my dad's words, and I can imagine him sitting on the couch with a glass of Chardonnay. He's off today, so he's probably catching up on old episodes of Dr. Phil.

"Actually, I was with a different counselor. He's new," I tell him, absently twirling the cord of the landline phone in Rhonda's office. My snake bite got me special phone privileges. I was tempted to call and gossip with Christina or check in with Manny.

Geoff doesn't respond and I hear the good doctor's southern drawl in the background. I feel like a prison inmate getting my daily phone call. Time is running out and any minute now, the automated voice of Dr. Phil will come over the phone and tell me I have thirty seconds left.

"Where's Dad?" I ask him.

Geoff snorts and I hear him gulp down his wine. "He's in Baltimore."

I suck my teeth and chuckle. "You know that's his job, right? You married a pilot. That's the life you chose."

"He's having dinner with Carrie. She has an art show out there or something," Geoff replies in a bland tone.

"So?" I scrunch my face.

"I've got to go, Junior." He's annoyed with me. "Dr. Phil is interrogating an extremely culturally inappropriate teenager. It's getting good. Be safe, and no more injuries!"

I sigh. "I love you, Dad. Miss you."

"Miss you too, baby girl." I can hear the smile in his voice. "And you know I love you to the stars."

"You're my shining star!" I sing out before hanging up the phone. I contemplate picking up the receiver and dialing Manny, but Rhonda pokes her head in just as I'm about to reach for it.

"So, that nature hike was a success. I mean, despite one minor hiccup." She pauses and motions toward my bandaged ankle.

"It's all the kids are talking about!" She tries to give me an encouraging smile. She's about to ask me not to quit. I never planned to.

"I heard a few of the kids discussing a possible..." She pauses again and frowns before collecting herself. "... lawsuit."

I laugh and shake my head. *Dammit, Jonah!*

"I'm not going to sue you, Rhonda. It was a joke. Jonah has an interesting sense of humor," I assure her.

She audibly sighs in relief and runs her hands down her face. "Great news! Now, how do you feel about switching gears and overseeing lake time?"

Why? So I can get bitten by a water moccasin?

Of course, I nod my head and agree to the proposition. I'd much rather swim than hike the trails right about now.

"Awesome! You and Jonah seem to work well together, so I'll ask him to help you. Travis likes scorekeeping more anyway!" Rhonda's got this extremely country accent and grayish-colored teeth. I've caught her smoking in her car a few times, which might explain her painfully raspy voice.

I can't help but smile at the thought of working with Jonah again, and I hate the feeling. Sure, it's nice to have a cute guy interested in me; but the way my life works, I don't have much space for a cute boy.

? ? ?

I'm placed on lunch duty for the next two days until my ankle feels better. Campers can swim in the lake on Wednesday of the second week of camp. Rhonda actually hires professional lifeguards for that job, so the counselors are just there to lead activities with the campers.

Jonah walks up to the group with a plastic bucket full of water balloons cradled in his long arms. He's got a lopsided grin plastered on his face. We haven't spoken much since the nature hike; I was on kitchen duty, and he's been helping Travis with sports.

"What are those for?" I ask. One camper asks if we're having a water balloon fight and they all get excited.

"Something like that," he tells them, setting the bucket down, and plucking a light blue water balloon from the top. There's something written on it in black Sharpie.

He tosses the balloon around in his palms as he explains the activity. "So, I figured we'd play a game that actually builds self-esteem and character." He turns to me with a sheepish expression. "Unless you had something else planned. I don't want to take over your group activity."

I shrug and shake my head. I had nothing planned. Most of the other senior counselors are just swimming and kayaking today, so I'm interested in hearing what he's come up with.

"Cool, so here's the plan." He turns and addresses the campers like he's that cool big brother they can look up to. "Each of you guys will pick a water balloon from the top of the pile. They all have something encouraging written on them." He holds up the balloon he's been tossing in the air as an example. "You'll read the words on it. For example, this one says *someone I want to get to know better.* Then you throw it at the person you think it pertains to." With that, he swiftly launches the water balloon at me. It hits my chest and explodes all over me.

I shriek and tense up from the impact of cold water. *Did he really just do that?*

The campers start laughing and fidgeting excitedly. Jonah lines them all up and instructs them to pick a balloon one by one and throw it at someone.

"Someone with a strong spirit," Ethan reads out loud and immediately throws the balloon at Shelby. I half-expected him to hit Paisley with that one.

"Why'd you hit me?" Shelby asks, looking around at the rest of the group, obviously embarrassed.

Ethan shrugged. "You're quiet, but that doesn't mean you aren't strong," he says between heavy breathing.

Paisley picks a balloon that instructs her to select someone who is confident. She throws it at Ethan and says, "I mean you *have* to be confident to be that big and still swim without a shirt."

"I'm not sure that was a compliment, Paisley." Jonah shakes his head.

"I'm just happy she chose me for something!" Ethan beams, and I swear I see hearts in his eyes as he watches her walk back to the line.

I have to hand it to Jonah, he picked a pretty awesome activity. It's the first time since we've started this summer that I feel like we're actually helping the kids.

"How about you do the last one, Camp Counselor Bo!" I'm glad to see Shelby coming out of her shell, but I don't want to take part.

"Good idea, Shelby," Jonah says. He's smirking at me with his arms snaked across his chest and his feet planted as he sways from side to side.

I sigh and walk over to the bucket. The last balloon is bright orange, and when I turn it in my hand it says: *CHICKEN FRIED DATE TONIGHT?*

A laugh sips from my throat, and I bite my lip to contain the rest. I look up at Jonah, and he winks at me.

"Well..." Paisley sucks her teeth. "What does it say?"

"It says, *someone who needs a haircut*," I lie, and then toss the balloon at Jonah. I aim for his head, but it falls short and explodes on his chest as he laughs.

"We've still got half an hour left." I pull my tank top over my head, leaving me in my swimsuit top and shorts. "Let's go swim!"

The campers take off, running towards the shoreline of the lake and jumping in.

I turn to Jonah and smile. "That was smooth."

"It took a lot of strategizing. I'll tell you more about it over dinner tonight," he replies, walking beside me towards the lake.

"I never agreed to that," I remind him.

"I meant what I said earlier with the water balloon." He looks at me with a genuine smile. Upon further inspection, I notice a small chip in his front tooth. An imperfection. It adds to his cuteness.

I internally kick myself for thinking that. I barely know this guy, and my hormones have my stomach flip-flopping whenever he's around. This isn't good. I can't like someone now.

"I really want to get to know you better," he finishes, snapping me out of my thoughts. I hope I wasn't staring at him with the goofy, puppy dog face I'm imagining.

"Why?" I ask him, turning my head towards the campers in the lake splashing each other. I'm wearing my water shoes, so when we reach the water, I walk right in.

"You seem like a cool girl." I'm not facing him, but I'm pretty sure he just shrugged while saying that.

I don't respond. The campers are a few feet away, splashing around, so I take the moment to float on my back and lose myself in my thoughts. I never hear Jonah get into the water, so I assume he's sitting on the bank watching me.

The sun is hiding behind the clouds now, making a cool shadow across the lake. I close my eyes and let out a deep sigh. My thoughts are always the same whenever I don't have my usual distractions.

Jonah says he wants to get to know me better. But how can that possibly happen when I don't even know myself?

Chapter Six

J onah is waiting for me outside of the lunch hall as if he already
expected I'd show up.

The entire camp is usually fast asleep by 10:00 p.m. Still, I waited
until 11:00 p.m. before changing into my gray sweatpants and
tennis shoes, and sneaking out of the girls' cabin I'm in charge
of, appropriately named *Dotted Gayfeather*. They named all the
cabins after native flowers or plants from our state. The kids get a
kick out of that one because kids think words like *gay* and *butt* are
hilarious.

"This better be the best chicken-fried steak ever," I warn him as
I stop a few feet away, my arms folded across my chest.

"I thought you were going to stand me up," he tells me sheepishly, planting his laced hands behind his head and bouncing on
the balls of his feet. He's wearing another pair of basketball shorts
and a plain white t-shirt that rises slightly with his raised arms.

"I seriously considered it," I tell him with a smirk. "But I'm
dying to have some real food. Especially fried food." Geoff hates
fried food, so he never cooks it. Mark is from the South, so he
loves fried chicken and anything else fried in grease he can get his
hands on. That being said, we usually eat fried food whenever
Geoff works late, and Mark is home.

"Let's go. The diner is just off the highway." He beckons for me to follow him as he walks up the trail that leads to the dirt parking lot that the staff uses to park their cars for the summer.

The camp counselors aren't allowed to leave camp without permission from Rhonda, so I've always left my car at home for the month. Geoff drops me off and picks me up.

There are about fifteen cars in the dirt lot, which is nearly half a mile away from the camp. I'm surprised when Jonah pulls out his key fob and chirps the lock on a shiny blue Camaro. It looks brand new and expensive.

"Nice car," I murmur as we approach the fancy ride. The moonlight and stars illuminated two black stripes on the hood and black-on-black rims on the tires, contrasting with the metallic blue color.

"Thanks," Jonah replies with a smile. He opens the door for me and waits for me to sit in the passenger's seat before jogging around to the driver's side.

The interior of his car is all black leather. There's a screen on the dash and interior blue lights on the floorboards. I'm guessing blue is his favorite color. I note the Davis High School parking pass hanging from his rearview mirror.

When he gets in, he's wearing that huge grin of his. "Ready?"

"Hopefully, you're not a crazed maniac," I quip, fighting a smile. He's too damn cute and charming.

"Nah, just a guy who likes fast cars and pretty girls," he winks and then starts the engine. It purrs awake, and I say a silent *"thank you"* that it's not one of those loud racing engine cars that roars when you drive it.

We take the dirt road that runs north of the campground until we reach I-35 and drive south. He's a safe driver. I always have to beg Manny to wear a seatbelt when we're driving around. The diner he's referring to is just off the next exit, and there are only two cars parked outside.

"I take it you don't sneak out much?" Jonah laughs at me as I look around the diner for any familiar faces. This place doesn't seem like the type of eatery Rhonda would be caught dead in, but I still can't risk getting caught. This job is going on my resume for college applications.

"No, I don't," I tell him. The server greets us and seats us next to the window right in front of the Camaro. Jonah orders a root beer float, so I order the same. The server asks him if he wants the usual, and he tells her yes for both of us.

"Spoiler alert. It's not real ice cream," he whispers from across the table. I laugh and nod. I wouldn't expect a greasy highway diner to have quality ice cream, anyway.

"So, you volunteer for the camp every year?" he asks me with an amused look.

"Yes, ever since I was a freshman." I nod.

"You must like it a lot."

I shrug. "I enjoy helping kids, even though Rhonda's methods are a bit skewed," I add the last part with a snort and a headshake.

"You've got that right," Jonah laughs. Sue, the waitress, brings our floats and drops off napkins and silverware. "What about you? Why are you volunteering this year?"

He shrugs and sips his float. "My mom was on this whole *giving-back* kick. So, I donated my last high school summer break to mentoring kids who think they're depressed; but really, they're just in middle school, and life sucks when you're in middle school."

I nod and spoon vanilla ice cream and root beer from my glass. It may be fake ice cream, but it's a relief to have something other than the over-baked brownies the camp cook makes every other day.

"I'm glad I did, though," Jonah adds, smiling at me. His dimples are back on full display.

"Do you race that car?" I ask, looking out the dusty diner window. There's a flickering streetlight in the parking lot that makes the gleaming blue color glow periodically.

"Nah, my mom would kill me," he tells me, following my gaze. "My best friend has an Acura that he swears can beat my Camaro, but I signed a contract with my mom, so we'll never know."

I giggle. "People race Acuras?" I'm not car-savvy at all. For my 16th birthday, my parents surprised me with a brand-new Acura. I would have been fine with a used car, but Geoff insisted I get a new car so that they could *be done with it.*

This time Jonah laughs. He seems genuinely amused by my ignorance, but not condescending.

"Yeah, it's an Integra; very popular in street racing," he tells me.

I shrug, "I drive an ILX. But I do not know cars. It was a birthday gift from my parents."

"Nice." He grins.

Sue comes back with two plates of the most massive chicken-fried steaks I've ever seen. They are slathered in country gravy and cover the entire plate, barely leaving room for the mashed potatoes.

"This... is a lot..." I say while eyeing my plate.

"I know, just try it! It's delicious!" he tells me with a mouth full of food. He's already digging in while I'm trying to put together a game plan for eating this thing.

Jonah was right, this is the best chicken-fried steak I've ever had. I have to bring Mark here one day.

"You can always tell when food is really tasty." Sue comes over and brings us both a glass of water. "You two were pretty chatty before, but now you've gone all quiet while you're eating," she teases. She's got a deep country accent like most people out here.

"It's delicious." I nod my head and wipe my mouth with my napkin. She passes Jonah the paper receipt, and I try to protest, but she cuts me off.

"Always let the man pay for dinner, Honey." She winks.

"This is *not* a date," I tell them both. "This is actually two irresponsible camp counselors breaking the cardinal rule of their job." Sue just laughs and walks away with the cash Jonah has handed her. I shoot him a mean look.

"I could have paid for my dinner," I tell him, pushing the plate away from me. I feel bad that he's paying for food that I can't possibly finish. There is still a large portion of steak left, but that's not saying much considering how large the patty was.

"I'm sure you could have, but this was my treat," he responds with a shrug. He's on track to clean his plate completely. I work on my melting float again.

"So, where are you from?" he asks me.

"I'm from the city," I tell him, referring to Oklahoma City.

"I figured." He chuckles. "Irrational fear of rattlesnakes."

"Being afraid of rattlesnakes is not *irrational*," I huff. "Where are you from?"

"Ten minutes down 77." He points north. "Local boy," he adds with a wink.

"In Davis?" I ask him, and he nods. "I didn't peg you for the small-town type."

"Why is that?"

Sue comes and collects our plates as I shrug, not really having an answer. "We'd better head back," I say instead.

Once again, Jonah opens the door for me and jogs around the front of the car. He drives relaxed and reclined in the leather seat, bobbing his head to a song on the radio that I've never heard of before.

"What's the plan for tomorrow's excursions?" he asks me, looking over briefly as we merge onto the highway.

I shrug and smile at him. "You did so well with that balloon activity today." Technically, that was yesterday, I guess. It's after midnight now. "I figured you could take over for now."

"I'm fine with that." He nods. "I've got a few ideas up my sleeve."

"As long as they don't involve snakes, I'm open to anything," I tell him with an eye roll.

When we make it back to the campsite, Jonah insists on walking me back to my cabin. The boys' cabins are on the opposite side of the lunch hall from the girls' cabins.

"Thanks for coming with me." He seems shy for the first time tonight, and I'm happy he can't tell that I'm blushing.

"Thanks for dinner. I'm not looking forward to eating the lunch hall food again," I tell him in a whisper, only half-joking.

"Well..." he hums, holding onto the 'L' sound mischievously.

"You're a troublemaker, I see." I fold my arms across my chest and shake my head.

"I prefer the term thrill-seeker." He feigns offense. "Besides." He pauses and smirks at me again. Only one dimple on display this time. "You owe me dinner now."

I let out a little giggle and shake my head before telling him, "Good night, Jonah." I silently pray that the squeaky screen door doesn't wake up the campers as I sneak back into the cabin. The last thing I need is Paisley, or one of the other girls, waking up and ratting me out to Rhonda.

I settle into my bunk and wrap myself up in the thin blanket. It's a habit, despite the sticky summer heat. It's well after midnight, but I'm wide awake. Thinking about Jonah, and what can't be.

Chapter Seven

Allowing Jonah to take the reins on camp activities was the best idea I've ever had.

For starters, he's a natural with the kids. He's got so many great ideas that actually pertain to self-esteem and learning. Like the obstacle course he came up with that made the kids use teamwork and communication to get to the finish line. Then there was the giant Connect Four game he made using one of Rhonda's shower curtains. He'd spray-painted it yellow and for the red and black pieces, he painted paper plates from the kitchen. The kids loved it!

Jonah has taken matters into his own hands. It gives me a chance to relax and enjoy the summer, instead of combating eye rolls and snake bites. But mostly, I enjoy being able to hang out with him. Travis has permanently taken over the sports scoring, so Jonah is my partner for the rest of the summer. There's one week left in camp, and while I'm excited to be away from mosquitoes and humidity soon, I'm kind of sad for camp to end.

In past years, by the end of these four weeks, I'd had all I could take from the angsty preteens, Rhonda's lack of organization, and Travis' perpetual freak-outs. I'd be ready to get home to Manny and hang out with Christina.

Now there's Jonah to factor in.

"We should do some extensive planning tonight," Jonah says while we're chaperoning lake time. "For our last activity, you know?"

"Okay, let's plan," I reply, smirking at him. We're sitting on the bank of the lake, while the campers float a few feet away in tubes. I'm wearing my plain yellow bikini top and white shorts over my bottoms. If Jonah was stealing peeks at my body, he's hiding it well.

I, however, can't help the occasional glance at his toned frame under his tank top and swim trunks. He's lanky, but not super skinny, and the sun has transformed this smooth skin, giving its natural brown a glow. I absently compare the exposed skin of our thighs next to each other. My sun-kissed bronze to his mahogany. It's oddly calming.

"I meant over a late-night dinner," he chuckles, winking at me, and leaning back on his elbows. I tuck my feet under my butt and bite my lips as his long body stretches out in the sand, a peak of his stomach showing when his white tank top rises slightly. I ponder his request just as Paisley screams and falls out of the inflatable tube she's floating in.

"Paisley! No screaming!" I yell at her. She sucks her teeth and rolls her eyes at me before standing up in the waist-high water and getting back on her flotation device.

"She reminds me of all the girls I go to school with, dramatic," I groan. Beside me, Jonah laughs.

"Yeah, we've got plenty of those at my school, too. Where do you go?"

"North Creek."

"Really?" He looks surprised. He's doing that grinning smile thing with the dimples, and I'm going to melt. "I figured you'd say some kind of private school."

I laugh with him. "No way. My dad is always going off about paying for college. He wouldn't fathom paying for high school!"

We share another laugh and fall into our newfound comfortable silence. We watch the campers float around in the tubes that Rhonda splurged on this summer after I suggested the old ones were lawsuits waiting to happen last year. Lawsuits are Rhonda's biggest fear.

In five days, the camp will be over, and moments like this will be a memory. This is my last year working at the camp. Next summer, I'll be preparing to go to college.

I chance a peek at Jonah, who is smirking at me.

"What's on your mind?" he asks me. I guess I had my thinking face on. It's like a mixture of a scowl, a smile, and a sad face if that's even possible.

"I was just thinking that a milkshake would go great with some late-night activity planning," I tell him. But I'm not bold enough to look at him, so I turn back towards the lake as I speak.

I can hear the grin in his voice when he says, "See you at eleven."

? ? ?

Jonah and I split a giant chicken-fried steak this time. I'm also finding myself partial to the fake ice cream. I ordered a vanilla milkshake this time.

"I never share food with anyone besides my little sister," he tells me as Sue walks away with our order. "Consider yourself special."

"I'm flattered," I giggle. We're once again two out of five patrons in the small diner where Sue is our server.

There's some country song playing out of the old radio on the counter. I hate country music.

"I hate country music," Jonah groans. "Please tell me you hate country music."

"I was literally just thinking the same thing," I laugh.

"What kind of music do you like?" He leans closer and rests his elbows on the table.

"I thought this was a final activity planning dinner?" I shoot back with a cocked eyebrow.

He waves off my statement. "I've already got that covered. I just needed a reason to get you to come out again."

I fight the smile that's trying to take over my lips and look out the window. The light outside is still flickering away over Jonah's car.

"So?" Jonah presses. "Your taste in music?"

"I like everything, except country," I reply, still looking out the window. I can't look at him, because I want to smile. Not a simple, cheerful smile. I want to give him the cheesiest, smitten, giddy schoolgirl smile.

"What's your favorite?" he asks me.

"I like R&B, and I listen to a lot of jazz with my dad. He's from New Orleans." Mark and I frequent the Jazz Lab whenever he's home for a reasonable length of time. Geoff tags along sometimes, making for a perfect family night. Mark says jazz isn't just music; it's an essence of life.

"Interesting." He grins and nods, as if he's hiding what he's thinking.

"What?" I ask him, wondering if I should be offended.

"Nothing, I've never met a girl my age that likes jazz," he elaborates.

"Well, I'm not like most girls, unfortunately." The words slip out in a mumble.

"Unfortunately?" he repeats in a questioning tone. "How about *most fortunately*?"

"I didn't mean it like that," I murmur. "But I do like pop music and rap, and I listen to a lot of Top 40."

I wait for Sue to walk away after dropping off our single steak to share before continuing the conversation. "What do *you* listen to?"

"Mostly rap and indie/alternative," he tells me as he cuts the chicken-fried steak in half. He puts his half on an extra plate that Sue left for us and then passes me the rest. She's thrown in individual mashed potatoes for both of us.

Geoff doesn't care for rap music. He says it's degrading. *"Especially to young women of color,"* he always adds when he catches me and Christina listening to a rap song in my car. *"It's not good for your self-esteem."*

Ha! If only he knew!

Jonah's got that weird smirk on his face again. I can't tell if he's silently judging me, or he's holding in a fart.

"What now?" I ask him suspiciously.

He shrugs, "Just an observation,"

"And just what did you observe?" I ask him, placing my fork down on the table.

"Eat your food before it gets cold," he mocks. I give him a challenging look and cross my arms, sitting back against the booth.

"Relax!" He snorts and laughs simultaneously. "I'm not judging you or anything, I promise."

I eye him for a few more seconds before finding it hard to resist the freshly fried steak smothered in gravy in front of me.

"I like artists and bands that most people haven't heard of," he reveals through a mouthful.

I chew my bite and swallow, wiping my mouth on the napkin. "So, you're a hipster?" Now it's my turn to tease him.

Instead of being offended, he gives me a hearty laugh. "No, I'm not a hipster. Indie artists just have more to say. They haven't sold out to the mainstream yet, so their music has more depth."

We talk about music and cars for another hour. Well, he talks about cars, and I listen. It's nearing one o'clock when we realize that it's time to head back to camp. The ride is quick, but Jonah insists he plays his favorite song by one of his artists.

"It's called *Confusion.*"

"I like it." I make a mental note to add it to my playlist when we get our phones back. My body sinks into the leather bucket seat and I sigh absently.

We don't talk. Just listen to the haunting lyrics of the song about how confusing life can be, but still living it. It should speak to me on a spiritual level.

Too bad I can't shake the feelings in my heart.

Chapter Eight

The day before our scheduled final activity, Jonah is nowhere to be found. It's a free day for the campers, so I'm a little bummed that he's not around to spend the leisure time together.

I sit at the scoring table with Travis and Melanie and watch a few of the boys play basketball while my campers are all running around doing God-knows-what.

"Where's that new guy?" Melanie asks me as we watch the game. This group of boys are willingly playing basketball, so they are a lot better than the regular groups who have to be forced to play.

I shrug, not bothering to hide my pout. "Haven't seen him all day."

"You're lucky you got paired with him." She side-eyes Travis. He's drumming his fingers on the desk, obviously not interested in the game either. At least he's not freaking out, though.

"Yeah, trust me, I know." I giggle.

Melanie nudges me and points behind me. "Speaking of which."

I turn just in time to see Jonah casually walking toward us. He's looking around the camp at all the kids running rampant, seeming utterly content with life. I envy his carefree spirit.

"'Sup, Freckles." He nudges me and takes the last seat beside me. "Hey, Mel." He leans over and waves at Melanie, who waves back.

"Is that your thing?" I ask him with a smirk. "Nicknames?"

"I guess so." He grins. "Miss me?"

My insides temporarily turn to mush.

"Didn't even notice you were gone," I lie. Melanie snorts, and I elbow her side. I've been searching for him like an obsessive girlfriend, which I'm not and can't be.

"So, I scheduled another nature walk for our last activity," he tells me casually.

I snort and roll my eyes. "Count me out!"

"Me too!" Travis chimes in. It's okay, no one will *ever* invite him on another nature walk.

Jonah chuckles. "I'm kidding, I swear," he tells us, throwing up his hands. His smile is captivating, and his charm is inescapable. I've never had these thoughts about a guy before.

"How about one last chicken-fried date before the summer's over?" he whispers. Melanie's attention is back on the game, while Travis is probably mentally freaking out, thinking of all the ways one might contract a flesh-eating bacterium during lake days.

My insides are immediately screaming, *Yes!* but I can't seem desperate. I can't let Jonah know the level at which I'm interested in him. Even though I'm pretty sure he's feeling the same way.

I nod, and he makes this small victory fist-pumping motion and sits back.

What's it matter if I play hard to get? We can't date, anyway.

? ? ?

Jonah's last activity is both fun and terrifying at the same time.

"Messy Twister!" he announces proudly as we all stare at the globs of matching paint on the *Twister* mat's colored circles.

"What's this do for our self-esteem?" Paisley asks, folding her arms and pouting. "We're going to get all gross and messy."

"That's the point," Jonah replies smugly. He's wearing a black t-shirt and another pair of basketball shorts; these black and red.

"We'll say it's supposed to help them break their comfort zone?" I ask him. It's definitely going to break mine. I'm wearing my jean shorts and a tank over my swimsuit again. After the final activities, there is one last lake time, and then the end-of-camp fireworks display. Tomorrow, we pack up and return home. Goodbye, Jonah.

His shoulders flop up and down in a shrug. "I figured we've done a lot of self-esteem stuff. Now it's time for some fun." He turns to the campers and holds his hands out. "Who wants to go first?"

Ethan volunteers to go first, and Jonah volunteers for Paisley to join him. She sucks her teeth and rolls her eyes, but she complies. Paisley wins, but they're both covered in paint from sticking their hands and feet in big mounds of blue, red, yellow, and green. The last round once again strategically pits me against Jonah, and I wonder just how he pulls these stunts off.

Jonah pours fresh paint on a few of the circles that have lost a good portion, and then slaps his hands together and ushers me towards that mat.

Paisley spins the dial and calls out, "Left foot, red."

I follow her instructions, and then it's Jonah's turn to put his right hand on a green spot.

We're keeping a safe distance until Paisley calls out "Right hand, blue" on my third spin. This calls for me to reach under Jonah's body, which is contorted in the green and blue spaces, and place my right hand on the nearest blue spot he's not occupying. Now I'm positioned partially under him, and he's looking down at me with a grin.

"So, this was totally my plan." He grins at me.

I laugh softly and shake my head, momentarily losing my balance before regaining it. "I can tell."

"Jonah, right hand, red!" Paisley calls out. My body breaks out in shivers at the realization that the red spots are on the other end of the board. He'll have to reach over me. When he reaches across, I feel the cold dripping of paint on the nape of my neck.

"Sorry." Jonah suppressed a laugh when I let out a shriek.

Paisley now tells me to put my left hand on the red space. So I take my hand out of the green paint and flip my body over so that I'm in a crab walk position, successfully swiping paint all across Jonah's shirt.

"Sorry," I mock him as I squish my hand in red paint.

Our chests are inches apart as he hovers over my body in an 'X' formation. I'm breathing heavily, and I have to admit that I'm nervous about how close we are, but I'm having fun.

Paisley's next command has Jonah attempting to maneuver his body back over mine so that he can place his left foot on the green circles. He's nearly made it when he slips and comes crashing down on top of me. He quickly recovers and lifts his weight off of me, but remains hovering over my face.

"This was definitely one of my greatest ideas ever," he says so that only I can hear him.

I smirk and swipe my hand across the mat, picking up globs of paint and wiping it across his face.

He laughs and ducks down, repaying me by smearing blue paint over the line of my freckles. I try to wiggle away from him, but the mat is so slippery with paint that I end up squirming in place.

We're both laughing and briefly in our own little world when we hear someone clearing their throat.

"Umm... Can we go to the lake now?" Ethan asks us. The other campers are all giggling and looking at us with amused faces. I realize this is a highly inappropriate scene for them to be witnessing. I hope no one reports back to Rhonda.

Then again, it's the last day I'll ever work at this camp and the last day I'll see Jonah. So, to hell with Rhonda!

"Everyone needs to grab a life jacket before you go in," I warn them, and then they take off toward the lake.

Jonah stands up and then extends his hand out to help me up from the ground. We're both covered in paint that is drying on our skin and clothes.

I peel off my tank top and toss it on the Twister mat to be discarded with the trash.

There's blue, green, yellow, and red paint in my hair and on my face. Even though I was wearing a tank top, there's paint on my stomach where the shirt rose while I was rolling around with Jonah. I glance at him to find he's in a similar state, with paint smeared across his cheek and matted into his curls.

We walk down to the pier in silence, but it's not uncomfortable. The entire camp has assembled on the bank, eating hot dogs and swimming. There's an end-of-summer firework show that happens every year at the end of the last day.

"I'd be lying if I said I wasn't going to miss this place a little." I'm leaning back on my arms again, but this time I stretch my legs out and cross my ankles. Jonah is beside me, sitting with one leg propped up and his arms and chin resting on his bent knee. The other leg is dangling off the side of the pier, skimming the water and causing ripples to move across the surface.

"Yeah, I thought this was going to be way worse than it ended up being," he muses too, lifting his head. "I actually had fun."

We're quiet again, and I feel like there's something more he wants to say to me. There's definitely more I want to tell him. But seeing as I've only been in one *"relationship,"* and I'm currently *"in"* that relationship, I don't really know how to conclude these past few weeks with Jonah. I want to see him again. Maybe, exchange numbers and continue to be friends outside of this summer camp experience.

Who am I kidding? I want to be more than friends. For the first time ever, I think I like this guy.

The sun disappears into the distance. Rhonda's making the same end-of-summer announcement I've heard three times already, so I don't mind missing it to sit in content silence with Jonah. She's thanking the counselors for their hard work and wishing the campers a fun school year, telling them she'll see them again next year. I scoot my body up to sit right next to Jonah. I dangle both legs over the pier, but fail to come close to touching the water.

And then the fireworks begin.

I have to admit it's probably my favorite part of the entire summer. The fireworks light up the sky in explosions of color that remind me of the paint smudged across my face and body. They bang and crackle back-to-back, and the kids that are now floating on rafts are cheering and singing a chorus of *"oohs"* and *"ahhs."*

I think about my life back home as I watch the giant flowers appear and then dissipate in the sky. Tomorrow, everything goes back to normal, if you even want to call it that. I definitely wouldn't call those components of my life *normal*. I guess I just mean that the routine will be back on.

Another year of being Bowie Phoenix Monroe. Whatever that means.

"So, you really don't have a boyfriend?"

Jonah's sudden words stun me, and I turn to face him, gauging his face for any plausible explanation for why he would ask me that.

He's still looking up at the illuminated sky. A blue and green Pyro-flower is just disappearing, falling into the lake below and sizzling. He's watching it, but it's almost like he just needs a place to focus his eyes while he waits for me to answer him.

I consider his question for the umpteenth time since I've met him. I'm still unsure of how to tell him the truth.

"No." I shake my head after a few more silent seconds. He gives out a sigh that seems to be one of relief and nervousness.

The pink light of another brocade firework illuminates his face as he turns towards me and leans in, pressing his lips to mine. I don't push him away, and when my lips respond, he weaves his hands into my sticky hair and deepens the kiss. I'm not sure how long we'll stay this way, but I know that when we're finished, it will be the most disappointing feeling ever.

Because if I thought I would hate parting with him before, I was mistaken. I probably would have gotten over it quickly before this. But now that we've kissed... Now that we're *still* kissing, I know that my life will be a lot more mundane without him.

Chapter Nine

I breathe out a sigh of relief as I make it to the upper floor of my high school. I've spent the last ten minutes looking for a parking space and being pushed around by nervous freshmen as I attempt to make it upstairs to the senior hallways.

Christina, Manny, and I used to fantasize about loitering in the private senior hallways, away from the chaos of the junior and lowerclassmen floors. Even our lunch is separate from the three lower grades. Even *I'm* getting a big head at the thought of being on top of the social class of high school!

I pass the junior halls and turn down the first sub-hallway of the senior section, in search of my locker.

"Hey, Bo!" I hear Christina before I feel her wrapping her arms around me. I continue to walk towards my locker with her hanging on me.

"Did you miss me?" I ask her, leaning my head in the crook of her neck.

"You know it!" she swoons. "I've got so much to tell you!"

"Yeah, me too," I mumble as I glance at the locker numbers. I find my locker and test out the combination to make sure it works. Christina snatches my schedule out of my hand and compares it with hers. She sucks her teeth and shoves the paper back toward me after I close my locker.

"We've only got three classes together. I bet you and Manny have every class together again."

I shrug and chuckle softly. We make our way toward our first classes, which aren't together but are in the same hallway. We nod and greet our fellow senior classmates, some of whom we've known since elementary school. There is no real social hierarchy in our class; we're pretty much just seventy-five acquaintances. Everyone knows everyone like we're in some small town instead of a metropolitan public high school.

When we walk past Chris Monte, a star basketball player in our class, I feel strange energy radiating between him and Christina. Well, actually, Christina keeps glancing over at him while he gives his undivided attention to his teammates.

"What's that all about?" I quiz her with an amused smile, motioning between the two of them.

"That's what I needed to tell you about, girl!" She's sheepishly biting her bottom lip. "Chris and I kind of spent the summer together."

"You didn't!" I gasp.

"We did. A few times," she admits, almost giddy now. They had sex. While I was out experiencing my first crush, Christina was losing her virginity to Chris Monte.

"I didn't even know you guys were dating." I look at her, still in disbelief.

"We had our first date the day before you left for camp, remember?" I remember her leaving with Manny because she had a date, but she never said it was with Chris Monte. I glance back at Chris and his friends. If there were a social hierarchy, he'd be high on the list; star athlete, perfect teeth, and smooth dark-brown skin.

"So, is he, like, your boyfriend?" I look back at my best friend curiously. "That's going to be weird. You're going to be *the Chrises.*"

She shrugs and shakes her head. "We're avoiding titles, I guess." I give her a skeptical look, and she ignores it, babbling on about the different dates that they went on; the last three ending with them in the back of his car.

"I may have, sort of, met someone..." I tell her nonchalantly, as we turn the corner towards our first classes.

She stops in her tracks and gasps. "What did you just say?" Her eyes are wide, and she's grinning from ear to ear. "Girl, I need details right now!"

"Well, his name is Jonah, and we met at the camp," I tell her quietly, but the sound of rambunctious boys making their way down the hallway interrupts us.

"'Sup ladies," Bryson greets us as he approaches and wraps an arm around Christina. "Have a good summer?" He looks down at Christina and smirks suggestively. "I mean, I heard *you* had a great summer."

Christina screws her face up in a frown. "What's that supposed to mean?"

"What about you, Bowie? Have fun at your fat camp thingy?" He chuckles and nods toward me.

"Of course, she didn't." I'm interrupted before I can answer that I did, in fact, have a fun summer at camp this year.

"She missed her man." And with that, Manny Herrera walks right up and wraps his arms around me, shoving his tongue down my throat.

"Hey babe, let's get to class," he says, and then drags me away from my friends.

"See you love birds later," Bryson calls out. Manny throws a wave at them, and I look back at Christina with a weak smile. She's just smiling knowingly and shaking her head before turning her attention back to Bryson and the other guys.

"There's everyone's favorite couple!" Haley Felix coos as we walk past her. Never without her yearbook camera, she snaps a pic of us and grins. "A shoo-in for the cutest couple in the yearbook!"

Manny smiles and then plants another kiss on my lips. I smile as well and kiss him back.

He is my boyfriend, after all.

Chapter Ten

I met Emmanuel Herrera on the first day of seventh grade. Christina and I had already been friends for years when Manny entered the picture. His family was from Puerto Rico, but Manny and his parents had lived in Orlando for most of his life before moving here.

Manny walked into our class on the first day of school and sat next to Christina and me, and we've been inseparable ever since. At first, we only saw each other at school until I invited him to my thirteenth birthday party at my house.

The first time Manny saw my dads embrace each other, he seemed to be in awe. I didn't really think much of it at the time; everyone loved my dads. They were fun and lax, and my birthday parties were always the highlight of the school year for my friends.

But Manny always wanted to visit. He seemed so comfortable at my house. His parents are very religious and strict. He'd visit for hours, eating dinner with us most nights, and staying for family movie night. We didn't mind, because we loved having Manny around.

Then, during the first week of our freshman year of high school, everything started making sense.

There was this new kid, Dillon Wilkenson, who we'd met in the last few weeks of middle school. On the first day of ninth grade, Dillon walked over to Manny, grabbed his hand, and attempted to kiss him on the cheek. Manny flinched slightly, and before he could move away from him, our other friends were all over Dillon.

"What the hell are you doing?" Bryson yelled at Dillon, pushing him hard in the chest; his grip on Manny's hand was lost. "Manny's not a little homo like you!"

I remember watching Dillon's eyes widen with fear and feeling sick to my stomach. Bryson was always at my birthday parties. Was that how he felt about my dads?

"M-Manny, tell them," Dillon pleaded with my best friend, who was standing next to me, staring at the floor.

"Manny?" I whispered, but he never responded.

"So, what is it, Manny? Are you a little fairy, like Dildo here?" Cole Reeves taunted harshly.

Manny shook his head vigorously. His fists were clenched at his side, and he was shaking. "No. He's lying. C'mon guys, you know me," he spat out through gritted teeth.

And with that, Bryson, Cole, and two other guys beat the crap out of Dillon. Bad. So bad that the school suspended Bryson, Cole, and two other guys from school for two weeks, and Dillon's family moved him to Iowa or something.

I cried for two nights thinking about the way those boys beat up Dillon, all because he was gay. The derogatory words they called him rang in my ears for days. I imagined someone hurting Geoff that way, and it made me even sicker. My dads tried their best to explain to me that some people were just afraid of people who were different. A small irrational part of my brain considered how different I was. How hard it was to understand why everything about me was made up, just like explaining why Dillon liked to kiss boys.

Only, no one would savagely beat me for being adopted.

The next week Manny was spotted walking down the halls with Mercedes Howard, and they were supposedly an item. I overheard her talking in the lunchroom with her friends, telling them she and Manny were planning to have sex that upcoming Saturday. It pissed me off. Not because I was jealous of Mercedes, but because Manny found time to plan a romantic outing with her. Yet, hadn't spoken a word to his own best friend since the first day of school. He hadn't returned any of my calls or texts and bailed on hanging out with Christina and me all week.

"Maybe he's just embarrassed by that whole Dillon thing," Christina tried to reason. I wasn't sure what the reason was, but I was about to find out so much more about my best friend.

Saturday night, while Manny was supposed to be losing his virginity to Mercedes Howard, I was at home in bed after another family movie night with Geoff and Mark. I was asleep when I heard someone crawl through my bedroom window. My room is on the second floor, so there was only one person who would take the time to climb through it.

Manny was there, sitting on the window sill.

"Manny?" I called out to him groggily. "What are you doing?"

He didn't respond, only walked over to my bed and climbed on top of me.

I didn't scream, because I didn't want to wake up my parents. I pushed him off of me and when I had him at arm's length, I could see that he was crying.

"Manny? What's wrong?" I asked him, crawling entirely out of his grasp and sitting with my back against my headboard. Manny stood up and paced the floor.

"I couldn't do it," he cried in a panicky tone. "She was right there, under me, and I couldn't do it. It... It wouldn't work!"

"Couldn't do what?" I scrunched my face. He was rambling, and I was too tired to comprehend anything he was saying.

"Mercedes. I couldn't..." He trailed off again and frowned deeper.

"You couldn't do *it*?" I asked him, and he looked at me with round, frightened eyes. "I don't see what's wrong with that?"

"No matter how much I tried to think about it, about *her*. It just wouldn't happen. I wasn't... able to..." His tone was quick, with tears still falling. I stuck my tongue out in disgust at the thought of Manny confessing to me he could not get a hard-on during his first time.

"I think that's normal the first time," I shrug. "Just try again another time—"

"It's not that! I just didn't want *her*!" he cried out. I shushed him and glanced at my cracked open door. He was going to wake up my parents down the hall.

"So, why did you come here and jump on *me*?" I asked him, folding my arms across my chest. It was late, after midnight, and I was only wearing my nightgown.

"I thought that maybe if I did it with you, someone I care about, then it'll happen," he explained in a voice laced with hope.

I shook my head in disbelief. "But *why* does it have to happen? Just wait until you're ready."

"No!" he cried out, and I glanced at my open door again. "You don't understand. If I can make it happen with Mercedes, or... or with you, then..."

"Then what?" I pressed him after he trailed off again.

"Then all of that stuff with Dillon... It won't mean anything," he finally whispered.

I sighed and sat forward as Manny came over to sit on the edge of my bed. "Look, I know you're embarrassed, but Dillon had no business making up stories about you. No matter how big of a crush he had on you, we all know you're not gay. He can't just walk up and try to kiss you like that." I tried to comfort him, but the entire time I spoke, he just kept shaking his head.

"We went on a date last month. We went on a lot of dates."

"Who?" I furrowed my brows and leaned forward to hear him better.

"Dillon and me," he sobbed.

"So then... You are gay?" It came out as a question, but I meant it as a statement. "Jesus, Manny, what the hell?"

"Please don't hate me, Bowie, I'm trying to fix it." He was pleading desperately, confusing me even more.

"Fix what? How?" I asked him, screwing up my face in confusion.

"If I have sex with you, then I won't be gay anymore, Bo!" he explained, and I think he meant it. That he genuinely believed it.

"I don't care if you're gay, Manny," I hissed at him, "But you just stood there while those guys beat up Dillon for telling the truth. Who cares if you're gay? You're a coward!"

"Bowie!" I heard Mark's voice at my door, and when we looked over, he was standing there in his robe and flannel pants with his arms crossed disapprovingly.

"I'm sorry, Mr. Monroe, we were just—" Manny stammered and stood to walk towards the window.

"Use the door, Manny," Mark scolded him, stepping out of the way and pointing into the hall.

As Manny passed, Mark grabbed him by his shoulders and embraced him. "It's okay to be yourself, son," he told him softly.

The next morning, Manny rushed through our front door, grinning happily and looking refreshed. A complete 180 from eight hours prior.

"I can't stay for long. I've got church with my parents in a few," he panted, leaning across from me and my bowl of apple cinnamon oatmeal on the kitchen island.

"I've got the greatest idea!" He was smiling so brightly, and I raised my brows expectantly, waiting for him to just spit it out.

"You'll pretend to be my girlfriend. Just until we graduate. That'll throw everyone off of my trail until I can move far away and start my new life," he quickly explained. I could tell he'd spent all eight hours of our separation last night conjuring it up.

"Funny, I thought your bright idea would be just to be yourself and be happy." I shrugged, scooping a spoonful of oatmeal into my mouth and eyeing him.

"C'mon Bo, you saw what they did to Dillon. I wouldn't stand a chance of making it through the next four years," he told me. The look in his eyes once again told me he believed that statement.

"Don't you feel bad about what happened to him?" I asked, pushing my oatmeal away. Geoff hated wasting food, but I suddenly wasn't that hungry anymore.

"Please, Bowie!" He clasped his hands together and shook them in front of his chin. "I need you, Bo."

"Why *me*? Ask Christina to do it!" Christina was way more outgoing than me. The type of girl that would make a believable girlfriend. I'd never even kissed a boy, so I certainly didn't know how to date one.

"Because you'll understand!" Manny yelled and motioned around to my home. "Look at your life, at your dads! If anyone can understand what I'm going through, it's you, Bo!"

"My dads aren't hiding who they are," I reminded him, picking up my bowl and dumping the cold oatmeal in the trash. "Mark was right, you know. It's okay to be yourself."

"This sounds like an intense conversation," Geoff commented, walking into the kitchen. I wondered how much Mark had told Geoff about the events that had occurred the previous night. We never kept things from each other. Well... except.

"Manny wants me to pretend to be his girlfriend so that people don't find out he's gay," I told my dad nonchalantly, folding my arms across my chest.

"A part of that agreement would be that you *didn't tell people about it,* Bowie!" Manny rolled his eyes and said in an exasperated tone.

Geoff made a *'pssht'* sound and brushed Manny's words off. "Kid, you spend every waking moment in this house. There are no secrets around here. You know that."

Manny sighed and dropped his head, and for a moment, I felt sorry for him. I wondered if it was this hard for Geoff when he came out. I'd heard bits and pieces of Mark's experiences to know that it wasn't the most pleasant transition. Transition, because before he'd met Geoff, Mark had dated women.

"That's just it," Manny whispered, staring at the marble countertop of the island. "When I first met you all, it made me feel better. I didn't feel like I was wrong for feeling the way I felt. I didn't feel like a sinner like our priest at church says about other... people like me."

Geoff snorted and went over to grab a glass from the cabinet for his orange juice. "Kid, that shirt you're wearing is more sinful than falling in love with someone who has the same hardware as you." I laughed, and Manny looked down at the checkered button-up he was wearing to church.

"As for this little plan you two are discussing," Geoff paused and took a sip of his orange juice and downed his daily vitamins with it. He pointed between the two of us and shook his head. "I'm totally against it. That's not fair to Bowie to tangle her up in your lies. And it's not healthy for you to hide who you are for the next four years."

Mark walked in just then, clad in his work uniform minus the hat. "I agree, but it's their decision. We agreed to stay out of it." He leaned in and kissed Mark goodbye, and then walked around and did the same for me. Then he wrapped Manny in a tight, fatherly hug and left.

The short version is that I agreed, but not before giving him a long lecture about loving yourself for who you were. Which was completely hypocritical of me. Geoff and Mark were against the arrangement. But they've always maintained a rule of not interfering with my social life and letting me make my own decisions and mistakes.

Besides, like summer camp and my mental diary, keeping Manny's secrets helps distract me from my own.

Chapter Eleven

I left Christina on a cliffhanger with my news about meeting Jonah. She'd tried to get me alone at lunch to hear the rest of it, but Manny wasn't having it. We had an image to uphold. People expected to see us together every step we took, holding hands, kissing, and seemingly in love. It's exhausting being someone's fake girlfriend. Especially a gay teenage boy who will stop at nothing to make sure everyone believes that he's straight.

"Okay, spill!" Christina tells me, flopping down on my bed after school. "I've been dying to hear about this special guy who has miraculously swept you off of your feet!"

We're at my house alone since Geoff is working at the hospital, and Mark is on a flight to Atlanta and then to Memphis.

"What makes you think he's special?" I muse, fighting a smile. Jonah is definitely special to me, but I don't want Christina to get carried away. Jonah's off-limits because of my arrangement with Manny.

"The fact that you brought him up." She smirks. "Now, talk!"

I take a seat next to her and crisscross my legs. "Okay, so his name is Jonah."

Christina pulls her cell phone out and starts typing like she's received a text message. "Last name?"

"Taylor," I tell her, "Why?"

"Keep going," she says instead. She flips her long braids over her shoulder and continues to type on her phone, and I wonder how much she's actually listening.

Christina is gorgeous. A warm, light brown skin tone and hazel-green eyes that remind me of a cat's eyes. She's slender, but curvy, with a round face and high cheekbones. But the most beautiful part of Christina is her unwavering confidence. She's not arrogant because of her physical appearance, but she's confident in who she is, and she loves herself.

"He's tall and really funny. I think he's pretty cute." I shrug because my description of Jonah doesn't do him justice. He's too much for words, if you ask me. "It's hard to describe him, but he's just..."

"Jonah Taylor-Richardson, maybe?" Christina interrupts me, brows scrunched.

"Umm, maybe." I shrug, confused. "He only gave me Taylor."

She turns her phone and shows me the profile picture of a guy's Facebook page that she's just searched.

It's Jonah!

I can't fight the smile when I see his face, smiling as he leans against his bright blue Camaro. "Yeah, that's him!"

"Look at your face! Oh my God, that's so cute!" she teases me and then turns the phone away from me and seems to scroll through Jonah's pictures. "Girl, he is *cute*!" She puts a hard emphasis on cute, so that it sounds more like *kay-yoot*. "Nice car too. Is that his car?"

"Yeah, it's nice. It's got this cool, all-black interior and lights on the inside. He drives like a pro," I tell her absently as I think back to the three times I'd ridden with Jonah in that car.

"Wait, you've been in his car?" She snaps her eyes up at me and grins wider, loving the details of my first male encounter. I nod and recount my summer with Jonah, leaving out the part where he kissed me because I want to keep that to myself.

"I can't believe this, Bowie!" she squeals, "You finally met someone you like! When do I get to meet him?"

I shrug and shake my head. "We didn't exactly make plans to meet again."

She frowns and sucks her teeth. "Did you at least exchange phone numbers?" I shake my head. "What? Why not, Bo? He was obviously interested!"

"Yeah, but what about Manny, Chris?" I remind her.

"What about me?" Manny asks, traipsing right into my room and taking a seat next to Christina on my bed.

"How did you get into my house?" I eye him suspiciously.

"I walked in with Geoff." He shrugs and looks down at Christina's phone. Snatching it out of her hand, he examines the screen and says, "Who is that? He's hot."

"That's Bowie's new boyfriend," Christina tells him in a taunting voice, and I shoot her a look that screams, *"Why!?"*

Manny gives me a confused look and tosses Christina's phone back to her. "Boyfriend?"

I shake my head. "We met at camp. I barely know him."

"Whatever, so today went well! Everyone seemed excited to see us together. We're definitely going to win Cutest Couple!" He rambles on, and Christina gives him a look of disgust before looking back at her chiming cell phone.

"And the Ainsley twins' party is coming up soon. So, you know we have to make an appearance," Manny continues, walking over to my closet and shuffling through my clothes. "Wear that pink dress that Geoff bought you last year for the Spring Fling. Remember the one you didn't wear because you said it was too short?"

I remember. The dress wasn't too short. I actually don't have a problem with wearing skimpy-ish clothing since I'm shorter than most girls, but Manny insisted I wore the pink dress so that he could wear the new pink button-down that he loved. He'd planned to blame the choice in color on me wanting him to match my dress if anyone questioned his sexuality. I'd tried to tell him that in the 21st century, wearing pink had become highly acceptable in men's fashion.

"Wow, he tells you how to dress, too?" Christina snorts, and I throw her a look that pleads with her to stop. Keeping the peace is what I'm all about, even if that means sacrificing my sanity. Refusing to wear the pink dress last spring was a rare moment of defiance for me. Usually, I give in to whatever Manny wants.

My friends stick around until it's close to dinnertime, and then Manny agrees to drop Christina off at her house on his way home.

"You know my password if you want to do some more snooping on Jonah's page," Christina tells me as I walk them to the front door. Manny's too preoccupied with his phone to comment. He's probably organizing a task list of all the things we need to do this school year to maintain our image as the perfect couple. That's what he does; he plans out our entire fake relationship with little feedback from me.

After dinner, I take Christina up on her offer and log onto Facebook using her profile. I've never been one for social media, much to Manny's despair, since he can't use Facebook and Instagram to boost our image further. Jonah's at the top of her recent search history. I click on the profile picture of him and his car and scroll through his photos and posts.

He's obviously a car fanatic, as there are pictures of him at race tracks and car shows. There are photos of him with his friends goofing around. He's also tagged in a lot of pictures, mostly with girls. He's pretty popular, I take it.

I zero in on one picture of him dressed up in a funny-looking costume. I'm not sure what he's supposed to be, and the date at the bottom isn't from Halloween. He's with a group of the same boys from the other pictures who are all dressed similarly. The next picture is one of him with a little girl on his back. They appear to be outside, at a park maybe. The camera is close to their face, and they're both cheesing hard.

I roll onto my side and continue to scroll through the pictures until I feel my eyelids grow heavy. He doesn't post a lot of statuses, mostly photos and funny memes.

He's one of the most exciting people I've met. Cute and funny and seems to be popular, but something tells me he's kind of a nerd too. He's about twenty things all in one lanky, curly-headed body. I envy his easy-going personality while being fascinated by it.

It must be nice to know yourself so well that you can easily *be yourself.*

Chapter Twelve

Falling back into my faux-relationship with Manny is always seamless after school starts again. It's easy, just kiss him a lot in public, talk about fake dates we went on, false arguments we had, and the pretend making-up that we do.

Manny keeps pressing for us to stage an epic event in which everyone knows that we've finally had sex, like going upstairs and making cheesy moaning sounds or allowing him to tell people that we have. It's not that people know that I'm a virgin; I'm sure they assume that Manny and I are doing it. But Manny thinks they need a little more proof that we are; which we're not, but again, they may or may not know that.

Confusing, right?

When we're not showing off in front of our peers, we're hanging out at my house by the pool or in my room. Christina always has somewhere to be after only a few hours of hanging out, and even though they never interact during school hours, it's usually to meet up with Chris Monte.

That leaves Manny and me alone to hang out, which usually results in more planning and one-sided brainstorming about the fake romance we share. It gets old, but it helps me from getting trapped in my thoughts. When my friends are happy, I'm happy. Or at least I think I am.

? ? ?

I'm watching one of those trashy reality shows on the TV when my cell phone rings. It's Christina.

"Hello?" I answer, glancing at the large clock on the wall of the living room. It's after 9 p.m., and Geoff and I have just finished eating dinner.

"Hey girl." Christina lets out a frustrated breath. It sounds like she's outside. "Are you busy?"

"Not really," I tell her without thinking about the answer. I mean, I *am* enjoying relaxing on the couch, and it is a school night. I'm never too busy for my friends, though.

"Think you could pick me up?" she asks. "I'd walk home, but I'll probably break curfew at this rate."

"Sure." I stand up from the couch and walk over to the door to retrieve my shoes. Geoff has a strict rule about removing your shoes at the door as soon as you enter the house. He even put a mudroom in the foyer to store shoes and coats upon entry.

"He went to Japan for two weeks twenty years ago, and suddenly we couldn't wear shoes in the house anymore," Mark commented, one time after Geoff chewed Christina out for walking into the living room with her sneakers on. We don't have carpet in the house, so I'm not sure what he's hoping to accomplish with this rule.

"I'll be there in ten minutes," I tell her because my house is that close to the mall where she works with Manny.

"I'm not at work," she tells me with a huff. "I was over at Chris' house."

"Oh." I pause, slightly confused. "Well, send me his address, and I'll pick you up." I wonder why Chris isn't giving her a ride home.

"Just pick me up at the CVS," she tells me. I hear the door chime as she walks into what I assume is the store.

I hang up the phone and jog upstairs to tell Geoff that I'm stepping out, holding my tennis shoes in my hand.

"Hey, I'm stepping out for a minute. Chris needs a ride home." I cringe inwardly when I call her Chris, because that's her new boyfriend's (or whatever he is) name, and it sounds weird. Geoff is relaxing on their California king-sized platform bed, clad in powder-blue satin pajamas.

He lowers the book that's masking his face and looks at me over his reading glasses. "I guess I'm supposed to say something parent-y like, *'You know it's a school night'.*"

I chuckle and roll my eyes playfully. "I'll be back before sunrise."

"Drive safely and don't do drugs," he calls out in a bored tone.

Christina is standing outside, leaning against the building of the CVS, when I arrive about ten minutes later. She's tapping her foot impatiently, and she looks pissed.

"Hey, sorry you were waiting," I apologize.

She waves off my comment as if to say that it's not me she's pissed at. "Thanks for coming to pick me up, Bo. Manny was at work, and I couldn't call my mom. She'd kill me."

"Where's Chris?" I ask her as I pull away from the parking lot and turn towards her house. Christina lives with her mother, older sister, and nephew. Their neighborhood is a few miles away from the more affluent area where I live.

Christina grunts and jabs her thumb behind us towards the neighborhood behind the store. "He's at home."

"You guys have a fight or something?"

"Yeah, after he got what he wanted, he was done with me for the rest of the day. He kicked me out when his parents came home. Didn't even bother to offer me a ride." She doesn't sound sad, as much as angry.

"Ouch. What a douche." I grimace. "I guess you're done with him?" When she doesn't answer, I look over at her, and she shrugs. She's looking out the window with her arms crossed.

"Or not..." I draw out in disbelief.

"No offense Bo, but I refuse to take relationship advice from someone who's never even liked a guy, let alone had an actual boyfriend." Christina huffs.

"Well, from the looks of it, you're not really in a relationship either," I shoot back nonchalantly.

"I mean, you have this incredibly cute guy who you like." She ignores my statement and throws her hands in the air in frustration. Now I think it's towards me. "And you didn't even give him your phone number! You haven't even mentioned him in weeks. And I know you really liked him. You've never met a guy worth mentioning."

She's right, to an extent. I haven't spoken a word about Jonah since the first day of school, and here we are almost a month later, and I've not even said his name out loud again. But that doesn't mean I haven't been thinking about him or stalking his Facebook and Instagram frequently. I figured out that his profile is private, that's why I can only see pictures and not any statuses. I scrolled down far enough to see that on January 21st, one hundred and thirty-six people wished him a happy birthday. And that last summer he went to some tropical island.

"What's the point? Can't have a boyfriend when you already have a boyfriend," I tell her with a shrug.

I hear her suck her teeth, but she doesn't respond. Christina has expressed multiple times to both Manny and me that she's against the plan. She says it's not fair to me. I tell her it's okay; that I don't mind helping Manny out. If I can't date now, there's always college. High school boys are too much trouble. Case and point our current situation, in which I'm giving my best friend a ride home because the guy she's having sex with kicked her out of his house with nowhere to go.

Of course, I keep that last part to myself.

"Jonah was a moment," I tell her after a few seconds of silence. "An experience. He lives like an hour and a half away, and if he wanted to stay in touch with me after camp ended, he would have asked for my number."

I park in front of her house and turn towards her, waiting for her to say something to me finally.

"I love you to death, Bo, but you seriously need to get a life outside of this *thing* that you've got going with Manny. You're just enabling him," she tells me before hugging me and then climbing out of the car. "Thanks for the ride, girl. I'll see you tomorrow."

I wait for her to go inside before I pull off, all the while considering her words.

My whole life revolves around helping Manny keep his secret, hanging out with Christina, listening to Geoff bitch about Mark, and our occasional family movie nights when Mark is home. The summer camp is really the only thing that's *mine*. But what's wrong with all of that? Who said having a boyfriend was so important?

I try to shake the thoughts out of my head. It's not that I'm angry with Christina. I just don't understand her logic. I put myself in her shoes, and imagine what it would be like to like a guy so much that he could be disrespectful to me, make it blatantly known that he only wants sex with me; yet, still, I want to be with him.

I like Jonah. I like him a lot. But if by some strange happenstance we got back in touch with each other, and by some miracle dated, would I deal with him being mean or insensitive to me? Dating has never been a big deal for me, so it doesn't bother me. I've dedicated my high school years to being Manny's fake girlfriend when I could instead waste my time with a potential flop.

By the time I make it home, I've got a headache from overthinking, and I know it's only a matter of time before I'm stressing over my supposed mundane life again. I don't want to be alone in my thoughts tonight, so I change into my pajamas and crawl into bed with Geoff.

He's still reading his book, but I notice he glances over at me as I curl up beside him and close my eyes. I feel him kiss me on my forehead before laying his book down and switching off the light.

Chapter Thirteen

Every year Tyler and Trevor Ainsley's parents go on a cruise for the Labor Day weekend, leaving the twins alone in their giant house to throw the biggest party of the year.

"You've got the nicest car so you're driving, Bo. Plus, you don't drink, and we'll need a DD," Manny tells me. He's looking himself over in the mirror, doing some last-minute primping.

If any of our classmates were to spend time with him outside of school, here at my house where he's always his truest self, they'd know for sure he was gay. This is the Manny I love the most, the one that takes so long to get dressed for any kind of event, be it a party or a trip to the mall, that you want to strangle him. When we're alone and he's comfortable, Manny drops the facade.

"Aren't you going to style your hair a little differently?" He turns up his nose at me and eyes my cropped hair that is tossed around in its usual style. "You know? For the occasion?"

"No, I'm not." I don't even bother entertaining his request. My hair is the darkest shade of black. I keep it cut short, framing my face in layers that stop just above my chin and the nape of my neck. No part, because I spend a lot of time running my fingers through it when I'm anxious. A bad habit, according to Geoff and Christina.

Manny rolls his eyes and goes back to shaping his pompadour. Christina laughs but doesn't look up from her text conversation.

"Just a heads up, Bo; when you actually start dating for real, you might want to dress to impress a little more," Manny throws out bitterly.

"I'm wearing the stupid dress like you asked," I shoot back in an exasperated tone. I'd rather be at home tonight, not at a party where I'm going to be the only sober teenager. Mark left yesterday, and we're not expecting him back until Tuesday night. That leaves Geoff here all alone. He's okay with it, but I'd choose movie night over this party any day.

"I'll be sure to find a guy who likes me for me," I add, even though I barely like me for me.

"Like Jonah," Christina pipes up in a childish tone. I throw her an evil eye and shake my head.

Manny snorts, "I forgot all about that."

"What's that supposed to mean?" I'm defensive, though I'm not sure why.

"Exactly what I said," he responds nonchalantly. "Okay, so maybe we could make it totally obvious that we're going upstairs to the bedroom, sit there for like an hour, and then come down with your hair all messed up. I mean, especially since you're not curling it or anything," he suggests, looking me over again with disapproval.

"I already told you *no*, Manny." I cross my arms and flop down on my bed. "Besides, you strike me as more of a minute man anyway," I add the last part with a smirk.

"Damn!" Christina eggs on from her place on the window sill. "Burn!"

"Shut up, Chris," Manny mumbles.

"Everyone already believes you're straight, Manny. Why do we need to change anything?" I ask him. He steps away from the mirror and gives me a look that's dripping in attitude.

"Let's go," he demands, storming out of my room without answering my question.

Christina chuckles again and walks over and links her arm with mine. "Our little diva." I nod and laugh with her, letting her lead the way out of my room and downstairs.

"You kiddies have fun! Don't do drugs!" Geoff calls out to us as we stop at the front door to put on our shoes. After a back-and-forth battle with Manny, I relented and wore four-inch pumps, even though I hate walking in heels for any prolonged amount of time.

The Ainsley party is in full effect when we arrive. I have to park down the street because the driveway and curbs in front of the house are all taken. Right before we start our trek across the lawn, Manny wraps his arms around my shoulder and pulls me into him. He's in boyfriend mode. It's amazing how we're able to turn it on and off.

When we enter the house the music is blaring. I wonder how the twins have done this every year since ninth grade without getting the cops called on them by the neighbors. Manny and I debuted our fake relationship at this same party three years ago. It was a smaller crowd back then, but now there are over sixty teenagers in the mini-mansion that the Ainsley family calls home. We never get too rowdy, but it's certainly not quiet, and a fool could tell that underage drinking is happening tonight.

Red cups are pushed into our hands as soon as we walk into the kitchen, and I politely place mine back on the table. I don't enjoy being drunk, not after I drank tequila in tenth grade, and ended up throwing up and crying all over Mrs. Ainsley's marble bathroom floor.

"We didn't think you guys were ever going to make it," Bryson says as we enter the living room. People are dancing on the makeshift dance floor, which they created by pushing the furniture against the walls. We're standing off to the side in the space that connects the kitchen to the living room, near the patio door.

"You know how girls are." Manny jabs a finger toward Christina and me. "They take forever to get dressed." That's a lie, considering Christina and I had finished dressing forty-five minutes before he finally finished styling his hair.

Bryson gives me a once-over. "Well, it was definitely worth it," he comments, taking a swig out of a glass beer bottle.

Christina punches him in the arm. "What about me? I spent hours at the mall looking for this outfit!" She twirls around slowly to model the fitted jeans and crop top she's wearing.

"Beautiful as always," Bryson replies, but he says it in a playful tone that earns another fist from Christina.

Manny pulls me in closer, placing a hand on my lower back and kissing me softly, "I think Bryson just hit on you," he whispers, but he says it teasingly, and I try not to laugh. The holding and kissing are all for show so that people can think we're speaking sweet nothings to each other. When, in reality, we're cracking jokes like the best friends that we are.

"Only because he thinks I'm your girlfriend. Guys have this weird fascination with stealing girls from each other," I reply with a smile.

Chris Monte walks by and makes eye contact with Christina. She all but teleports away with him, and Bryson walks away to socialize some more, leaving Manny and me to finish our conversation with a little more privacy. Well, as much privacy as you can have in a crowded house. Manny takes another swig of his red cup and positions himself behind me, pulling me close again and whispering in my ear.

"I've got another date with that guy who goes to OU tomorrow," he tells me excitedly, placing his hands on my hips and swaying back and forth with my body. He's so good at this whole sensual-touching thing. He's studied it so much that he's perfected it so that we never get called out for faking. I don't discredit our classmates' sanity for believing our façade. From the outside looking in, we appear to be in love.

"Does he know you're in the closet?" I ask him with a smirk. He pinches my side, and I squirm.

"I told him my family is very religious, so I'm private about my sexuality," he tells me in a snarky voice before taking another sip.

"AKA, *in the closet*." I look up at him and roll my eyes. He leans in and kisses me again, and I want to puke at the taste of passionfruit vodka on his lips.

Manny downs two more cups of vodka and fruit punch and goes from romantic and almost sexy to obnoxious and belligerent. Kayla McMurray has always made it her goal to get with Manny behind my back and is now on the dancefloor grinding on him. If only she knew she was barking up the wrong tree.

I take a seat on one of the leather sofas against the wall. Victoria Lovelace, the alternative Black girl who scored her dream job at Hot Topic this summer, is occupying the opposite end. She looks skeptically between Kayla and me.

This is the part where I'm supposed to play along and look angry or jealous that another girl is all over my boyfriend. I throw Kayla and Manny a pout and then pull out my phone to occupy my time. I'm reading a new book that I'm dying to finish, so I pull up my e-reader app.

I'm only reading for about five minutes when a text message appears.

> **580.555.1205:** Hey Freckles, I hope this wasn't some sort of prank and this is really your number.

I furrow my brow, and my heart beats faster. Five-eight-zero is an Oklahoma area code, but not in the city. Rhonda's camp has a 580-area code, and the person texting called me *Freckles*. No way is my luck this good.

> **Bowie:** Umm… who is this?

> **580.555.1205:** Jonah.

I'm caught in a vortex, and the surrounding music seems to slur and slow down. But my heart? My heart flutters and my head fills with air as I float away. It's Jonah. Jonah is texting me!

Bowie: How did you get my number?

580.555.1205: A little birdie. Though I'm still skeptical that this is really Bowie.

Bowie: You texted me, but you're the one that's skeptical?

580.555.1205: Touché.

I'm just about to respond with a clue to tell him I am indeed Bowie when my phone alerts me that the mystery number is trying to FaceTime me.

I quickly shuffle through my purse for my AirPods before answering the video call. It's dim and loud in the living room that I'm in, but I can see him clear as day. He's smiling brightly, as if happy to see that it's me. He's lying on his back, propped up on the armrest of a couch, I think.

"So, it really is you," he says as his grin widens. I smile shyly and nod.

"How did you get my number?" I ask again, and he scrunches his face and brings his phone closer to his ear to hear me better.

When he pulls back, he smirks a little and asks me, "Are you at a party or something? I can't really hear you."

Nodding, I put my index finger up, signaling for him to wait while I stand up and weave through the crowd of dancing teenagers toward the back door. I run into one of the twins and lean in to talk in his ear. "Hey Trevor, if you see Christina or Manny, tell them I stepped out."

Trevor shakes his head and laughs at me, "Four years later, and you *still* can't tell us apart, Bo? I'm Tyler."

I laugh with him and then continue out the sliding door into the warmth outside. There are a few people walking around the pool and making out on the patio furniture, but mostly, it's quiet. Mrs. Ainsley has a huge maze-like garden to the right of the pool that has stone benches in the center. I like to come out here sometimes and hide from the party-goers when I've had enough of their drunken antics.

"Okay," I breathe out, taking a seat on the cement bench and giving Jonah my full attention. "Better?"

"Much," he replies, relaxing back again. "I didn't pin you for a party girl."

"I'm not. I'm just here with my friends."

"So, how's life post-Rhonda?" he jokes, and I can't help but laugh.

"It's been pretty boring, actually," I reply, still laughing. He looks so handsome relaxing with his arm bent behind his head and his other hand holding his phone above him.

"I've missed your face, Freckles," he tells me suddenly, and I can't fight the blush that I'm sure he can't see. I hope he can't see it. I'm not sure how to respond, so I turn my face away and bite my lip so that I don't release the giddy smile that's threatening my face.

"Aww, you can't take a compliment? That's so cute," he teases, and I shake my head.

"How did you get my number?" I ask again. Same answer.

"I told you, a birdie."

I scoff and shake my head again. "A birdie named Christina Harris."

"I'm sworn to secrecy." He makes a zipper motion with his lips, followed by a key turning in a lock and then being thrown away.

"I hope I'm not interrupting your fun. I was just laying here watching TV and finally mustered up the courage to text you," he says in a genuine tone.

He was nervous about texting *me*?

"No, it's fine," I assure him, running my hand through my hair and pulling it to one side. It slowly, piece by piece, falls back to the other side, so I do it again. "I'm not big on drinking, and everyone is pretty hammered. I'm just the designated driver." It's partly a lie, but I don't even think about it.

"Everyone around here went to the lake, but my little sister isn't feeling well, so I stay home with her while my mom works," he replies. The camera shifts around a lot as he switches positions and is now lying on his side.

"That's really sweet," I smile at him. I'm leaning forward with my elbows resting on my knees, but when I look at myself in my little forward-facing thumbnail screen, my cleavage is on full display. I quickly straighten up and put the camera directly in front of my face.

"Oh no, please do that again," Jonah says suggestively, but the playful tone behind it tells me I shouldn't take offense.

"I almost had you pegged for a pervert after that round of twister," I chuckle. "I guess I was right."

He shakes his head and denies my accusations, and I'm momentarily mesmerized by his dark curls and dimples. His dark-brown eyes seem brighter as he talks about school and hanging out with his friends. I have little to contribute to the subjects, but I'm enjoying just listening to him talk. I like how he doesn't mind taking over the conversation. He's just talking to me so casually. It's like he really wants to talk to *me*.

He's in the middle of telling me about the restaurant his grandparents own when my phone alerts me it's about to lose power. I check the clock and find that we've been talking for over an hour.

"Good thing that birdie gave you my phone number." I smirk at him on the dimming screen of my phone. "If you hadn't texted me, I'd still be sitting on the couch reading and trying to avoid having liquor spilled on me."

"Is that an invitation to call and text you again?" he asks me with an equally flirtatious smile. Except for Manny, I've got almost zero experience in flirting with guys. Yet, for some reason, everything comes so easily to me with Jonah.

I smile at him and nod shyly. "Definitely."

Chapter Fourteen

On the last Sunday of every month, Geoff and I attend church with Christina and her mother. We used to attend a different church when I was younger until a deacon made a spectacle of our non-traditional family in front of the entire congregation.

He told my parents that, *"Even though God may frown upon their lifestyle, it was very noble of them to care for me as their own."*

AKA: *"You're going to Hell, but maybe adopting an abandoned orphan will soften the blow."*

My parents were mortified, and I was confused. We weren't faithful Catholics by any stretch, only choosing that church because Mark had been raised in a similar church. We aren't even religious, but Geoff liked the idea of giving me the option to explore organized religion. I studied enough to know that God supposedly frowned upon all sins. So why was homosexuality such a colossal crime against humanity? Needless to say, we left in the middle of mass and never went back there.

Christina's mother, Ms. Shonda, invited us to attend church with them a month later, after a gossip session with Geoff divulging the homophobia that was spewing out of our previous place of worship. Ms. Shonda's church was massive. Made up of a predominantly black congregation, and a lot of friendly faces and powerful sermons, according to Geoff.

"Black folks can be just as judgmental, but at least they're quiet about it in church," Christina's mother joked. We've gone every fourth Sunday ever since. After church, we all meet at the Hunan Wok for lunch, a tradition that's been going on for years now, and one that Mark usually misses due to work.

"I've never known you to be the type of girl that's glued to your phone, Bowie," Ms. Shonda teases as we sit around the table with plates piled high with Chinese cuisine. "And look at that smile. Must be talking to someone special," she adds with a wink. I blush and place my phone on my lap just as it vibrates.

"Mmm hmm…" Geoff hums while blowing on a spoonful of Egg Drop Soup. "She's been like that for a month. She's met some boy, I bet."

Beside me, Christina makes a *'hmph'* sound, and I swiftly kick her under the table. I haven't mentioned Jonah to Mark and Geoff, not because I'm afraid they'll care, but because I want to see how far this is going before I bring him into my personal life. The minute I tell my dads about Jonah, I know they'll want to meet him.

Ever since the Ainsley party, Jonah and I have talked every day. Mostly through text messaging, but we've had a few FaceTime sessions, and we talk on the phone maybe once a week. He's told me almost everything about him, like how he lives with his mom and little sister, Mia. His grandparents are from the Caribbean, Sint Maarten, but have recently moved to Davis so they can help Jonah's mom with Mia after Jonah leaves for college. He hasn't mentioned his dad, but he told me he was changing his last name from Richardson to Taylor, which is his mother's maiden name. He wants to attend Oklahoma State University in the fall and major in mechanical or automotive engineering. Of course, he wants to work on cars. We were on FaceTime during that conversation, and I could see the excitement on his face when I told him I also planned to attend OSU. The stars seem to align, and everything so far is telling me that *this*, whatever it is between Jonah and me, is right.

"I bet you're right." Ms. Shonda smirked. "Christina's been lovesick over that basketball star at their school. I'll tell you like I tell her, Bo, be careful with those boys. Don't want to end up like Destiny over here. Pregnant before you even get a chance to live life." Christina's older sister sucks her teeth and wipes sweet and sour sauce away from her kid's mouth. She's two years older than us, and when she was sixteen, she had her son. The father split, leaving Ms. Shonda to help raise the baby.

"Don't get me wrong." Ms. Shonda raises a finger to signify that she's not finished and will continue once she's done chewing her lo mien. "I love my baby, and I love my grandson. But I wanted more for her, and I want more for you two." She points her fork at Christina and me. "Be smart."

Geoff nods in agreement. He and Ms. Shonda have a best friend bond, even though they only see each other consistently once a month. I want to tell them they don't have to worry about me getting pregnant. Unlike Christina, my crush lives almost an hour away, and we haven't even remotely hinted at seeing each other in person again.

After Christina found out about our FaceTime during the party, she immediately requested Jonah's friendship on Facebook and followed him on Instagram. He accepted. Now I'm able to sneak on his profiles and see so much more than before. Now I can put faces to the names whenever he tells me he's hanging out with his friends.

"Bowie's always pretty honest with us, but she's so reserved at the same time," Geoff comments. "She gets that from Mark's side."

I scoff and side-eye him. "I'm adopted. I don't share any DNA with Mark."

Geoff cuts his eyes at me and groans. "She gets that backtalk from him, too."

Everyone at the table laughs, and I shake my head. There's always been a silent war between Mark and Geoff. Well, actually, Geoff is in a silent war with Mark. Mark is pretty oblivious to it.

All the things Jonah and I have talked about so far have been pretty innocent. We talk about our schools, and he talks about cars and the restaurant his grandparents own where he works after school. But mostly we play these silly *"would you rather"* games. I guess they're our version of icebreakers.

Ms. Shonda asks Geoff about his work at the hospital just as my phone vibrates again.

> **Jonah:** Invisibility or Super
> Speed?

> **Bowie:** Super Speed.

That way, I can run from all of my problems.

Chapter Fifteen

I'm lounging in the living room on our sectional watching a boring documentary on the Alaskan wilderness when Geoff calls out to me. Not that I'm not interested in Alaska; it's actually on my bucket list of places I want to visit before I die. But I'm still waiting for Jonah to respond to my text. `Would you rather spend twelve months in the Alaskan tundra, or one hour on a nature walk with Travis, Ethan, and Paisley?` I sent it to him thirty minutes ago. We've been having a pretty steady conversation all afternoon, and now he's just gone silent on me.

"Bowie? Why is there a boyishly handsome young man in an electric-blue Camaro walking up to our door?" Geoff calls out from the kitchen. The glass front door and giant windows across from the kitchen provide a view of the open atrium walkway and circular driveway in front of the house.

I gasp when the doorbell sounds. Geoff looks over at me and narrows his eyes mischievously. "Is that *him*?"

I nod in response with a pitiful smile. Geoff makes a beeline to answer the door, and I pad across the room to hide behind the wall that separates the living room from the foyer. Geoff swings the door open swiftly, and I hear him dramatically dig into Jonah.

"Do you drink? Do you do drugs? And do you intend on impregnating my teenage daughter?" Geoff rattles off quickly. I can imagine him standing there with his arms crossed and his hip slightly jutted to the side, leering at Jonah. He can be quite the drama queen sometimes, and I love it!

Jonah, however, doesn't miss a beat.

"Not when I'm driving. Only socially. And probably not today," he answers Geoff's questions in their exact order. I can't fight the giggle that escapes.

"Hi, I'm Jonah." And I'm pretty sure he has extended his hands out for a shake.

"Hmm... You've passed the test, Jonah. Come inside. I'm Dr. Geoff Denton-Monroe. Bowie's father." Geoff steps aside and allows Jonah to enter the house. "Shoes off and in the cubby," he adds.

While Jonah is sitting on the cubby's bench kicking off the Nike tennis shoes he's wearing, I decide to make my presence known. I walk around the corner and lean against the wall opposite of the mudroom.

When he looks up at me, I can't tell if he is smirking or suppressing a smile. He looks gorgeous in a pair of loose-fitting gray sweatpants and a black compression shirt. His hair is pulled into a bun, showing off the tapered sides that the curls had hidden all summer.

"I'd definitely take that Alaskan Tundra over anything that has to do with Travis and hiking." His mouth has now formed into a smug grin.

"Did you know that in Alaska it's illegal to whisper in someone's ear while they're moose hunting?" I ask him, crossing my arms across my chest. Now my expression is one of a suppressed smile.

"Bummer," he chuckles and stands up.

Geoff makes a *'tsk'* sound and shakes his head. "She finally brings home a guy, and he's as strange as she is," he groans and throws his hands up, walking away. Jonah laughs, and those damn dimples nearly melt me!

"In my defense, I didn't *bring him home.* He just showed up unannounced," I call out to Geoff's retreating form. I chuckle again, and Jonah does the same. "Let me guess. Christina gave you my address."

Jonah nods. "I didn't even ask. She just sent it in a message."

"So, you just randomly decided to visit me?" I ask him skeptically.

"Well, actually, I was in town running an errand for my mom, so I figured now would be a great time to visit," he tells me, sheepishly. "I hope that's okay?"

"No!" I shake my head frantically. "I mean, yes! I mean—" I pause and take a minute to collect myself. He's here in front of me and so far I've been able to keep my composure, but inside I'm combusting.

"I mean, no, I'm not upset that you popped up. Yes, it's okay you're here." We're stuck in an awkward vortex of silence.

"Bowie, maybe invite him a little further into the house?" Geoff calls from the kitchen where he's finishing dinner preparations.

"Umm, yeah, I can show you around if you want?" I tell him, running my hands through my hair.

"Jonah, I insist you stay for dinner." It's more of a demand than an offer coming from Geoff.

"Oh, I don't want to intrude." Jonah holds his hands out in protest. "It's bad enough I just showed up unannounced."

"I won't take *no* for an answer, Jonah. Call your parents and let them know you'll be eating dinner with us." See, I told you! *Demanding Geoff.*

Jonah laughs and nods his head in agreement. Or maybe surrender.

"Bowie, give Jonah the grand tour. Dinner will be ready in an hour. Why, we're even expecting a special dinner guest!" Geoff states in mock excitement. "Mark is supposed to be home tonight."

I laugh and shake my head at him, motioning for Jonah to follow me out the back door.

I give Jonah a brief tour of the backyard, showing him the swimming pool, pool house, and the small stone garden seating area, that Geoff had the landscapers create last year. The late October air is chilly, so we don't stay out long.

After giving Jonah my best impression of a grand tour, we go into the kitchen to help set the table. I keep sneaking peeks at him, and each time I'm met with his dark brown eyes. He's stealing glances at me, too. The little flutters in my belly that I usually get every time he texts me have intensified now that he's standing in my presence. I ask him how he managed to get away on a Saturday. On Saturdays, he's usually working at the restaurant that his grandparents own in his hometown.

"I told you, I had official mom errands to run." He winks and passes out the forks and knives on each placemat. I would assume most families in the 21st century just grab plates from the cabinet and serve food from the pots and pans on the stove before sitting down at the table. Geoff, however, still finds it necessary for everyone to be seated around the table while he serves the entrée and sides.

I feel a vibration against my wrist, and when I check my watch, I see that it's Manny calling me. I ignore the call, not wanting anything to ruin this moment with Jonah here in my home. Knowing Manny, he was calling with some scheme to get me out of the house tonight to play pretend. As soon as the vibration stops, a text message comes through.

> **Manny:** Everyone's meeting at Harkins tonight to see that new scary movie. Pick me up at 8. We're going to Fridays after.

I look over at Jonah, but he's preoccupied with talking to Geoff about tonight's dinner, so I take a moment to sneak into the living room to retrieve my phone.

> **Bowie:** Can't. Plans with my dads tonight since Mark's home. I'm sorry!

> **Manny:** What do you mean "can't"? I can't show up alone! Everyone is

bringing a date! Even the Chrises
are coming together.

Manny: Eww, the "Chrises" Gross
right?

Manny: Bowie, you HAVE to come.

I sigh and groan. Why can't he just take no for an answer? Usually, I'd jump at his every request, except for a few extreme ones, but not today. Not while I finally have Jonah here, face to face after almost two months of texting each other. He's *here*, in the kitchen chatting with my dad, and preparing to eat dinner with us!

Bowie: Sorry, Manny, I can't. We
rarely get time with Mark. You
know that. And yes, I despise
calling them the Chrises too!

Manny: Fine! I'll just tell everyone we're doing our own thing!
That's still believable.

I want to ask him why he thinks it's necessary to divulge every detail about our *"relationship"* to everyone. I want to explain to him that normal couples keep some things private. That telling everyone every aspect of our fake life together actually makes it *less* believable. As if he's overcompensating for something. Instead, I decide not to reply. Just as I'm about to place my phone on the ottoman, it vibrates again.

> **Christina:** Whaaat? Let me find out you're taking a stand against Manny!

She and Manny both work part-time jobs at the mall; Manny in a sandwich shop in the food court, and Christina at JCPenney. I'm sure they're carpooling home from work together, and he's bitching to her about our text exchange now. I just pray they don't decide to drop by and attempt to convince me to go.

> **Bowie:** Jonah's here. I'd rather hang out with him. DON'T TELL MANNY!

> **Christina:** OMG! You're kidding! Do ya thang, girl! But I want the details on Monday! And of course, I won't tell Senor Grumpy Pants!

I laugh at Christina's nickname for Manny and text back a *thank you.* I'm not sure what details I'll have for her on Monday, but I'm hoping the rest of this evening is eventful enough.

"Hey, Geoff wants us to start dinner. Something about Mark being perpetually late and a no-show." I jump slightly at the sound of Jonah's voice.

I chuckle and shake my head. "Sorry, Geoff can be a little... much," I tell him, tossing my phone down on the ottoman and facing him. He's smiling at me, the same smile I keep giving him.

I'm not sure what to say to him. Am I supposed to tell him I think he looks incredibly handsome standing there in the space between my living room and kitchen? That seeing his smooth, full lips again reminds me of the kiss we shared months ago at the lake. That I want to kiss him again, badly.

I've never had thoughts like this. Besides movie stars and other famous people, I've never swooned over a guy. Jonah has evoked thoughts and feelings inside me I've never felt before. Hormones, maybe? It's got to be hormones.

We take our seats at the table. Jonah and I sit next to each other, and Geoff sits across from me, leaving Mark to sit across from Jonah whenever he arrives.

"I'm sure you kids are starving. We can eat without him!" Geoff huffs, and I know he's just putting on a show for Jonah. He wants Mark here, just as bad as I do. Geoff misses Mark whenever he's away, and he'll never admit it, but he worries about him too. There's always been an unbreakable rule that Mark has to text us every time he takes off and lands his plane.

"We can wait, Dad. It's fine," I protest with a laugh, and Jonah nods his agreement.

"I'm fine with waiting." He shrugs.

Before Geoff can make his rebuttal, we hear the locks clicking on the front door.

"Geoff, I know we discussed the number of miles Bowie was putting on the Acura, but did we really need to buy her a brand-new car *today*?" Mark jokes.

"That's *Jonah's* car," Geoff says in a suggestive voice, and I groan and run my hands over my face. Cheeky-Geoff is not who Jonah needs to experience for his first Monroe family dinner. "Get in here, you're late!"

"Jonah, huh?" Mark calls out in his native New Orleans drawl, and I assume he's removing his shoes at the cubby. "Who is *Jonah*?" He appears in the dining room and takes in the scene. He looks exhausted, but still the ageless, handsome man I've known my entire life.

"*This* is Jonah," Geoff motions to Jonah with a flick of his wrist. "The reason Bowie is glued to her phone lately."

"Seriously, Dad?" I whimper desperately. "We're really doing *this*?"

Mark chuckles and loosens his tie. He murmurs an apology and then bends down to kiss Geoff on the lips.

It's the moment of truth. I haven't told Jonah anything about my family, especially not about my two dads. I'm not ashamed by any means. It's just something I wanted to tell him in a setting where I could gauge his reaction. I wanted to see if he was really as amazing of a guy as he seemed to be, or if he'd be an ignorant, homophobic douchebag at the discovery of my same-sex parents.

But when I look at him, he's watching my gay dads peck each other on the lips, wearing only a small grin that I can tell is from finding amusement in Geoff's banter.

"Go change, so we can eat and finally get the chance to embarrass our daughter! This is so exciting!" Geoff says in a giddier tone now, clapping his hands obnoxiously.

Mark leans across the table and extends his hand out to Jonah. "Mark Monroe, Bowie's father."

"Nice to meet you, I'm Jonah Taylor." Jonah shakes my dad's hand.

By the time Mark returns, freshly changed out of his uniform, Geoff is serving everyone dinner.

"I hope you like parmesan-crusted tilapia, Jonah," Geoff sings out as he places a fillet over the bed of brown rice he's already placed on the plate in front of Jonah.

"It smells delicious!" Jonah grins.

"So, where did you two meet?" Mark asks us, and I fill the next couple of minutes recounting the now hilarious antics of my first nature walk as a senior counselor.

"Wait, you're telling me you convinced our *Bowie Phoenix Monroe* to break the rules and sneak away from camp?" Geoff drops his fork on his plate and looks at Jonah sternly.

"Umm... yes sir, but it was all in innocent fun. The mess hall food was really terrible," Jonah replies nervously as if he thinks he's in trouble with my parents.

Geoff looks over at Mark and winks. "I like this kid." Mark only shakes his head and Geoff continues, "Bowie never breaks the rules! She's made parenting so boring. Did you know she actually *told* me when she was going to ditch class with her friends to go to the fair?"

"I don't see the issue here," Mark protests, scrunching his brows in concern. Desperate to change the subject from recent acts of defiance, he asks Jonah about his family.

"Well, my mom is a real estate agent, and my grandparents recently moved here from Sint Maarten and opened an authentic Caribbean restaurant in Davis. That's where I work after school usually," Jonah explains while shoving his mouth with baked fish and brown rice.

"Hmm... so you can cook a Caribbean dish?" Geoff asks suggestively. "I think we should have you cook for the next dinner."

Did Geoff really just invite Jonah to dinner again? I try to read my fathers' faces, and I see it there. They like Jonah! I mean, I'm not surprised; he's funny and personable. I'm just curious to know if they really like Jonah for *Jonah*, or if they're just excited to see me partaking in normal teenage behavior. Something that has nothing to do with covering for Manny's being gay.

After dinner, Jonah offers to help me do the dishes, something that impresses Geoff and Mark even more.

"I don't really do much of the cooking at the restaurant, just serving and dishes," Jonah whispers as I pass him the dry towel. I laugh and start scrubbing the dinner plates.

We're just finishing up when Mark and Geoff come downstairs, bickering in hushed voices.

"This is a terrible idea!" Mark whispers frantically, "We just met this boy!"

Geoff shushes him and throws us a phony smile, and I instantly know he's up to something. They're both wearing their coats, making it clear they're leaving.

"Where are you going?" I ask them both in a mix of confusion and mortification because I think I know what's happening and I'm not sure I'm ready for it. While I've been silently dreading the moment that Jonah announces he needs to head home, a part of me knows I'm not ready to be alone with him.

"Oh, we're just going to catch a movie. We were planning on inviting you, but you've got company so..." Geoff trails off and gives me this look that I'm sure you're only supposed to give your girlfriends when setting them up on a blind date. Not when you're leaving your teenage daughter alone in the house with a boy you all barely know.

"I can leave if you want to go to the movies with them, Bo," Jonah offers sincerely, walking up to stand tall next to me.

"No, you kids enjoy yourselves." Geoff waves his hand lazily, and I hear Mark groan beside him, earning an elbow from his husband.

"Oh okay, I guess I'm supposed to say something fatherly like, *'Stay on opposite sides of the room,'*" Geoff waves goodbye and retreats.

Mark stops and regards both of us seriously. "Jonah, it would be respectable for you to be leaving by ten o'clock."

Jonah nods vigorously and waves goodbye, and then we're alone and the walls of my spacious house seem to close in on us as if fate is literally trying to bring us closer. This night can go one of two ways: it can be the greatest night ever, or I could screw it up by saying or doing something embarrassing.

Life was so much easier when I didn't care much about the opposite sex.

Chapter Sixteen

In the spirit of making sure that everything about this night is as awkward as possible, I suggest we go upstairs to my bedroom. Call it a test maybe?

I lead him up the staircase to the second level of the house and into my bedroom. My heart is pounding so loud that I can barely hear him commenting on the collection of photos that Geoff has hanging on the staircase wall. Pictures of me aging from newborn and up, with a space at the top where my eighteenth birthday photo will go.

He looks around my room, seeming interested in the photos of my friends and parents, and the wall made entirely of bookshelves that Mark built for me when I was twelve.

"*Bridge to Terabithia*? I loved this book in middle school." He grins, fingering the worn spine of the paperback. "And *A Wrinkle in Time*!" He smiles at me and I blush.

"I'm a reader. Nothing special," I shrug. I'm sitting on my bed with my back against the headboard, fidgeting with the frays on my patchwork quilt. It was a gift from Carrie when I was a little girl.

"Yeah Freckles, but you have books on your bookshelf that they forced us to read in school," he chuckles. He pulls my copy of *A*

Clockwork Orange from its place among the more mature selections on my shelf.

"Do you like to read?" I ask him. I can feel myself relaxing, even though the sun is almost completely setting outside and I've never been alone in my bedroom after dark with a boy besides Manny.

"Just comics and graphic novels," he replies nonchalantly. "I'm more into movies." He waves the tattered copy of *A Clockwork Orange* at me and recites, "1971, Stanley Kubrick, Malcolm McDowell."

I raise an eyebrow and shake my head. "Anthony Burgess, 1962."

"I've never read the book, but the movie was great," he says placing the book back in its home. "I heard it's written in that weird slang they use in the movies."

I nod, "Nadsat. I had to download a special dictionary just to get through it."

He takes a few minutes to admire my book collection some more. They're all older beat-up copies. Geoff and I spend our daddy-daughter outings in stores like *Half-Priced Books*, buying up as many of our favorite reads as possible. Geoff enjoyed picking out books and challenging me to read them.

"Reading is therapeutic, Bowie. I never want to catch you without a book in your hand."

After he's finished ogling my bookshelf, Jonah walks over, and to my surprise, he flops down across the foot of my bed. He's just lying there on his back, grinning at me.

"So?" I bite my lip. "How do you feel about everything?"

"What do you mean?" He grins harder and I'm a slave to the dimples. I kick them out of my mind for the moment because I have more important matters to focus on.

"I mean my *two dads*?" I elaborate, dropping my hands on my lap. At first, I think he's playing dumb until I see his grin lower and he shrugs nonchalantly again.

"I think you have two cool dads that love you and each other. That don't abandon their family and cheat on their amazing wife for some young paralegal." There's venom in his voice at the mention of the last part of his sentence.

"Okay, so that's pretty specific." I give him a sympathetic look and go back to pulling on the frayed edges of the blanket.

Jonah sighs and stares up at my ceiling. "My parents got divorced back in January. He cheated on her and everything was a mess. The divorce was ugly, but my mom finally won. Well, she doesn't like to call it *winning*. She says *she survived the storm*."

"She sounds like a strong woman," I smile reassuringly, even though he's not looking at me.

He nods. "The day the divorce was finalized, my mom took me to the dealership and told me to pick out whatever car I wanted and customize it, however I pleased. Then she went back to work selling houses. All the while, my dad is shacking up with this woman he cheated on her with, expecting my sister and me to treat her like she's our stepmother. I decided I didn't want anything to do with him anymore. That's why I'm changing my last name."

"I hate you had to go through that, Jonah," I tell him sincerely. I want to reach out and touch him; reassure him, but I don't want to do anything inappropriate. I curse myself for being seventeen and having no idea how to act around the opposite sex.

He seems to shift his mood instantly from solemn to his usual jovial self, sitting up and laughing it off. "It's no problem. We've never been happier."

"That's good," I give him a small smile, averting my eyes downward.

"So, which one is your dad?" he asks, leaning back on his elbows.

"They both are, silly," I say playfully. I know what he means, but I wonder if joking around will help me loosen up some.

He gives a sarcastic laugh this time. "You know what I mean. Which one is your biological father?"

I shake my head. "Neither of them."

"Oh, so you're adopted?" He doesn't sound sympathetic or judgmental. It's a general observation and I love it. I nod.

"Do you know your birth parents?" That question stings, and I do my best to hide my reaction in my face. It's not his fault. He doesn't know how I feel about the subject. Nobody knows.

I shake my head.

"So, how'd you end up with Mark and Geoff?" he presses. He's looking at me with that boyish smile, so innocent and oblivious to the sore subject he's digging into; not because he's nosy, but because he actually wants to know things about me.

"There was a solar eclipse. Mark and Geoff were outside watching it with those stupid protection glasses, and then Geoff looked over at a park bench, and **BAM!** There I was!" I tell him with a smug smile.

"*Little Shop of Horrors*, 1986, Frank Oz, Rick Moranis." He laughs and gives me a look that says *"cut the bullshit."*

"If I'm prying, you don't have to answer. I was just trying to get to know you better. I guess to make up for that unnecessary sob story I told you earlier."

I consider his words and think back to the last two months we've been talking. He's told me so much about him, and I've remained vague and secretive. Here he is, this cute guy, interested in my strange life, and I've got the nerve to want to keep him in the dark.

"A hospital worker found me wrapped in a thin blanket behind a dumpster at Integris in the middle of an ice storm. They estimate I was about eighteen hours old."

Jonah is quiet for a long time. He just looks at me with this hard-set look on his face, like he's taking everything I just said in and analyzing it. I don't tell it like that to gain sympathy from him. I just want to be as open as possible.

"Damn. I'm not sure what to say." He rubs the nape of his neck, even though I'm pretty sure he's not sore.

"Do me a favor?" He looks at me in anticipation, and I sigh and continue. "Just don't say you're sorry."

"No, I definitely wouldn't say that," he tells me reassuringly with his signature chortle. "I mean, it looks like you've got a pretty great life." He looks around my room as if to prove his point.

"Yeah, I guess you're right," I tell him, even though I *know* he is. I'll never underestimate the life that I have been given. Geoff gave me my middle name, Phoenix, to symbolize my *"rebirth."* A new life with him and Mark. A happy life.

The look Jonah's giving me now lets me know that he's got something up his sleeve. It's the look he gave me right before he asked me to sneak away from camp to eat chicken-fried streak with him.

"I want to know something about you that nobody else knows," he states, flopping back down on his back, bending his arms up above him so that his head is resting on his palms. I allow myself about five seconds of viewing when his shirt rises to show just a sliver of chestnut skin just above the waistband of his sweatpants.

I turn towards my open bay window now and consider his question. I think about what he's asking me, and what my answer will be. What kind of person would I be if I told my secrets to a boy that I barely know when the people I've known my entire life don't even know how I feel about myself?

My only solace is in the fact that Jonah is so easy to talk to. When I'm talking to him, I come close to breaking out of my shell and opening up to him in a way I've never opened up to anyone. But then I always slink back into my shell and allow him to do all the talking.

"I'd volunteer to go first, but I'm already an open book." He holds his hands out and gives me a charming smile. "No pun intended."

I laugh heartily and shake my head, "Obviously. How about I just tell you a story instead?" He nods and then there's a brief silence as I gather my nerves and prepare myself to bare my bones.

"So, there's this girl, right? She's got everything a girl could ask for. More than most of her peers have in some aspects. Wealthy family, nice home, brand new car, loving parents, amazing friends, a college fund, nice clothes, you name it. She had a rough first day in this world, sure, but the last seventeen years have made up for it tremendously. Yet, on the inside, she's drowning and can't express it to the people she cares about the most because she *has* this amazing life and knows she shouldn't complain about anything."

I pause and examine his face to see if I can read some sign of boredom on his face.

"Why is she drowning?" he asks me, rolling on his side and propping his head up. I bite my lip to stop it from trembling. I'm so nervous that I can feel my body temperature rising and I run my hands through my hair. As usual, it bends back and flops back into place.

"What's your mother's name, Jonah?" I ask him instead of answering directly.

"Nicole," he tells me with a confused smile.

"And your father?"

"Vince," he says, with a hint of venom.

"What is their ethnicity?" I ask, instead of telling him to be lucky that he can answer that question, venom or no venom.

"They're Black." He shrugs. "Mom is Black and Native American. Vince was born in Phillipsburg. He's Caribbean."

"I understand why you feel so much animosity towards your dad," I tell him after taking a shaky breath. I'm not very good at speaking my mind, or telling people how I really feel. There are only rare occasions when Manny and Christina bring that out of me, so I pray I don't offend Jonah. I just want him to understand how I truly feel.

"But imagine if you knew nothing about him? About either of them? Imagine if you didn't know about your Black, Native, or Caribbean heritage? Despite the fact that colonizing white Europeans tried their hardest to wash that away," I muse absently, thinking about a conversation I'd had with my parents. This was after my World History teacher sent a letter home attached to my report on diaspora and the negative effects of European colonialism. He called it *radical and inappropriate for a sixteen-year-old.* Geoff framed it in the hallway.

To my surprise, he doubles over and laughs. Then he calms his laughter and waves me off. "I think I know what you're getting at."

I raise a brow. "You do?"

"Yeah, you're saying that you don't know your background. Everyone wants to know where they came from." He shrugs.

"That's only part of it. I mean, what ethnicity do you think I am?" I ask him seriously. "When you first met me, what did you think I was?"

He shrugs. "I don't know. I figured you were Black. Maybe mixed with Hispanic or something. I didn't really think about it." Of course he didn't, because he's normal. And normal people don't have an overbearing obsession with people's race and ethnicity. Not like me.

"Exactly," I frown, "*I* don't know. Nobody does." I add the last part quietly. "And it's not just that."

He sits up and waits for me to finish. I've got his full attention, something I rarely get from anyone. Mark's never home. Geoff is always complaining about Mark not being home. Christina's always talking about boys, and Manny only wants to talk about himself and the plan.

But Jonah's sitting here listening attentively to me blubber about how shitty life is, despite having everything I need.

"Everything about me is—made up!" I throw my hands up, losing myself in frustration. "They estimated my birthday, and everyone just swept my ethnicity under the rug!"

"But my biggest question would probably be *why*?" I say in almost a whisper after calming down a little. "Why did she abandon me?"

There's another silence and I wipe away a tear that's threatening to fall, hoping that Jonah can't see it. I've already made things awkward with my sob stories; I don't need to freak him out by crying, too.

"Sorry. I'm sure you didn't want to hear all of that," I tell him sheepishly, standing up and attempting to shake my embarrassment out of my fingertips.

Jonah follows suit and stands up too, towering over me. "I asked, didn't I?"

He's so close to me now that my heart flutters again. Despite the slight nerves over the subject and fear of saying the wrong thing, I feel so much more at ease being around him than I expected.

We're standing face to chest, and I look up at him, wondering if he's going to kiss me again. I'm praying that he kisses me again.

Instead, he asks, "You've never told anybody any of this?" I shake my head, no. "Why?"

I shrug. "My parents have done so much for me. I guess I feel like I'm being ungrateful if I complain about what I feel I'm missing. Like what they've given me isn't enough or something."

He makes a face that I'm not sure how to read, and then there's another moment of thought-filled silence.

"Honestly, race and birthdays and backgrounds are cool, but a person's character is everything in my book. And in terms of character, and especially looks, you're beautiful to me," he tells me with a straight face. When a smile finally breaks through, I think to myself, *I've fallen in love with Jonah Taylor.*

When he leans down and presses his soft lips against mine, I'm convinced that I have.

Chapter Seventeen

Christina slams her Coke can on the table along with a tray of nachos and her heavy backpack. It's Monday, and I'm still reeling from my very eventful Saturday.

"Woah, I wouldn't open that soda right away if I were you," I half-joke as she sits across from me at our usual lunch table. I'm here earlier than usual, so Manny and the others haven't arrived yet.

"Miss me with all the small talk, Bo." Her hazel eyes gleam to match her simper. Christina is the only person in her house with greenish-brown eyes and a light-brown skin tone. Ms. Shonda and Destiny are both a darker brown shade with brown eyes. Christina says she got her features from her father, who I've never met because he lives eight hours away in Houston, leaving Ms. Shonda to raise Christina on her own.

He sends money once a month that my mom puts in my savings account for when I'm in college. Other than that, we don't need him," she told me once when we were talking about her feelings about her distant relationship with her father. I wanted to tell her how nice it must be to not care about her father's abandonment, but I knew it wasn't right. I can't take my frustrations out on other people just because I'm so insecure about my identity.

"What's there to tell? You're the one who gave him my address, Chris. Glad he wasn't a stalking ax-murderer." I glare at her playfully. She pops the top on her Coke and it fizzes everywhere.

"I told you!" I laugh, handing her my extra napkins from my pizza order.

"Enough about this stupid pop. I want to know what happened Saturday. How'd your dads like him?" she presses me, wiping up the brown liquid before it can run across to my pizza slice.

"They liked him a lot. Geoff couldn't stop talking about his humor all day on Sunday, and Mark liked how respectful he was."

"We'll probably need to finish this conversation at your house; everyone's walking over and I know you don't want them all in your business." Christina sucks her teeth and looks past me.

"Geoff's home today. The last thing I need is for him to hear about me and Jonah making out in my bedroom," I reply absently, rolling my eyes at the thought of him gushing at my newfound love life.

"*WHAT*?" Christina screeches, causing everyone to glance over at me. I cannot believe I just said that out loud to her! I smack myself on the forehead for my stupidity.

"You guys made out? As in *kissed*?" she hisses.

"Of course they made out, Christina. That's what *actual* couples do." Kayla McMurray's words are obviously a stab at whatever Christina and Chris Monte have going on. She takes a seat next to me, which is weird because she never sits with us.

"What the hell is that supposed to mean, Kayla?" Christina challenges her, cocking her head to the side.

Kayla brushes her off and turns her attention to me. "I'm here to tell you that you win. Manny is 100% yours. I've met someone else. His name is AJ Mitchell. He goes to West Lake."

"Okaaaay." I give her an amused look. I'm not sure why she felt the need to tell me that, but I'll let her have her fun. This works for the plan, I guess, and Manny, Christina, and I will have a blast laughing at this later.

"Girl, if you don't move around with all of that." Christina shoos Kayla away.

Kayla flips her brown hair and stands up to walk away with her minions, who never even bothered taking a seat with her. They just stood there holding their lunch trays while she talked to me. So weird!

"Made out?" Christina grins at me. "On your bed?"

I can feel myself blushing and I bite my lip, nodding.

After the initial kiss, some unknown force (probably hormones) guided us onto my bed, where Jonah laid partially on top of me and we kissed, tongue and all. His hands stayed appropriately on my hips the entire time, even though my shorts were riding high on my thighs with every movement. At 9:47 p.m., he deemed it time to go out of respect for Mark's rule. He kissed me again, softly, in front of the door after putting on his shoes. Then he called me and we talked on the phone the entire time he was driving home.

"I feel bad," I tell her, scrunching my face up in shame. "Like I put out too much."

"It was just kissing. It's not like you had sex with him," she tells me nonchalantly, brushing off my indifference. "He seems like a nice guy, but even nice guys like making out with pretty girls."

I blush and try to suppress my smile. "He told me I was beautiful."

"Because you *are*, Bowie." She winks at me and then downs the remaining Coke in her can.

"Christina," I mutter as I watch the rest of our friends approach the table. She gives me her attention and a *'huh'* sound. "Do me a favor and don't tell Manny. I don't want him to know about Jonah yet."

"Your secrets are always safe with me, Bo." I can tell that there's more that she wants to say, and Christina is never one to hold her tongue, so it must be something serious.

I don't get to think about it for long before Manny walks up and kisses me on the cheek. It's time to turn on girlfriend mode.

? ? ?

"It's exhausting, I swear!" Jonah groans and runs his hands down his face. We're on FaceTime for the third time this week, and it's only Wednesday. It's been our new thing since his visit last weekend. This time I'm using my MacBook to video chat with him since I've got a paper due that I've been neglecting.

"Are you even good at playing basketball?" I giggle. This is the reason I've been neglecting my biology paper What's better than staring at a handsome guy and his dimples for hours? Certainly not microbes!

"I mean, I *am*, but that doesn't mean I want to play." He scoffs, and I laugh harder. "They've been trying to recruit me every year since I hit my growth spurt in seventh grade! It's just not my thing."

I calm my laughter enough to ask him, "Does your school have clubs for things you *are* into?"

"I'm not sure any high school in Oklahoma has a car club, or film club, or any type of club for blerds," he replies sarcastically.

"Blerds?"

"Y'know, *Black nerds*. Especially not out here," he adds sarcastically. "We're one of like seven Black families in town."

"I'm sure film club is a thing somewhere," I reassure him with a smile. "So, who is your favorite superhero?" I ask him while typing away at my paper. I've mastered the ability to talk on the phone and do homework from years of being friends with Manny and Christina, who are always calling me to dish out the latest drama while I'm trying to maintain my 4.0 GPA. With Jonah, it's a little harder, especially when I'm able to see him smiling at me and making his adorable faces.

"Batman, with Green Lantern as a close second," he replies instantly.

"Why?"

"Batman, because he's the most dangerous man in the world, and he doesn't even have superpowers. Green Lantern, because he's only limited by his own creativity. Kyle Rayner, the fourth green lantern, even became the White Lantern. He basically had no limitations."

"Hmm... I like that Green Lantern part. But couldn't Superman just blast Batman away or something?" I muse, shifting my eyes to see him chuckle.

"Batman would just get some Kryptonite."

"Where would he randomly find Kryptonite?"

"He's a billionaire! He'll buy some! Probably from Lex Luthor!" He laughs harder, and I can tell he's genuinely enjoying this topic.

"Fine," I fake pout and change the subject. "Who's your favorite director?"

"That's a tough question. It's like asking you who's your favorite author; depends on the genre."

"True, but I also don't believe in favorites. I believe in liking what you like, without placing everything in a box."

"That's funny," he chuckles, and I notice a hint of sarcasm in it.

"How so?" I ask him curiously.

"Stanley Kubrick," he says instead.

"Huh?"

"That's my favorite director. He can do no wrong in my book. *A Clockwork Orange* and *Full Metal Jacket* are my two favorites in case you're wondering."

"I've never seen *Full Metal Jacket.* Geoff hates gore, so we never watch movies like that for movie night." Again, he laughs.

There's a pause in our conversation when his mother calls him into another room. I take the few minutes that he's distracted to skim over my essay. I catch a few typos that are probably from paying more attention to the little box on the screen with Jonah's face than the larger one with my *Microbes in the Human Body* midterm paper.

"Sorry about that," Jonah says as he flops back down on his bed.

"No problem. I was putting the finishing touches on this term paper," I reply as I save the document and email it to Geoff. He'll proofread it from his bedroom down the hallway and send it back with any necessary corrections. With the document closed, my entire screen is now Jonah.

"So, you don't have favorites, but there have to be things you like?" he asks me with a humorous grin on his face. He's lying on his back with his phone propped at an angle that shows his head down to his t-shirt-clad chest.

I shrug, "I mean, I like books. Geoff has kept a book in my hands ever since I could read. We go—"

He laughs again, the same sarcastic *"observation"* laugh he did our second night at the diner and earlier in our conversation. I'm growing irritated with this secret joke he's got about me.

"Why do you keep laughing at me?" I say with a little more force. I won't take *"Nothing"* or *"Just an observation"* for an answer anymore.

"Wait, don't take it the wrong way," he pleads, sitting up so that his face is closer to the camera. I'm finding that his charming smile is going to be an issue in whatever future we may have together. He'll be able to tear down my walls with it and get me to forgive him for anything. That's not good if he's the type of guy that knows how to abuse this hidden power.

"I've just noticed something about you," he continues. "I've listened really closely to everything you've said to me since we met, and I've finally realized something."

"Do tell." I cross my arms and wait for him to explain his findings like I'm some sort of animal on a wildlife show that he's been following around for months, and now he's ready to tell the world about my mating habits.

"You don't have favorites. You listen to jazz because your dad likes it. You listen to rap because Christina likes it. You don't watch certain movies if your parents aren't picking them for movie night. I thought maybe books were your thing, but you only seem to like those because Geoff loves to read. Is there anything that you like because *you* really have an interest in it?" When he's finished talking, he stares at me expectantly.

I consider his statement. He's not being condescending. He was giving me a genuine smile as he spoke. I explain to him that I listen to all music, which slightly skews his opinion of my choice of music. I will adjust my station to match those around me. But I'm not being a poser or anything like that, am I? Is it so wrong to listen to John Coltrane or visit the Jazz Lab whenever Mark is home, simply because I love to hear my dad talk about his passion for the genre? Or to rap Megan Thee Stallion lyrics and sing car karaoke Beyoncé songs with Christina because she's obsessed with those two artists? Am I even the type of person who enjoys action movies? And do I read because it makes Geoff happy? Or do I enjoy losing myself in books?

It all goes back to the underlying problem here: I don't know who I am.

"I guess I've done a terrible job of describing myself to you." I sigh, biting my lip and searching the air for my next thought. "It's hard to describe something you know nothing about."

"You may not know who your parents are or what ethnicity you are, but you know yourself, Bo," Jonah chuckles, and again, it's not patronizing.

"I do enjoy reading," I tell him instead because I don't feel like it's necessary to sully this conversation with my stupid insecurities.

"Yeah, well, I enjoy kissing you," he replies. He says it the way Geoff tells me what's for dinner, as casual as a conversation about the rain in April. I groan in embarrassment and hide my face in my sleeve like an eight-year-old girl.

"Am I the first guy you've kissed?" he asks me in an amused tone. Still hiding my face, I don't even think twice about nodding my head. "You're kidding." I can hear it in his voice the moment his grin widens, and if I wasn't hiding my face, I could probably see those dimples I've grown to fantasize about.

I shake my head. It's technically not a lie. Kissing Manny doesn't count because it's all a façade. I've never kissed a boy in any real romantic encounter before Jonah.

Geoff pops his head in my room and gives me a thumbs-up to signify my paper looks good. When he sees me giddy, sitting crisscross on my bed in front of my laptop, he steps further into my room to see what's going on.

"What are you doing?" he asks slowly, like I'm an unstable mental patient.

I laugh and motion toward the screen. "Talking to Jonah."

"Hi Mr. Monroe," Jonah calls out through the screen and waves as Geoff comes around to sit next to me on the bed. He's wearing a fluffy white bathrobe, and for a brief moment, I feel a twinge of embarrassment. I'm turning into a *normal teenager*.

"*Dr. Denton*, but call me Geoff. How are you, Jonah?" Geoff replies in an overly prestigious tone, and Jonah and I both laugh.

"I'm great! I was just telling Bowie how much I miss her." The words flow out of Jonah's mouth so informally that I wonder if he's forgotten he's talking to my dad.

Geoff's eyebrows shoot up in amazement, and he looks at me and then back at the box with Jonah's smiling face. "Is he always this alluring?" I laugh out loud and nod my confirmation. Geoff smirks. "Well, I guess I'm supposed to do that parenting thing

where I tell you it's a school night and you two need to wrap it up."
He looks at Jonah again and narrows his eyes. "Pun intended."

Jonah sits up due to the fit of coughs Geoff has just sent him into, and my face would probably be as red as a cherry if I were only a few shades lighter. Geoff stands to leave, but pauses at the door with his hands on his hips, facing me expectantly.

"Can I just have five more minutes to say goodnight?" I humor him by playing along.

"Two," he snaps back, but then his pearly white smile breaks through and I know he wouldn't care if I stayed up all night talking to Jonah. As long as I was happy and acting like a normal teenager.

After he closes my bedroom door, I turn my attention to Jonah, who has recovered from his Geoff shock. "Sorry about that. Geoff likes to do this thing where he acts like he doesn't know how to properly parent me."

"Why does he do that?" Jonah asks with a confused laugh.

"He says I've never given them a reason to *properly parent*. I don't date, and if I stay out late, they know that I'm with my friends and that I'm not drinking, doing drugs, or getting knocked up. I do well in school. I literally wrote an entire paper while we were talking tonight."

"What, are you trying to beat some kind of good girl record?" he teases.

I shrug. "Doing the right thing is just easy. Why lie when you can be honest and just do things the way they should be done?"

The moment the words leave my mouth, I want to vomit. What a hypocritical thing to say. In the Hall of Hypocrisy Fame, I should have my plaque and bust.

Bowie Monroe: Most half-lies told in a single (non) relationship.

Chapter Eighteen

Our daily lunch table usually consists of Manny and me constantly sucking faces, Cole and Bryson being loud and belligerent about everything, and Christina putting them in their place. Aside from the five of us, there is a revolving door of random seniors who will decide to sit with us. Today, Christina is nowhere to be found and I'm left to listen to Bryson recant his story about catching his parents having sex last night.

It's lunch period and I want so badly to spend my free time texting Jonah, but I can't risk Manny seeing it. Plus, I have to spend the entire forty minutes with Manny's tongue down my throat.

"I mean your mom *is* hot," Cole shrugs and laughs obnoxiously, "I wouldn't mind—"

"Bruh, shut up!" Bryson's face screws up with disgust, and he shoves Cole roughly.

"Everyone has caught their folks going at it." Cole laughs. "It's like a teenage rite of passage."

"You sound oddly excited about that, Cole." Manny scoffs, and the entire table laughs.

"I guess I'd be more traumatized if I had Bowie's parents," Cole snickers, and I swear I hear someone fake-gag.

"Why is that?" I say in a challenging tone. I sit up and lean against the table, breaking Manny's embrace around my shoulders.

"Just saying, it would be weird seeing two dudes going at it." Cole gives me a snarky laugh and takes a sip from his Gatorade.

I narrow my eyes at him and then at Manny, who's staring back at me completely void of any emotion toward the subject. I hate when he does this. When he acts like he's got no backbone because he's too afraid to be called out by our peers for anything.

I turn back to Cole and he's still laughing at the thought of my parents' love-making. Geoff and Christina would tell me to fight fire with fire; remind him that spring, Eric Trembley walked in on his dad screwing Cole's mom, and that's why they're archenemies. I'm not confrontational like Geoff and Christina. Though I've got a hell of a lot more backbone than Manny sometimes.

"There's nothing traumatizing about married, *faithful* parents having sex, Cole. Grow up!" Now it's time for everyone to snicker at what I said. While I didn't call him out directly on the events of last April after junior prom, I alluded to the fact that Cole's mom is a cheater.

I grab my backpack and stand to leave, but Manny grabs my hand. "Babe, where are you going?"

"I need to talk to Coach Parker before class," I lie, because I'm getting pretty good at it lately. "I have some questions about the test today." Another lie, because I'm positive I'll pass that test with flying colors. Teachers always go easy on us the week before Thanksgiving break because they plan on brutalizing us the week before Christmas.

"C'mon Bo, Cole's just being an asshole." Bryson tries to reason with me, but I refuse to sit here another minute with them laughing at my parents.

"See you guys around," I murmur, bending down to kiss Manny on the lips before storming out of the cafeteria.

On my way to class, I see Christina and Chris Monte in the hallway. He's got his arm wrapped tightly around her waist and she's pretending to push him away, giggling the entire time. I've seen him do this with about three other girls in our class, but Christina doesn't seem to mind. Or so she says.

"Hey Bo!" I hear her call out to me just as I'm rounding the corner in the opposite direction. I pause and wave, allowing them to catch up to me. "Why aren't you eating lunch with Manny and the others?" Christina asks me. We've been friends longer than anyone in this school, I'm sure, and it's like she can read me so well. Still, sometimes I need her to see through my fake smiles and ask me, *"What's really going on, Bo?"* Because we all know I'll never divulge my secrets to her or anyone. No one cares when the girl who has everything feels like she's got nothing on the inside.

"Eh, Cole pissed me off, making fun of my dads." I try to shrug nonchalantly, but I see the fire in Christina's eyes. Since they've approached, the arm that was draped around her has dropped, and now Chris Monte simply stands next to her.

"Oh, hell no!" Christina sucks her teeth and exclaims, "I know he's not talking about *anyone's* parents. Not while his momma is running around town in *everybody's* bed!" Her greenish eyes gleam with anger and I can't help but smile. Leave it up to Christina to say everything that I'm too afraid to say.

A teacher comes out of one of the freshman classes and shushes us, motioning for us to move away from her class before slamming her door shut.

"You always so damn loud!" Chris shoves Christina softly and chuckles. He turns to me and smiles, and I see that he really is handsome. He's tall, smooth dark-skin, with a flirtatious smile. I can see why she's so obsessed with him, but that's no excuse to let him be an ass to her.

"She's right though. Don't take that shit from Cole. Your folks always been mad cool, Bo," he tells me, and I thank him quietly.

"I'll let you guys get back to whatever you were doing," I tell them, backing away to continue around the corner. "See you around."

I make it to Coach Parker's classroom ten minutes before the bell is scheduled to ring. The door is locked, so I sit down on the floor and rest my back against the first locker next to the classroom. When I pull my phone out, I see that I've received several text messages from Jonah.

Jonah: If I was the first guy you've kissed, I guess it's safe to say you're a virgin too?

Jonah: I'm sorry that was really inappropriate. Sometimes my body reacts before my brain. You don't have to answer that!

Jonah: Oh great, you're not responding. You probably think I'm
some type of perverted creep, huh?

Jonah: ☹

All the messages were sent fifteen minutes ago, while I was sitting there listening to Bryson describe walking into the kitchen for
a late-night glass of water and seeing his parents getting busy on the
counter. He had a packed lunch today and all I could think about
was his mom spreading mayo on the sandwich bread right there
on the very countertop she was moaning on.

I laugh at Jonah's overreacting messages and quickly respond.

Bowie: You're a little creepy, but
I don't think you're a perv at all.
Sorry about the lag, I was eating
lunch. Yes, of course, I'm still
a virgin.

Bowie: I didn't peg you for an
emoji user.

Coach Parker returns to his classroom while I'm waiting for
Jonah's reply, smelling like Chinese takeout from the Chinese

restaurant in the shopping center next to the school. He unlocks the door and ushers me inside. "My favorite student, always on time. Where is Herrera?" Even our teachers believe we're that perfect couple!

I take my seat, which is strategically placed in the back of the class next to Manny's, and check my new message. He claims that sitting in the back of the class makes everyone assume we're fooling around and that we don't want the teacher to see us. He says it'll make everyone wonder what we're doing back there, so that's where we sit in every class. I often want to point out how much I doubt everyone cares *that* much about our relationship.

    Jonah: Only in dire situations
    will I resort to emojis.

    Bowie: What about you? Have you
    ever…

I blush at the thought of the words Jonah and sex. He's so confident and handsome that I'm sure he's done it lots of times. The girl friends on his socials are always tagging him in pictures and posting cheek-to-cheek photos that make me want to vomit. He's not even my boyfriend, and I'm already jealous of every girl he's ever been around.

    Jonah: I'm a seventeen-year-old
    boy in a town with a population

of 2,000. There's really nothing
better to do here lol.

Bowie: I figured as much.

I'm not sure if dejection can register through text, but I can't help but respond that way. What else am I supposed to say? *"Congratulations" "Way to go!"*

Jonah: But I'm not a man-whore or
anything! I've only done it a few
times. And only with one person.

I'm not sure that makes it any better, because now I want to know who she is. And why only her? Did he love her? Does he *still* love her? I don't ask him any of this, of course. Instead, I reply with:

Bowie: What's the deal with the
term MAN-WHORE? Why is the default
gender for a whore, female?

Jonah: Are you a feminist?

Bowie: Haha no, just a thinker.

Jonah: I want to see you this weekend. Can I come over?

Bowie: Not if you plan on making me number two on your list of conquests.

Jonah: I'd hardly call them conquests. If my friends knew I was one step away from virginity, they'd laugh at me.

Jonah: I was actually hoping we could have a Kubrick marathon.

The bell rings as I ponder his request. Geoff and Mark will be gone most of the day on Saturday, a perfect day to spend time with Jonah alone. I'll run it by them at dinner tonight, but I know they won't care.

Bowie: Saturday. As early as you can.

Jonah: Bet! I can't wait!

Bowie: But you have to read A Clockwork Orange before you come over.

Jonah: How am I supposed to read that book in three days???

The classroom begins filling up, so I send him a winking-face emoji and slip my phone into my pocket. I'll spend the next three days dreaming about spending an entire Saturday with Jonah alone, watching his favorite movies in my living room.

? ? ?

"Where are Geoff and Mark?" Jonah asks me on Saturday after I let him in. It's ten o'clock in the morning and I predict that we've got a good five hours before my parents get home.

"They left for a funeral about ten minutes ago." I shrug non-chalantly. "Geoff wanted to get there early to get a good seat."

"A good seat? At a funeral?" Jonah raises a brow.

"Knowing Geoff, there's probably some kind of juicy drama he's waiting to unfold at the service." I laugh and lead him into the living room where we settle down on the sectional. I pull up a streaming app on the TV that has a Stanley Kubrick film collection category and ask Jonah which movies he suggests.

"*Full Metal Jacket, The Shining,* and of course *A Clockwork Orange.*"

I scroll to the thumbnail of *A Clockwork Orange* and smirk at him. "Did you actually read the book in three days?"

He chuckles and then tortures me with his dimples. "I read six chapters."

I shake my head, but I'm laughing with him. "Pathetic. Let's watch this one first."

"I brought popcorn, got a bowl?" He waves the package of microwavable popcorn in my face. I grab it from him and jog into the kitchen.

"I also brought you Twix. Oh, and M&M's to pour in the popcorn," he tells me as I flop down with the bowl of popcorn.

I give him a weird face. "M&M's with popcorn? Before noon?"

"Don't knock it 'til you try it." He winks at me, and I feel bubbles in my belly.

When the movie starts, we're seated on the sectional, a whole cushion apart. I'm trying to focus on the eerie opening scene of the movie, in which Alex and his droogs are staring into the camera, drinking milk with loud sinister music playing in the background.

The bowl of popcorn is on the cushion between us. I briefly think about the mini heart attack that Geoff would have if he knew I was eating buttery popcorn on the leather couch, risking grease streaks.

I'm intently watching Alex being subjected to sexual and violent videos while strapped to a chair when Jonah moves the popcorn bowl and scoots closer to me. He places his arm around my shoulder and I reflexively tense up.

"Is this okay?" he asks me sincerely. I inwardly scream at myself to calm down before I scare him off.

"Yeah, it's fine." I smile reassuringly and allow myself to sink into his embrace. Now we're snuggled close, but casually, with Jonah's long legs stretched out and resting on the ottoman. My body is angled into him with one leg resting on the floor and the other running the length of the sofa.

He smells clean, like fresh soap and shea shampoo that I'm sure is coming from the curls that occupy the top of his head. Despite how lanky he is, he's comfortable to lie against. Somewhere near the end of the movie, I absently bring both of my legs up to curl on the couch and lay my head comfortably on his chest. It's a move he wasn't expecting. I know because I can hear his heartbeat quicken as I do so.

I miss most of the end of the movie in favor of listening to his heartbeat and thinking about what life would be like to have something like this casually. To have a normal boyfriend. To have Jonah as a boyfriend.

"I can change the movie if you want or I can get some more snacks out," he speaks up after a while and I startle at the sudden vibration of his chest. When I look at the TV screen, I see the credits are ending and my face heats with embarrassment. Did I seriously just lay here silently swooning over him while he was waiting for me to switch movies?

I need a quick escape, so I tell him I need to use the restroom and that he can choose the next movie. Then I bolt up the stairs and into my bedroom.

Christina answers me on the first ring. "I was just about to text you, girl! Are you busy? I need a ride home from work. Maybe we can go get fro-yo?"

"Chris, I'm freaking out!" I scream at her in a hushed tone.

"Why? What's going on?"

"Jonah's here. The dads are gone, and we're on the couch watching TV," I whisper loudly, making my way through my bedroom and into my private bathroom. The further away I am from Jonah, the less likely he is to hear my meltdown.

"Umm... Okay?" she draws out with a curt laugh.

"And well... We were kind of cuddling," I elaborate.

Again, she laughs. "I don't see the issue here, Bo."

"I think I really, really like him, Chris!" I reveal dramatically. I was never the type of girl to reply to anything dramatically. What is happening to me?

"Well duh! Of course, you do!" Now she is cracking up on her end like it's the most obvious thing in the world. "Are you worried about Manny? Is that what's freaking you out?"

"No, I just... don't know what to do," I sigh. "I feel like I'm embarrassing myself."

"Where are you? Where's Jonah now?" she asks me. I can tell she's texting and has me on speaker, probably looking for another ride home. I feel a pang of guilt that I'm not able to help her.

"I'm in my bathroom. He's downstairs starting the next movie."

"Okay, first of all, get out of your bathroom and go back down-stairs!" I can tell she's suppressing a laugh, but then she snuffs it and speaks more seriously. "And then just be yourself, Bo."

That's terrible advice when it's meant for me, but I don't tell her that.

"You are amazing, Bo. That's why he's there now. Just be your-self. Call me tonight because I want details!" She adds the last part with a feisty tone and then hangs up.

I stare at my phone and sigh. How am I supposed to *"be myself"* when I spend twenty-four hours a day trying to figure out what that means? I've been thriving on being someone I'm truly not. From seventeen years of answering to a name that was given to me weeks after my birth, to being Manny's fake girlfriend. It's what has gotten me through my teenage years without having a nervous breakdown.

Jonah's sitting on the couch scrolling on his phone when I finally come downstairs. He looks up and smiles at me when he sees that I've returned. I take a seat on the couch next to him and try to formulate a decent sentence to break the awkward silence.

"That movie was great. I still like the book better, though," is all I'm able to come up with.

"Did I do something wrong?" I snap my head towards him at the sound of his confused tone. There's a whole couch cushion between us again. I didn't notice that I sat on the other side of the sofa again.

"No!" I shake my head and run my hands over my face. "It's me, not you. And yes, I know that's very cliché, but it's the truth."

"I have a habit of getting my signals crossed." He shrugs, and I want to die right here on the couch or melt onto the floor in a puddle of humiliation, only to be mopped up by Geoff and his honeysuckle floor cleaner, his newest odor obsession.

"Your signals are fine," I give an uneasy laugh. "It's just... I'm not... used to *this*." I motion between the two of us and the sofa.

He nods his head and chuckles a bit. "I understand, but I think you're overthinking it."

"How so?" I raise an eyebrow curiously.

"You seemed pretty relaxed for a while until I told you the movie ended. Then you ran upstairs like you'd seen a ghost or some-thing."

I groan, and this time I do actually sink onto the floor, minus the liquid state. I'm pretty sure girls like Christina and Kayla don't go through this when they're with their male interests.

Above me, Jonah laughs, "You're really cute, you know that?"

"*Hamster*-cute? Or *pathetic, inexperienced seventeen-year-old girl*-cute?" I ask blandly, and he laughs harder. I love that laugh.

"*Really pretty, freckled-faced, rhyming name girl that I'm trying to refrain from kissing*-cute, actually."

My heart skips a beat, and I feel my face heating up again. Besides Manny, no one has ever expressed the need to kiss me. I want to be the confident girl that says in return, *"Don't refrain, just do it. Kiss me!"* Of course, I am not that girl.

"Can you please come back over here and sit with me, Bo?" he asks, and I don't feel like his words are laced with bullshit. Just like everything else, he makes this seem so easy. I slide my butt back on the couch cushion before sliding down the length of the sofa and into his space again.

"*Full Metal Jacket*?" he asks casually. His arm is stretched across the back of the couch and his other is on his lap, gripping the remote. I settle into him again, resting my head near his heart and folding my legs up.

This movie is graphic and I have to bury my face in Jonah's chest when the soldiers beat the overweight guy with bars of soap in towels.

"Note to self, *Full Metal Jacket* is not a film to show if you're trying to set the mood," Jonah jokes, and I find comfort in feeling his chest rumble with laughter.

"Definitely not." I shake my head, but I'm laughing with him.

We're midway through *The Shining*, which I've seen once with Mark when I was younger, when we hear the front door open. Jonah pauses the movie, and I sit up and respectfully put the one couch cushion between us again; scooting away from Jonah but giving him a reassuring smile that tells him my parents won't care that he's here.

"*Oooh weee*! Bowie, you missed the funeral of the century!" Geoff calls out from the mudroom.

"That's typically not the first thing a person says after leaving a funeral," I call back to him. I hear Mark laugh as he rounds the corner first.

When I told them I'd invited Jonah over, they were slightly apprehensive. Geoff eased up a little more than Mark after I assured them that everything between Jonah and me was completely innocent. Geoff, a firm believer in the necessity of dating, was the first to give the okay. Mark felt it necessary to suggest we have *the talk* again, to which I reminded him that neither of them actually had *the talk* with me. That was Carrie.

"Hey Jonah, how are you?" Mark greets Jonah after surveying the scenery. There's a respectable two-and-a-half-foot space between our bodies. The TV is paused on little Danny riding his big wheel down the hallways of the Overlook Hotel.

"I'm great, Mr. Monroe. Nice to see you again. Sorry about the loss of your friend." Jonah immediately stands up and shakes Mark's hand. Not out of nervousness, but heedlessly, like he was always taught to shake a man's hand when he enters a room.

Geoff snorts and waves off Jonah's comment as he enters the living room. "John was hardly a friend. We only attended the funeral out of pure amusement. He was an old college roommate of mine."

"No, *you* only went for amusement. I genuinely liked the guy," Mark huffs before adding, "Sometimes."

"Well... What happened?" I laugh, still sitting on the couch. Jonah is standing with my parents on the other side of the couch, with his hands in the pocket of his sweatpants coolly.

"Kid, I can't make this stuff up." Geoff waves his hand. "First his wife spoke, and she was crying and brought the entire room to tears and whatnot."

"She was always nice." I smile sympathetically, even though I know Geoff is far from finished.

"Then they ask for two-minute eulogies from those closest to him." Geoff pauses and pinches the bridge of his nose. "First his mistress stood up, then his girlfriend, and then his girlfriend's girlfriend. All of them were going to *miss his big personality and heart.*" Naturally, Claire was mortified!"

"That poor woman!" I scrunch my face. "Dad, that is not funny!" I scold Geoff when he cracks up laughing.

"I tried to tell him he's going to Hell." Mark shrugs. "You'll have to excuse him, Jonah. He means well." Jonah waves off the comment, fighting his laughter.

Geoff defends himself. "Oh please, I'm not laughing at *her*, just the situation. I tried to warn her in college that he was a dog."

"C'mon Mark, let's go change for dinner, and let these lovebirds watch their creepy movie." Geoff grabs Mark's hand and drags him towards the stairs.

"Jonah, you're more than welcome to accompany us to dinner," Geoff calls back, "We're having Greek. Our treat."

"No thank you," Jonah replies. "I'll need to get back home before the dinner crowd at the restaurant."

My spirits drop at the thought of him leaving and I inwardly curse myself for wasting so much time freaking out over how to act around him. I've now trained myself on new silent breathing techniques I can perform to calm my nerves whenever he's near me.

"Maybe next time, you can come see me?" he adds quietly with a wink, and then there it is...

A ray of hope!

Chapter Nineteen

For the past ten years, Carrie Fontaine has served as my unofficial godmother. Before she brandished this title, and many years before my birth mother stuffed me behind a hospital dumpster, Carrie was engaged to Mark Monroe.

They grew up in the same New Orleans suburb and were childhood sweethearts until Mark met Geoff and called off his engagement with Carrie in their early twenties. Supposedly, the emotional toll of not only losing the love of your life, but losing him to another man was so hard on Carrie that she went on to live a lonely, single life as an artist on the east coast.

After the *"Which one of you is my mommy?"* fiasco following Christina's seventh birthday party, Mark and Geoff introduced me to Carrie. They made it clear Carrie was *not* there to act as a mother figure, but to help my dads out by teaching me things that normally a mother would teach her daughter. So, despite the love/hate relationship Geoff and Carrie have sometimes, she always seems to turn up conveniently whenever I've reached a milestone in my womanhood.

When I had my first period, Carrie flew in from Baltimore to talk to me about what it meant to be a young woman. Of course, my dads had already made me sit in with Ms. Shonda when she had the same talk with Christina and Destiny. When I was in the eighth grade, Carrie was tasked with the awkward job of teaching me about sex and condoms, and STDs, because while Ms. Shonda was very informative and no-nonsense on the subject of teenage sexual activity, there were some things Geoff and Mark did not want me to learn. Like the time, she reminded Destiny that oral sex was just as risky as regular sex while we were eating Sunday lunch at Hunan Wok.

While it's not uncommon for Carrie to pop into our lives at random with her wandering artsy spirit, I should have expected a visit from her after I started *"dating"* Jonah.

"What's with all the smiling?" Mark questions me as we sit at the dinner table. The week leading up to Thanksgiving, Geoff allows us to eat takeout every night since he spends an entire day and a half cooking Thanksgiving dinner. Some years we're accompanied by my parents' ragtag group of misfit friends who don't have other dining options for the holiday. But usually, it's just the three of us; yet Geoff sees it fit to cook every traditional dish possible.

"Nothing." I try to rid my face of the goofy smile, but it only spreads as another text message comes through.

"Oh, that's what we call the *Jonah face*," Geoff tells him. He's not even looking at me. He's just memorized my facial expressions whenever I'm endlessly texting Jonah. "You're never around to see that one," he adds in poor taste.

"Aren't we supposed to check her phone to make sure they're not, like... *sexting*?" Mark asks, and unlike Geoff, who likes to pretend he's new to parenting, he's seriously considering it.

"Well, I figure since she's at the dinner table eating lo mein, instead of locked up in her bedroom posing in lingerie, that wouldn't be necessary," Geoff retorts sarcastically.

"We're talking about how redundant it is that The Flash is always late, despite being the fastest person in the world," I tell Mark with a laugh while texting Jonah back.

Mark gives me a skeptical look and asks, "Is that code for something?"

I laugh harder. The doorbell rings and I volunteer to answer it. When I reach the glass door, there's a woman with honey-colored skin and curly brown hair standing there. She smiles brightly at me, and even though she usually looks like she's about to have a nervous breakdown, her smile always reaches her eyes for me.

"Carrie!" I squeal and throw the door open to hug her. "Oh my gosh, I didn't know you were coming!"

"Well, I was in the neighborhood and decided to pop in," Carrie tells me in her raspy voice. She slips her boots off and tosses them into a cubby and follows me back into the kitchen.

"What a surprise. Carrie is here, unannounced," Geoff states blandly. Carrie immediately walks over and kisses Geoff on the cheek, much to his pretend disdain. Geoff likes to act as if he and Carrie are enemies, but they secretly love each other. They share a bottle of wine and catch up late at night when they think Mark and I are asleep.

"Hey Mark." Carrie walks over and wraps her thin arms around my other dad and kisses his temple. He smiles warmly at her and returns her greeting.

"Carrie, are you staying for Thanksgiving?" I ask her happily, returning to my seat at the table.

"Nah." She frowns sheepishly. "I'll probably go visit my parents, or just go back to Baltimore."

"How was your show in Denver?" Mark asks, referring to an art showcase she had.

"You had a show in Denver? Is that why you're here?" Geoff asks, popping a wonton in his mouth. "Mark never divulges the contents of your many secret conversations."

"*Secret conversations*?" Carrie laughs. "You're hilarious, Geoffrey. But yes, I figured I'd just fly here on my way back home. I missed my favorite family."

"You're more than welcome to stay and have Thanksgiving dinner with us, Care. There will be plenty of food," I tell her, using Mark's nickname for her, *Care*.

"Bowie, you can't just randomly invite people to holiday dinners!" Geoff huffs.

"Since when?" I throw him a look and shake my head. "If John Haskell wasn't dead, he'd be here too, with his three girlfriends and wife!"

Geoff ponders my words and then picks up another wonton. "*Touché* Junior… *Touché.* Besides, Carrie *is* family, I guess." He adds the last part before smiling mischievously and popping the fried bread in his mouth.

"I guess it's better than listening to my mother remind me for the thousandth time how much of a failure I've become in life." Carrie shrugs. Mark gives her a sad look, but she returns his look with one of reassurance.

"So, what's new with y'all?" Carrie asks, looking between Geoff and me. She's seated across from us next to Mark, picking at an egg roll that Mark passed her.

"I'm still aging gracefully," Geoff replies, tossing imaginary hair over his shoulder, and we all laugh. "Bowie has a boyfriend, though."

Carrie's jaw drops and her eyes light up. "Oh, my gosh! Like an actual boyfriend? Is that Manny-thing over?"

I shake my head and glare at Geoff. "No, I'm still helping Manny. Jonah's just a friend."

"Mmm hmm, a *friend*. Whatever you say, girl." Carrie eyes me, knowingly.

At the mention of his name, I'm reminded that I was texting Jonah before Carrie showed up. I send him an apology and explain to him I've got company and that I'll talk to him later. Carrie and I excuse ourselves from dinner and go upstairs for girl talk.

"Let me see a picture of him?" Carrie asks, sprawling across my bed.

Pulling out my phone, I log onto Christina's Instagram. I sift through the best-looking picture of Jonah, which is tough because all the pictures he takes are good. I don't think he's capable of taking a crappy picture.

I show her a selfie of him he must have taken just before handing his phone over to Rhonda last summer. The sun is shining behind his curly head and his dimples are on full display as he gives a thumb up to a caption that says: *Ready for an entire month of babysitting! #Sarcasm*

"Oooh, he's cute, girl!" Carrie coos in her southern drawl. Mark told me once that her mother is of French descent and her father is Haitian and Native American. A smorgasbord of ethnic backgrounds like me. Only she knows her true roots.

"I think so too. And he's really sweet and kind. He's a nerd and hilarious. He's just..." I halt my gushing when I catch her smirking at me.

"Go on..." she quips with her head hoisted on her palm.

"I don't know. It's weird. I've been around guys my whole life, and out of nowhere, this random boy just comes around and jumbles up my world," I tell her with a nervous laugh.

"Falling in love does that," she sighs. I ponder her words. "It's puppy love for sure," she continues, seemingly reading my mind. "But all great love stories start as puppy love. The ones that kick it off intensely usually end in tragedy." She shrugs and flops down on her back.

We spend the rest of the night chatting about Jonah and her recent art shows. She tells me she's working on something top secret to show in a big art contest she's entering this spring. When Carrie goes the guest room to finally get some sleep I'm left with thoughts of Jonah and our puppy love. Maybe we are destined for greatness?

? ? ?

On her last day in town, Carrie tags along with my friends and me for a little Black Friday shopping at the mall. We're sitting in the food court eating takeout from my favorite place, the *Cajun Grille*, which is run by a Vietnamese family and serves lo mein and meat dishes that strangely resemble Chinese food.

"Ya'll know this is *not* what authentic Cajun food is like, right?" Carrie eyes our plates suspiciously. She opted for a gyro at the Greek place next door.

"It's still delicious, Care." I shrug, laughing at her disgusted face, sucking a single noodle through my puckered lips. Beside me, Manny is sitting coolly with his arms across the back of my chair. He's checking our surroundings, probably scouting for classmates to show off for.

"You know, Manny, life would be so much easier if you just relax and be yourself," Carrie tells him. He's probably heard that from all of us who know his secret about a million times now.

Manny sighs and gives Carrie a questionable look. "Can I ask you something personal, Carrie?"

Carrie nods and shrugs. "Sure, shoot."

"When Mark... you know... told you..." He stumbles over the words a little and Carrie frowns. Christina and I look on curiously. "Well... how did you take it?"

Now it's Carrie's turn to let out a deep sigh and sit her mixture of lamb meat and pita bread on the table. She takes a moment. I guess, to draft her words.

"I didn't take it well at first," she finally tells us, taking the time to look at each of us as she speaks. "I said some pretty mean, hateful things to him. Things that no one should ever say to anyone, let alone a person who is discovering something... new about themselves." She looks really sad at the memory, pauses again, and looks down at the table.

"I guess I never really got over it, but I apologized for the way I reacted, and we've been able to remain friends. Family almost." She ends her statement with a wink in my direction and I smile.

"See, that's exactly why I need to keep this a secret until I leave for college. People are going to freak out if they find out. They'll crucify me!" Manny groans dramatically. "Especially my parents."

"Mark's parents were furious about his relationship with Geoff. But he's doing just fine, as you can see," Carrie reminds him. I want so badly to tell her that her words are in vain. We've all been trying for four years to convince Manny that high school isn't the be-all and end-all and that what people think about his sexuality won't matter as soon as we graduate and move on to bigger and better things.

Of course, I'm not necessarily the poster child of being true to oneself, so maybe I should just keep my mouth shut.

? ? ?

"This place is pretty neat," Carrie comments as she sits in the chair that Mark has pulled out for her. He takes her coat and drapes it over the back of her chair and then does the same for me. We're at the Jazz Lab, a usual hangout spot for Mark and me whenever he's in town.

"Mark said he'll take me to the real jazz club downtown after I turn twenty-one," I tell her with a nod. "But this place is awesome, and the food is good too."

We order appetizers and casually talk under the dim lighting in the small room. Carrie and Mark order drinks and reminisce about listening to jazz music and their younger years.

Our usual server approaches with our food and smiles brightly at our group. She's a student at the nearby college, maybe twenty, and I always get a kick out of watching her smile flirtatiously at Mark.

"Is this your mom? You guys look like twins!" she gushes, pulling a few loose blonde strands behind her ear and standing up straight with her tray under her arm.

The thought of someone looking at Carrie and me and saying we look like twins is a stretch. Carrie has sandy-colored curly hair and light brown eyes, in contrast to my dark hair and dull brown eyes. We're about the same skin tone, I guess. This foreign feeling rises inside of me and the words are leaving my throat before I know what's happening.

"Yeah, usually it's just me and Dad." I don't flat-out confirm Carrie is my mom, but I don't correct the server, whose name is Tinsley, that Carrie isn't my mom, just a family friend.

After Tinsley walks away, the air is thick with awkwardness. I'm sure that Mark and Carrie have exchanged confused glances with each other, but I'm too ashamed and confused myself to look at them. Why would I do that? I feel like I just took a huge crap all over Geoff. I have never been ashamed of my parents. Not when Cole points out how gross their bedroom life must be, or when everyone stares at me whenever a same-sex couple kisses in a movie we're all watching. I've never cared about that. I love my parents. So why would I, for one brief moment, give in to a fantasy about Carrie being my mother?

I chalk it up to the need to be identified. Carrie has her French heritage and her Haitian roots; though she simply identifies as a Black woman and is frequently featured as a leading Black artist in magazines and articles. But she has an identity, and if Tinsley looked at her, then looked at me and saw the same person, then I would have an identity, too.

Right?

My head is pounding by the time we get home. Mark and Carrie go into the living room to continue visiting, so I rush upstairs. As I pass my parents' room, I see Geoff relaxing in bed, reading. I change courses and immediately go to him, collapsing on his chest and knocking the book out of his hand.

"I love you."

"Love you too, Junior." He snuggles me, not missing a beat. "Please don't tell me you're pregnant."

I snort and laugh, and he does the same, and everything is right again. *I think.*

Chapter Twenty

My birthday falls on a Tuesday this year, so it's easy to split my time between Manny, my fake boyfriend, and Jonah, the boy I want to be my real boyfriend.

At school, I'm bombarded with *"Happy Birthday"* greetings and Manny and Christina follow tradition, trashing my locker with balloons and candies. I'm eighteen. It's the age where we're legally adults, but still young enough to be misguided and confused about life. Like the fact that I'm an eighteen-year-old virgin, experiencing love for the first time with a boy who lives an hour and a half away; which is far enough away from my fake relationship with my gay best friend.

And that's about all I know right now.

Jonah was the first one to tell me happy birthday this year. He called me at midnight while I was lying in bed. Geoff had an overnight shift and Mark will be in Chicago until this evening. We could only talk a few minutes before Christina and Manny and Geoff called, but he's been texting me all day. He wants to come to the city to see me, but he has to work at the restaurant tonight and it's still a school night. That's fine because tonight Mark and Geoff are taking me and my friends to dinner.

Jonah: I have a birthday present for you. Can I visit after school tomorrow?

Bowie: You didn't have to get me a present, Jonah.

Jonah: Is that a no?

Bowie: Are you sure? I'd hate for you to have to drive back and forth so late.

Jonah: Bo…

Bowie: Okay, geez! Come if you want to.

Jonah: ☺

Bowie: I thought emojis were only
for dire situations.

Jonah: and whenever it's your
birthday, Freckles.

"Please tell me she doesn't spend every waking moment, smiling at her phone like that in class," I hear Mark grunt as I smile at Jonah's last text. I decided on a popular bar and grill restaurant in Bricktown for my birthday dinner. It's easy to appease everyone by going to a restaurant that has variety. Mark and I always order the catfish and sirloin dinner, while Geoff and Christina both love their ribs and Manny gets the chicken.

"No, she's too busy pretending to swap spit with Manny," Christina snickers and I throw her a look that says *"not cool."*

"What's going on?" Manny asks, looking at us in confusion, and I mentally slap my forehead. I haven't mentioned Jonah to Manny, and I assumed he hadn't noticed my sudden interest in constantly texting my newest crush. Now the cat's about to be freed from that bag, and he'll most likely throw a fit.

"You mean to tell me you don't know about Bowie's *real boyfriend*?" Geoff taunts him.

"Boyfriend?" Manny's eyes bulge and he looks at me as if I've betrayed him.

"Jonah's not my boyfriend." I roll my eyes. "He's just a friend."

"*Jonah*?" He nearly spits out his soda. "The guy from fat camp?"

"Okay, one, it's not a fat camp. It's a self-esteem camp." I raise my index finger before adding my middle one, "And two, yes, we've been in contact ever since the Ainsley party, thanks to Christina." I shoot my other best friend a look that now says, *There, now you're going down with me!*"

"I can't believe you haven't mentioned this to me, Bo!" he huffs out and folds his arms across his chest. He's pissed and I briefly wonder if it's because, as my best friend, he should know that I have a new love interest; or if it's because he feels like this will affect the plan.

I shrug and smile sheepishly at him. "I'm sorry, Manny. I guess I just figured you wouldn't care." He gives me an incredulous look and I can feel a rebuttal coming, but luckily, Mark interjects.

"I don't think that tonight is the right time for this conversation." He clears his throat, just as the servers bring our food. Once they're gone, Geoff steers the conversation in a different direction.

"Mark and I booked our cruise." He beams proudly over his half rack.

"What cruise?" Christina asks.

"It's a queer cruise," Geoff responds. "We've been dying to go on another one since before we adopted Bowie, but we've never had the chance to."

"*You've* been dying to go on one," Mark corrects him with a laugh.

"So, it's like a cruise for just gay people?" Manny is seemingly mesmerized by this information.

"For the most part," Mark responds, cutting into his steak.

"That seems like fun! Out on the sea with people who are like you," Manny gushes with stars in his eyes, grinning at my parents.

Again, Mark shrugs. He's more of the conservative type compared to Geoff. "They're fun, but I can do without all the craziness. All the dressing up and drunken antics aren't my thing. I'm only going because Geoff wants to."

"I have a question, but it's kind of personal," Christina says, looking between my parents.

"Well, go on," Geoff tells her after taking a sip of his margarita. "You know we're open books around here."

"Well, Mark, you used to date Carrie. Which means at one time you were attracted to women, right?" Christina asks him in her usual straightforward tone, and I wonder where this is going.

Mark chuckles and nods his head, choosing to finish the mouthful of catfish he's chewing before answering. "That would be correct," he tells her after finally swallowing.

"But now, you're 100% attracted to guys?" she asks him next, leaning into the table intently. Manny's zoned in now too, and I know for a fact that, for now, I'm safe from his wrath.

"I'm 100% attracted to Geoff now." He's purposely dancing around the actual answer to her question with a sly smile.

Christina sucks her teeth and laughs. "Well, of course, who wouldn't be?" She winks at my other dad.

"How cute," Geoff mocks her with an exaggerated smile that makes us all laugh.

"I guess what I'm trying to ask is... do you still find women attractive as well?" she finally outright asks him.

"Hmm..." Mark considers her words and looks over at me. I've never put much thought into the fact that Mark may still like women, because all of my life, he and Geoff are all I've known. I've never even fathomed the thought of either of them finding other men attractive.

"Like celebrities and stuff," Christina elaborates. "Not necessarily everyday women. But like, do you get anything sexually out of seeing naked women?"

I gasp now, "Christina!"

"What?" She laughs and looks at me. "I warned you it was personal. I'm just curious!"

"It's fine, Chris," Mark tells her. "But to answer your question, yes, I can still appreciate the appearance of a woman."

"So then, you're bisexual?" Manny asks in a confused tone.

This time Geoff laughs out loud. The waitress comes over to refill our drinks, but Geoff is still laughing and points at Mark, who is calm throughout this interrogation. Again, the conversation continues after the waitress is away from the table.

"I prefer to stay away from titles," Mark tells her, pausing to take a drink. "I fell in love with Geoff for who he was on the inside, not because he's a man. I fell in love because of the connection we made. He identifies as male and so do I, so I'm fine with the title of a gay man. But it's more than that for me."

Christina makes a face, but she's not judging him. She just seems confused.

"Confusing, huh?" Geoff chuckles.

"A little, but I think I get it. It's all about loving the person, not the titles or anything else." Christina smiles at Mark and he winks at her.

"Have you ever felt an attraction to women, Geoff?" Manny asks next.

"Nope. Never." Geoff shakes his head proudly. "My first crush was Timothy Newman in seventh grade."

"I really tried to like girls," Manny mumbles, "But it just wouldn't happen."

"Because you're gay, Manny," Geoff tells him, "And there's absolutely nothing wrong with that."

Mark and Christina and I all nod our heads in agreement. Still, I can see that words aren't fazing Manny at all. He's nowhere near closer to being true to himself and our peers.

? ? ?

I'm convinced Jonah may have skipped the last part of school to visit me the next day. I've barely made it home from dropping Christina off at the mall for work before he arrives at my house. Geoff is at work, but Mark is actually home.

I answer the door before he rings the doorbell and interrupts Mark's nap. At least this way we'll have some type of privacy.

"Hey, Bo!" He grins at me and I'm once again a slave to the dimples. He's holding a box neatly wrapped in colorful wrapping paper with a ribbon on it. I don't have time to examine it long before he swoops in to hug me tight and kiss my cheek. I giggle softly and squirm out of his embrace.

"What was that all about?" I step back and eye him, trying to fight the goofy smile that's threatening me. My face feels hot where he kissed my cheek, and my heart is pounding in my chest.

He shrugs and kicks off his shoes in the mudroom. "I guess I've just missed you."

I should probably tell him I've missed him, too. It's been a few weeks since our movie date, and our closest form of face-to-face interaction has been through FaceTime, which isn't as nice as being together in person. Thoughts like that scare me, because I've never longed to be around someone so badly, and I hate to imagine what we'd be doing if we lived in the same city.

"This is for you," he tells me, handing me the wrapped box. I thank him and take the gift from him and motion toward the living room. When we take our seats on the couch, I sit as close to him as respectfully possible, in case Mark wakes up and comes downstairs.

"You didn't have to do this, Jonah," I remind him again, fingering the pretty homemade ribbon bow. "Nice wrap job, though."

"My little sister did that. I suck at gift wrapping." He laughs and looks around. "Are your dads home?"

I nod my head. "Mark is upstairs, sleeping off the jet lag."

"Are you gonna open it?" he asks me, after nodding at my response. There's a hint of disappointment on his face, probably at the knowledge that we're not alone. Maybe he wants to kiss me again, and he thinks we can't do that with my dad upstairs. If he thinks he's leaving here today without kissing me again, he is terribly mistaken.

Christina and Geoff would be so proud of that thought I just had. I'm being a *normal teenager.*

I pull the ribbon strings apart to undo the bow and then tear away at the wrapping paper, careful not to shred it too much, and risk having to hear Geoff complaining about messes in the living room.

My gift is a white box with the words, ***ANCESTRY DNA KIT*** printed in bold blocky letters across the top. I furrow my brow and eye Jonah suspiciously.

I open the folded tabs on the box, and inside there's a sterile swab kit and a bunch of pamphlets and instructions.

"What is this?" I ask him, not completely confused, but still a little perplexed.

"Well, I'm not sure how I can help you find out anything about your birth parents. But I figured this could help you solve one of your problems," he tells me sheepishly, biting his lip and rubbing the back of his neck nervously. "I hope you're not pissed at me. I didn't mean it as a joke or anything. I thought you'd really like to know your ethnic background. I told you my heart acts faster than my mind sometimes."

I spend a few more moments staring between him and the DNA swab kit in my hands in complete shock. I've never revealed those insecurities to anyone, not even my parents or my two best friends. And yet, I felt the need to confide in this boy I'd only known for a few months. I told him my deepest, darkest secrets.

And he listened.

And to top that off, he actually cared.

"Jonah..." I breathe out softly, "Wow..."

He clenches his teeth together and groans, "Is that a good *wow* or a bad *wow*?"

I laugh, and without giving it a second thought, I lean over and press my lips against his. He's caught off guard and before he can get a chance to respond, I'm already pulling away from him.

"Thank you, Jonah," I tell him sincerely.

It's the strangest present I've ever received, and I'm apprehensive about actually following through with using it. It's the thought of him caring enough to want to help me that drives me to accept his gift the way I did.

"I'm glad I didn't screw this up because it finally hit me that buying a girl a DNA test probably isn't very romantic." He laughs and leans back into the couch some more. He's smiling and his dimples are teasing me.

"I mean, I'll definitely have to think about it. Using it I mean. Like what will that mean after I know what my ethnicity is?" I tell him honestly. Then I think about what this kit must have cost him, and I want to smack myself for even saying that.

He shrugs again. "I don't know, but hopefully it's a start to making you feel better about yourself." He says it so casually, void of any judgment towards me being whiny and insecure about my wonderful life. It makes me want to kiss him again, but I hear footsteps upstairs and I know Mark is awake.

I quickly gather up the box and wrapping paper and stuff them under a couch pillow. If Jonah finds this action strange, he doesn't mention it. He just straightens up his posture and sits as casually as possible as Mark makes his way downstairs.

While Jonah chats with my father, my mind silently wanders to the ancestry kit hiding under the throw pillow. Is self-discovery so simple that you can just find it with a thirty-second mouth swab?

Chapter Twenty-One

On Saturdays, I'm usually lounging around the house with whichever dad is home until my friends finish their shifts at work. I've tried convincing my dads to let me get a part-time job like Christina and Manny, but they insist on me enjoying my freedom before college. Today Geoff's home, but Mark will be here later and they've got some sort of date night planned. No parties or social events are happening this weekend, but I'm sure Manny will find something for us to do.

Until then, I decide to lose myself in my latest favorite pastime. Texting Jonah.

Jonah: It's Saturday, you should be out doing something.

Bowie: Nope, not yet. I need a definite plan of action. Like Batman!

Jonah: Lol. I like that reference, but you should really be a little more spontaneous, like Wolverine. Live a little Bo!

Bowie: That's not my style. How do you plan on spending this wonderful Saturday?

Jonah: Hanging out with my friends until Vince brings Mia home later, and then I'm on babysitting duty until my mom gets home from work.

Jonah refers to his dad by his first name as well, but unlike me, it's because he hates the thought of calling him his father. His dad has a new girlfriend as well; the woman they suspected him of cheating on Jonah's mom with.

"Who cares if your dads are gay?" he told me once after I told him about the comments some of my peers have made. *"At least they love each other and you enough to stick around."*

My phone pings. Jonah is sending another message.

Jonah: Otherwise my plans would have involved visiting you…

I smile at his words and bite the corner of my pillow, which I have pressed against my chest as I sit crisscross on my bed.

Bowie: You spend way too much gas and time visiting me.

Jonah: Doesn't sound like a terrible investment to me.

Reading his sweet words sparks an impulsive thought in me, and before I know it, I'm calling out to Geoff that I'm going out, and that I'll be home later.

"We're eating at Musashi's, so you're on your own for dinner tonight!" he yells back.

"No fair!" I reply, but I'm already slipping on my sneakers and coat and heading out the door with car keys in hand.

Within twenty minutes, I'm merging onto I-35 South with Cardi B as my emboldened theme music before I can even have time to talk myself out of what I'm about to do. I've just made it past Norman, the halfway mark, when it hits me. I'm driving an hour away to see Jonah, alone. I didn't even tell my dad. This isn't typical of me. Typical Bowie plans these things out first and never hesitates to tell her parents where she's going. Hell, I haven't even told Jonah that I'm coming to visit him.

I drive past the exit Geoff always takes to Turner Falls and I know that means I'm close. I see the exit sign for Davis just as the voice on my GPS tells me to take the next exit. I don't even have Jonah's address, or even know that he's at home.

I call him, and he picks up on the second ring.

"Hey, I was starting to think you didn't like me anymore after you didn't text back." He chuckles into the receiver.

Yeah, right, like that's going to happen anytime soon, I tell him in my head. But instead of saying it out loud, I just laugh and say, "Yeah, well, I decided to try that whole *"be spontaneous"* thing you mentioned."

"Yeah, and what were the results?" he asks me with what sounds like a mouthful of food.

"My spontaneity has brought me to the corner of..." I draw out the last part as I stop at a red light and crane my neck to read the street signs. "West Main St. and North 3rd St."

I hear him choke on his food, or drink maybe, and I stifle a laugh. "3rd and Main? Are you in Davis?"

"Yep," I tell him with a nervous laugh just as the light changes. "Where might I find you in this one-horse town?"

"Turn down 5th street, and you'll see my car parked outside of a little building on the left. It's a burger joint," he tells me, and I can hear the mixture of excitement and astonishment in his voice.

I see Jonah before I see his car and the look on his face slightly eases my nerves. He's genuinely happy to see me!

"Wow, Freckles. I thought you were joking for a minute!" he greets me after I've parked next to his car and gotten out of my own.

"Yeah, well, I figured I'd see what all the hype was about with this impulse thing everyone keeps talking about," I reply, trying to play things cool. But on the inside, I'm giddy with the joy of being around him again.

"I'm proud of you, Freckles." He's towering over me with his arms folded across his chest, nodding his head. We stand in an awkward silence for all of 15 seconds, where he smirks at me and I struggle to keep my knees from buckling in.

"So, I didn't really come here with a plan," I stammer out slowly. "I hope I'm not interrupting anything." I motion toward the hole-in-the-wall restaurant behind him.

"Nothing too important, just hanging out with my friends." He doesn't take his eyes off me, and I can feel the heat rising in my face. "Hungry? They make pretty good cheddar burgers there."

I decline, because I'm so nervous I may puke up anything I eat today. Jonah's friends come out of the restaurant and he introduces me to them. They seem friendly enough, and when they offer for me to tag along while they go play basketball at the middle school playground, I agree because, like I said, I didn't come here with a plan.

Jonah rides in my car and directs me toward the middle school a few blocks away from where we leave his car at the burger joint. I sit in the bleachers and watch as the boys play a game of Twenty-One. Jonah says he doesn't like to play organized sports, but he's actually pretty good at basketball.

"He's really not that good, Bowie," his friend on the opposing team comments, and I chuckle with him. "He's just trying to impress you."

Jonah laughs too and then tosses me a lopsided grin with a lot of charm. He shoots the ball, and it slides effortlessly through the chains of the hoop.

"Well, is it working?" he asks me and I swear I'm going to die from all the gushy teenage emotions he's forcing me to experience. He's the sexiest, most confident nerd I've ever met. He's like every stereotypical high school personality in one, and I envy his ability to just be *him*.

Jonah and his teammate lose the game. Partly because Jonah keeps getting distracted by me and his friends keep making fun of him for it. After their not-so-devastating defeat, Jonah walks over and joins me at the park bench.

He's sitting so close to me that our bent knees and shoulders occasionally touch, and I think he's doing it on purpose. I'm seventy-six miles away from home, alone with this boy, who may or may not be my boyfriend someday.

It's chilly outside, but he's got a light sheen of sweat on his forehead from running up and down the asphalt court. I pull my hands into the sleeves; not because I'm cold, but because I'm resisting the urge to reach out and brush my fingers across his loose curls that are framing his forehead now.

"We can get out of here. I'm sure you didn't come all this way to sit on a bench in the cold," he suggests, gifting me with the sight of the dimples again.

"I'm not sure why I came out here," I say more to myself, but I've said it out loud, so he chuckles.

"I think that's pretty obvious."

I'm fighting this goofy smile, so I turn away from him because I'm going to embarrass myself if I don't. Of course, now I notice his friends are watching us, and giving a silent commentary on our awkward interactions.

I hear Jonah chuckle lightly as he stands and stretches, "You're really cute when you play shy, Freckles."

"Maybe you can show me around," I suggest, standing beside him. "I've got plenty of gas in the car."

Jonah snorts. "Trust me, you won't need it."

We do climb in my car, but we only drive long enough for me to take him to his car, and then I follow him a few blocks into a neighborhood. We park both cars in front of a ranch-style brick house with a huge front yard and circle driveway.

I park my car behind Jonah's Camaro in the second driveway that leads to a separate two-car garage, and he gets out but doesn't walk toward the house.

"I'll show you *het huis van Taylor* later. Let's go for a walk," he tells me in a fake Dutch-Caribbean accent after he's opened my door for me and helped me out of the car.

We walk down his street back towards the main street at a casual pace. He doesn't seem to be in a hurry, and even though I've snuck down here without permission, neither am I. Mark will be overly concerned because I didn't tell them I was leaving town, but he won't be angry with me. Geoff will pretend to be furious with my actions, but it'll all be a ploy because on the inside he'll be ecstatic.

As we walk through the neighborhood, several people, young and old, call out to Jonah in greeting. He casually waves at them, but his attention is solely on me at the moment.

"I wish there was more for us to do. If I'd known you were coming, I would have had something planned. This place isn't that exciting."

I shrug. "I don't need an itinerary for *everything*, I guess. You always visit me. It's nice to see you in your natural habitat." I add the last part in a fake Australian accent, and he laughs at our inside joke. He knows my obsession with watching the Discovery Channel when I'm bored out of my mind and waiting for his texts.

"The Anoli theater plays older movies sometimes. But the nearest movie theater is in Ardmore. It's a small theater, though."

"Small theaters. There isn't any privacy," I blurt out with a giggle. Instantly, I'm mortified because I know how weird that must have sounded and I didn't mean it that way.

But Jonah laughs, not missing a beat. "Jordan Baker from *The Great Gatsby*, Baz Luhrmann, 2013."

"Try Jordan Baker from *The Great Gatsby*, F. Scott Fitzgerald 1925!" I shoot back with a laugh.

"You're right though." He laughs lightly, and I'm watching his dimples again. "About the privacy thing." He's poking fun at my awkwardness, but I don't mind it.

It's foreign, but I like the person I'm becoming whenever I'm around Jonah. She's more relaxed until she realizes it.

"Honestly, I'm perfectly fine just doing this," I motion around us. "Dates are just superficial titles that people use to make hanging out with someone you like sound fancier. A date can be anything."

Jonah considers my words and nods in agreement. "So then, this is a date?" he motions between us.

"Yes, an impromptu one, I guess." I nod.

"Good." He nods again, looking both ways at the streetlight, "Because I'm totally expecting a kiss after this."

I suck in a breath. I'm not shocked that he wants to kiss me, but I'm shocked at how badly I want to kiss him, and I'm far enough away from home that I can do as much of that and more if I want to.

That's scary.

Before Jonah, I never had these kinds of thoughts about boys. I read an article once by an anti-gay activist, that claimed that gay parents will raise gay children. Which is completely ridiculous. Mark is terrified of me becoming a woman and experiencing the world of romance and sex, whether it's with a boy or a girl. And while Geoff is pushing me into adulthood and dating, he's never specified which path I was supposed to take. When I didn't immediately take to dating boys as soon as I hit puberty, there was never a question as to whether or not I would be into girls. Dating just wasn't my thing.

Now I think I was just waiting for the right person. And Jonah is definitely the right person to have my first romance with. Too bad he came when I was already committed to a four-year-long fake relationship.

Chapter Twenty-Two

We dip into a coffee shop and order hot chocolates before heading back toward his neighborhood. He's given me a pretty decent tour of his immediate part of the small town. But I've been so focused on our conversations that I don't even realize how long we've been walking until Jonah's phone rings, and he grumbles something about meeting Vince and Mia at his house soon. His dad lives in Nichols Hills, about five miles from my house in Oklahoma City. So, they must be on their way back to Davis to drop Mia off.

"Nice home," I comment as I admire the rustic theme of the living room inside Jonah's house.

"Thanks. We've lived here my whole life. My mom was ready to fight tooth and nail before she let Vince take it from us," Jonah replies bitterly, flopping down on the plush, brown microfiber couch. "I doubt he misses it much, though. Not with his mini-mansion in the city." I walk along the mantle above the brick built-in fireplace. There are pictures on the mantle and on the wall above the fireplace. Pictures of Jonah and Mia mostly, but a few of what I assume are his grandparents and his mother. Nothing of his father.

I spot a picture of a young Jonah on the wall near the giant flat-screen TV. He's wearing large glasses with red frames and smiling wide with a toothless grin. There's a giant mass of brown curls on top of his head.

"Aww!" I gush and point at the picture, looking back at Jonah.

"Mom insists on making that picture the epicenter of our home." Jonah sucks his teeth, but I can tell he's fighting a smile.

"It's a really cute picture." I shrug and move around some more. There's a picture of Jonah's mom holding a younger Mia. I haven't met either of them, but judging from the pictures, they must look just alike.

"Everyone says my sister looks like the spitting image of Mom," he comments, as if reading my mind.

"And you?" I ask looking at a similar picture of Jonah and his mom next. He's a little older than Mia is in the other picture, maybe eight or so. Again, he sucks his teeth. I'm guessing he looks more like his dad.

"I'm sure I'm supposed to be showing you around the house or whatever, but I'd much rather kiss you on this ultra-plush couch we have here." His tone is serious. I bite my lip because I'm both enticed by his words and amused.

His long legs are stretched out in front of him and his arms are propped up behind his head. He seems so relaxed and chill, where my body is on fire and my heart is pounding like crazy.

It's hitting me that I'm alone with him again. And this time, we're more familiar with each other. There's no one here to stop us from taking things too far. I sit beside him and force myself to melt into his side. He brings one arm down and wraps it around me, pulling me closer.

"I'm really happy you decided to be spontaneous today," he tells me, and I feel myself relaxing in his embrace.

"This is one of the best ideas I've had in my life," I reply with a nod. I relish in the rumble of his chest when he laughs.

I feel him shift in his seat, and when I look at him, he's looking at me with this adoring expression that lets me know I'm trapped. I'm fine being trapped by Jonah, though. There are way worse places to be trapped. Like behind a dumpster.

"You're frowning," I hear him say.

"I am?" I reply dumbly. I guess my stupid dumpster thought registered on my face.

"Yeah, what's wrong?"

"Nothing," I semi-lie, because nothing *is* wrong. Everything is perfect with Jonah.

"Am I making you uncomfortable?" he asks, pulling away slightly. I pull him back and shake my head.

"No, this is perfectly fine," I assure him with pleading eyes. I want him to kiss me, and I hate that I'm ruining the moment with my stupid insecurities.

"You're perfect, Bo. Regardless of how you feel about yourself, I think you're perfect," he tells me sweetly. He's looking me straight in the eyes, and I think he really believes what he's saying.

I shake my head, though. "I'm far from perfect, Jonah."

"Why? Because you're adopted?" he asks me with a skeptical tone. He's being sarcastic, but not offensively so.

No, because I've been lying to you about having a fake boyfriend, I think to myself. Of course, out of respect for Manny, I don't tell Jonah this.

"I wish you saw the you that I see," he tells me nonchalantly. "You'd like her a lot."

"I do like myself. I'm just... confused about who that is some-times."

Most of the time.

"I can understand that, too." He shrugs. "I'm going to do every-thing in my power to make sure I'm nothing like my father."

At least he has a reference point...

"Everyone has insecurities, Bowie. Maybe you should talk to your parents about yours?"

No way that's going to happen, so maybe we should go back to plotting our make-out session. I'm not going to voice that to him either, but I will take the initiative to draw him in for a kiss.

Our lips barely ghost over each other when the sound of a car door slamming and a little girl's voice rings out from outside the picture window behind the couch.

Jonah pushes forward anyway and pecks me on the mouth. "That would be Mia," he tells me, standing up to open the door for his little sister. "Vince will just drop her off in the driveway. He won't dare step foot in the house."

I nod, even though the information is pointless for me to know. I technically shouldn't be here either.

"Hi, Jonah!" Mia greets her older brother as she skips through the screen door. "Dad and Lauren took me to the Science Muse-um. It was so cool!"

Mia looks up at her big brother with so much excitement and adoration. It makes my heart swell. I've never had anything close to a little sibling, and I'm not complaining, but I can tell Mia looks up to her older brother ferociously.

"Cool," Jonah responds, closing the door behind her. A car honks outside, but he doesn't even flinch as he helps Mia out of her coat.

I peek out of the living room window just in time to see a black Mercedes pulling away from the circle driveway. A gasp from Mia brings my attention back to the siblings as they enter the living room.

Mia's grinning at me, displaying a pretty child-like smile that most ten-year-olds have when their teeth are too big for their growing mouths.

"Are you Bo?" she asks me, and I cock my head in surprise. I nod and look at Jonah curiously. "I knew it was you because Jonah is always talking to you on the phone." She grins wider. She's got the same dimples her brother has, but her skin is a shade darker and her hair is only curled for style.

"Oh my gosh, you're so pretty!" she squeals, and I absently choke on my own breaths.

"I've heard a lot about you, Mia." I stand up and extend my hand to her, but she hugs my midsection instead.

"Sorry, we're a family of huggers around here," Jonah laughs and scratches the back of his neck.

I return Mia's embrace with a smile. "That's cool."

Mia sits next to me and begins telling me everything about their life. She tells me about her friends at school and about her grandparents' restaurant, where she gets to work as a hostess on the weekends.

"Have you met Cooper?" she asks me with another excited gasp like meeting Cooper is a rite of passage that I've missed out on.

"Jonah, I'm telling Mom you left Cooper in his pen all day!" She frowns at her brother and runs into the kitchen.

Seconds later, there is the sound of tiny nails on the hardwood floors. A little Yorkie comes bolting through the kitchen and living room and onto my lap.

"Mia, put the dog up!" Jonah yells at her while scooping the dog away from my face, where he's excitedly trying to lick me.

"Aww c'mon Jonah. He just wants to say hi to Bo!" Mia pouts, snatching the hyper dog from her brother. I giggle as the siblings bicker back and forth in the middle of the living room.

"Not everyone likes dogs, Mia!"

Mia huffs and stares at Jonah as if he's the devil for saying those words. She turns to me, wide-eyed with fear. "Do you hate dogs, Bo?" she asks me, and I can tell that the fate of our friendship depends on my answer.

I shake my head. "No, but I've never had one as a pet."

The locks on the front door click, and we all turn our attention toward the entrance as Jonah's mom enters the house. The dog wiggles out of Mia's grasp and starts running circles around the woman's feet.

"Hey guys, I stopped by the restaurant and picked up dinner," she calls out while dancing around the dog and carrying two sacks of takeout. I assume she means Jonah's grandparents' restaurant. He pointed it out today during our walk. Apparently, during his parents' separation, his paternal grandparents moved here from Sint Maarten to support their soon-to-be ex-daughter-in-law and grandkids. He didn't elaborate on the relationship they kept with their son, Jonah's dad.

"Hey Mom!" Mia runs over and hugs their mom after Jonah relieves her of the bags.

"Hey Mia, how was your day?" Ms. Taylor asks, returning the embrace.

"It was so fun! I went to the Science Museum with Daddy and Laur—"

"That sounds great, Honey," Ms. Taylor cuts Mia off. She heads into the living room and does a double take when she spots me sitting on the couch.

"Oh Mom, this is Bowie! Jonah's friend, remember?" Mia tells her with an excited bounce.

I stand and offer a short wave. There's a mischievous flicker in Ms. Taylor's eyes, but a friendly smile. It reminds me of the look Geoff gave Jonah when he first saw him walking up to our front door "Hello, Bowie. I'm Nicole Taylor. Everyone calls me Nic."

"Well, it's a good thing I grabbed extra chicken! It's nice to finally meet you, Bowie." Jonah's mom is beautiful; tall like Jonah, with shoulder-length hair that is highlighted with different shades of brown. Like Mia, her skin is slightly darker brown than Jonah's. She's wearing a designer pantsuit and carrying a leather briefcase.

Jonah walks into the living room and looks so excited at the mention of me staying for dinner that any thoughts that I had at declining the offer fly out of the window.

"Call your dads and tell them you're staying for dinner. We've been dying to meet you, Bo." Ms. Taylor, or *Nic* as she insists I call her, goes upstairs to change clothes, while Jonah and Mia and I set the table.

"Dads," I mumble in an amused tone. Jonah smirks at me as if to ask what I'm mumbling about. "Your mom. She told me to call my *dads*."

Jonah shrugs, "Yeah, you're no stranger in this house." My heart warms at the thought of Jonah telling his family about me. I take a seat at the table across from Mia, with Jonah and his mother at the end.

Aside from being beautiful, Jonah's mom is cool. She smiles a lot, even if she seems tired from what she calls a *"long day of pushing houses."* She listens to Mia recount her fun activities at the museum, but cuts her off every time she mentions Lauren, their dad's new girlfriend. She gives Jonah a hard time for not cleaning up the house before inviting company over, even though the house isn't cluttered much.

"So, Bowie, Jonah told me your dad is a commercial pilot," Nic states between bites of chicken. "Do you ever get to fly with him?"

"Which dad? You have two dads, right, Bo?" Mia chimes in eagerly. "Emily Neely at my school has two moms."

"Mia!" Jonah scolds her, throwing her a look that says she's embarrassing him.

"It's fine," I assure him with a smile. I turn that same smile onto Mia, who seems ashamed of her outburst. "Your friend is lucky to have two moms." She beams proudly at me and then turns her nose up at Jonah triumphantly.

"On my tenth birthday, Mark surprised me by letting me and Geoff fly to Orlando with him. He even announced before takeoff that we were all going to Disney World, too," I answer Nic's question.

Mia takes off on a tangent about wanting to go to Disney World and how much fun it would be. She's a natural at taking over a conversation, but I don't mind it. It's nice not having the spotlight on me and just enjoying the idea of eating dinner with Jonah and his family. I envy her ability to talk so confidently at such a young age.

She does most of the talking for the rest of the evening, with Jonah and his mother chiming in occasionally with jokes and banter. There are dimples all around this dinner table, and it's hard to paint the picture Jonah describes of their lives this time last year when their father was making his exit. They seem so close, just like Mark, Geoff, and me, despite missing a key component of the traditional familial setup.

I've lost track of time, until my phone pings with a text message from Geoff that reads: `Seriously Bo, Davis?`

The jig is up. I've been caught. Ousted by the dreaded location-sharing feature. We don't use it to keep tabs on each other. Geoff only made us activate it so that we always knew that Mark was arriving safely in each city.

"He could end up in the middle of the ocean and we'd know exactly where he was," Geoff explained one day during family dinner. Mark and I laughed. Mark doesn't fly internationally, so he wouldn't have a reason to be stranded in the ocean.

"I really should head back," I announce as I'm clearing my plate. "I can stay and help do dishes or something first, though."

Nic shrugs me off. "It's Jonah's night to do dishes."

"It's always my night to do dishes," Jonah mumbles. He nods his head towards the living room and I bid Mia and Nic farewell.

"Thanks for having me over for dinner. Even though I showed up completely unannounced."

"Nonsense." Nic waves my comment off and downs the rest of her red wine. "We've been dying to meet you. Jonah won't shut up about you. Drive safe and let us know you made it home. I can talk to your parents if you'd like."

I shake my head. "That won't be necessary." They won't be mad at me. Mia hugs me and makes me promise to visit again.

"Next weekend is my birthday. You should come to my sleepover," she gushes. I chuckle and nod my head. I doubt I can make that happen, but it feels oddly nice to be so wanted by Jonah's little sister. Maybe it's because I like him so much that I want her to like me as well.

Outside, Jonah and I are finally alone again. I'm leaning against my driver's side door and he is standing over me.

"So, how much trouble are you going to be in for sneaking down here?"

"How'd you know I snuck down here?" I ask him curiously.

"I didn't, but now I do." He grins. "I can't believe you lied to your dads to visit me. They're going to think I'm a bad influence. They'll ban us from seeing each other, and then we'll have to sneak around. It's a tragic love story waiting to happen."

"I never knew you could be so dramatic, Jonah." I smirk at him. To my surprise, he brings his face down and kisses me softly on the lips, pulling away before I can respond.

"I'll call you in a few minutes after I finish the dishes. We can talk while you drive home," he tells me, stepping away from me with a cocky grin. I wonder if he can tell that my cheeks are on fire, and my lips are still tingling from his kiss.

He calls me just as I'm getting on I-35N, and we talk about random things until I make it into my house. It's almost 11:30 p.m., and Geoff and Mark are having a family movie night without me. They're watching *Sleepless in Seattle*, Geoff's favorite.

"You're grounded until Sunday," Geoff calls out without turning around. He's in my usual spot, cozy across Mark's lap.

"I'm sorry I got you in trouble, Bo," Jonah sighs on the other end of the phone. "Maybe I should apologize to them?"

I laugh at his cluelessness. He's cute and honorable. "I'm not in trouble and if I was, it would be my own fault. Not yours. Sunday is literally half an hour away. So, I better call you tomorrow when I'm off punishment."

I hear him laugh as he realizes the joke. "It was great seeing you today, Bo. Good night."

After we hang up, I plop down on the chaise lounge perpendicular to my parents on the sectional. I can't fight the smile on my face, and neither can they.

"Have fun? You little harlot," Geoff teases, looking over at me. Mark shakes his head, but his eyes wander over to mine.

I nod. "It felt nice to do something spontaneous."

"You're eighteen now, but could you at least give us a heads-up next time? I haven't had the tires rotated on the Acura yet," Mark tells me, but the gleam in his eye tells me he's happy for me.

I nod my agreement, just as my phone pings again.

Manny: So, where have you been all
day? Chris and I both called you
and you were M.I.A! This is the

```
second movie date you've missed
Bo!
```

I think back to Jonah's words outside of my car earlier.
"It's a tragic love story waiting to happen."
He was probably onto something.

Chapter Twenty-Three

I 'm on unnecessary damage control for the next week, cuddling and kissing Manny excessively. He thinks people will think there is trouble in paradise due to me missing the group movie outing on Saturday.

Whatever. It was worth it.

I think back to the short kiss Jonah gave me outside of his house with longing. I want to feel his lips again. Not the short, chaste kisses we've come accustomed to. I want the intense kiss that we shared the first night he visited me.

And those thoughts scare me.

"You two are going to drown from the amount of spit you swap on a daily basis," Cole snickers at us.

"Stop hating," Manny retorts, kissing my neck. I'm sitting in between his legs with both of us straddling the bench seat at the lunch table. This break in kissing allows me a chance to take a drink from my water bottle.

"I'm not hating," Cole snorts. "Just hope you guys are wrapping it up tight."

I nearly choke on my water. "Watch your mouth, Cole. You don't know what you're talking about."

"So you guys *aren't* doing it?" Cole presses with a laugh.

"What the hell, Cole?" Christina barks at him, slamming her Sprite can on the table and shooting daggers at our annoying blonde tablemate.

Manny says nothing. This is his dream. For people to think we're having sex so that they don't suspect he's gay. Too bad I draw the line at my sex life.

"Not that it's any of your business." I glare at him. "But no, we're not *doing it.*"

"Yet," Manny mumbles in a playful tone, loud enough for our friends to hear. He tries to nuzzle my neck again, but I pull away from him in disgust.

"I'd rather you not refer to me like I'm a piece of meat," I scold him, hoping he can read the disappointment in my eyes.

"C'mon babe, it was just a joke." To everyone else, it may look like he's groveling. But to me, it's a silent plea to go along with his idea of an overly sexual straight couple.

I simply shake my head at him. I'm not bending on this. I don't care what my classmates think about my sex life. Manny and I are probably the last virgins in this school, so no one can judge me. But I still don't enjoy having my most intimate business, real or fake, displayed for everyone.

I think about Jonah, and how even when he's expressing how much he enjoys kissing me, he's never crossed the line or made me feel like he's only after one thing. I'm sure there is a small percentage of teenage relationships that aren't built for the sole purpose of having sex. Jonah seems to be a testament to that.

"The Ainsley twins are throwing another party this weekend. Their parents are going out of town," Bryson announces.

"Count us in!" Manny volunteers for both of us. I roll my eyes, but I don't protest, even though I'd rather drink Geoff's honeysuckle toilet cleaner than go to another high school party this year.

I glance over at Christina, but she's preoccupied. Chris Monte is across the room flirting with Chantel Grisby. Chris Monte will definitely be at the Ainsley party, and from the looks of it, he and Christina aren't on the best of terms. Or maybe they are. It's hard to tell since he's always flirting with other girls. Needless to say, I doubt she'll want to go to that party if he's already grooming Chantel to be his date.

I spend the rest of the day pretending like Manny's actions at lunch didn't piss me off. He's my best friend, I know that everything he does stems from confusion and fear. He loves me under all the selfish, shallow exploits.

"Bowie, what's going on? Why are you being so difficult lately?" Manny whines as we shuffle through racks at *Ross* after school. He needs a new pair of jeans to wear to the party. Manny's family isn't very wealthy, but he's the best-dressed guy in our school. He's a bargain-shopping guru, another one of my favorite things about him.

There are actually *a lot* of things I love about Manny.

He's hilarious, for one. Especially when it's just the three of us and he's not putting on a front for our classmates. He does the best impressions of Kayla and her cronies, even though I don't condone bullying or making fun of people. He's a total fashion buff, and he hates anything he deems tacky or unstylish. He can take a ten-dollar pair of jeans and an eight-dollar button-down, and you'd think he was wearing the most expensive of designer clothes.

"You wear the clothes; the clothes don't wear you." That's his life's motto.

When we were in the tenth grade, Christina had to have an appendectomy. Her dad flaked on making the drive from Houston to be with her in the hospital. He said it was a routine procedure, and that it wouldn't be worth it to make the long drive just for an hour of surgery. She got sick after the surgery and had to stay in the hospital a week longer than a standard couple of days. Christina tried to play it off like her dad's letdown didn't bother her. He'd never been around much, anyway. But we all knew it did. So Manny decided to throw her a get-well-soon party in her hospital room. We snuck in party favors and snacks, and all our friends piled in the room and played music from Manny's portable speaker until the nurses made everyone leave. It was short-lived, but Christina was so happy.

Sometimes he'll send me random text messages in the middle of the night with terrible riddles he knows only I'll appreciate.

> **Manny:** Why did the scarecrow win an award?

> **Manny:** Because he was out-standing in his field!

Then he'll call me and talk my ear off about his hopes for his new life on the East Coast after graduation. I always want to tell him how much I'll miss him when he leaves, but I don't want him to think I'm not happy for him. I can't wait for the day that he can live his life freely. I can't wait to see him truly happy.

"Jonah is what's going on," Christina snickers beside him. I shoot her a look that says *stop*, but Manny's already given me that look of betrayal.

"You can't flake out on the plan now, Bowie!" he scoffs. "Bros before hoes!"

"Or is it chicks before dick?" Christina laughs, and I notice Manny holding in his laughter, just as I am.

"Shut up, Chris!" Manny shoots her a look laced with daggers and then turns to me. "You said you'd help me through this, Bowie. You promised."

"I *am* helping Manny. Jonah's just a friend," I half-lie.

Christina sucks her teeth. "Why don't you just tell Jonah about your agreement with Manny?"

"Because I don't want some stranger knowing my secrets," Manny spits out in a hushed tone before I can agree with Christina. He looks around as if he thinks someone might be listening in on us. "What if he tells someone?" he accuses harshly.

I feel the heat in my chest and the need to defend Jonah's amazing character is strong. "Jonah wouldn't do that!"

"He doesn't even know *you*," Christina adds, rolling her eyes. She pulls a black and silver silk dress shirt from the rack and holds it up against Manny's chest.

"That is hideous, Chris! I'm not going to the disco!" He turns to me again and narrows his eyes.

"I can just explain to Jonah that we're best friends and that—"

Manny cuts me off. "It's *my* secret, Bo! And if I don't want anyone to know about it, then you have to respect that."

I open my mouth to say something but then decide against it. I want to tell him I can tell Jonah about the plan without actually divulging that Manny is gay, but I don't want to argue with him. It's not worth it.

Christina, however, is not having it.

"Wait a minute!" She snaps her fingers at him. "The last time I checked, Bowie was a part of this plan. So that makes it her secret, too."

Manny is annoyed, and Christina is ready to keep putting him in his place. We're all best friends. This argument is dumb and unnecessary.

"It's no big deal, guys." I muster up my best smile. "I don't have to tell Jonah anything. Like I said, we're just friends."

Christina sucks her teeth and shakes her head. Manny stares at me for a moment and then sighs.

"My life will be ruined if people find out about me, Bo," he tells me in a pleading tone. "I need you."

I smile sympathetically and nod. "I know, Manny. I'm still in this with you."

He beams back at me and mouths *"thank you"* before focusing on the rack of clothes again. Beside him, Christina is still visibly irritated, but I shake my head at her and give her a similar pleading look, begging her to drop the subject. She rolls her eyes again and then holds up a thin flannel button-down.

"Now, that's what I'm talking about, girl!" Manny gushes and snatches the shirt from her. "At least *pretend* like you love me!"

We share a laugh, and for a moment all is right with the world again. Manny, Christina, and I are the three amigos, the Musketeers, or Charlie's Angels, as Geoff likes to call us. Manny and

Christina are always at each other's throats, but there's never any love lost. They always have lunch together in the mall food court on the days that they work, and you'll never catch them separated from each other in a shared class.

We're a packaged deal.

? ? ?

On Friday, the entire lunch table is reeling with excitement over the upcoming Ainsley twins' party. They're all bragging about their hot outfits and who they're hoping to hook up with, and I'm just sitting here dreading it.

At least I get to see Jonah tonight.

Our plan is to meet halfway at the Warren Theater in Moore and catch a movie together. It works for both of us, as he can easily head home on the highway afterward, and I get the privacy I need since my peers all go to the AMC in the mall. It's been less than a week since I saw him last, but I'm still really excited to see him again.

In my last class of the day, my phone vibrates in my lap. We're supposed to be using the entire period to study for end-of-the-semester tests next week before Christmas break. However, I've been studying year-round in my free time waiting for Manny and Christina to get off work on the weekends or for Jonah's phone calls at night. So I use my spare time to read Jonah's text.

Jonah: So, my mom had to go to Texas this weekend for work… I've got to stay here with Mia.

So much for our movie date.

> **Bowie:** It's okay. Maybe tomorrow?

I realize after I hit send that I'm obligated to play tonsil hockey all night with Manny at the party tomorrow. Now I'll have to dig myself out of the suggestion.

Or not...

> **Jonah:** I wish… tomorrow is Mia's
> bday and she's having a sleepover
> with her friends. I'm on party
> duty since Mom's gone.

I sigh and put my phone down. I'm not upset with Jonah at all. It's actually really sweet of him to play host to Mia and her friends. I was just really looking forward to seeing him. It would make going to this stupid party so much easier if I had fresh memories of us cuddling in the top row of the movie theater in my mind as a place to escape to.

A thought hits me and I'm texting before my mind has a chance to talk me off of the cliff.

> **Bowie:** I can come down there
> again. Help out with the party?

> **Jonah:** You'd do that?

Bowie: Sure.

Jonah: I don't want you to get in
trouble again.

I chuckle silently because I know he's being sarcastic. Still, his words cause me to make the conscious decision to keep this little trip back to Davis, to myself.

My phone vibrates again, and Jonah has sent another message.

Jonah: But seriously, I'd like
that very much.

? ? ?

The look in Christina's eyes lets me know that she fully supports my plan. Not that I ever doubted she would.

"You've been covering for me our entire friendship." She grins mischievously. I picked her up from work tonight, and now we're sitting in her room on her bed, scheming for my big night tomorrow. "And now I finally get to return the favor!"

"It's not that big of a deal, Chris." I brush her off even though I'm giddy on the inside.

"Then why aren't you telling Mark and Geoff about it?" she asks knowingly.

"Because I know they'll try to convince me to stop helping Manny if they find out that I'm really serious about Jonah," I sigh. It's the classic *have your cake and eat it too,* except Jonah holds the entire cake. I don't get much out of my fake relationship with Manny.

"About that…" My best friend trails off and gives me a look that says I'm not going to like what she has to say next.

"One more semester and it's over, Chris."

"I'm not telling you to stop helping Manny," she cuts me off. "But I think you should tell Jonah what's up."

"But Manny doesn't want people to know. He wouldn't have told you if I hadn't cried and begged him," I remind her. I don't want to have this conversation with her right now. I'd much rather be talking about Jonah.

Christina makes a *'pssht'* sound and rolls her eyes. "Girl please, I would have figured it out eventually."

We laugh together at our best friend's expense. Christina always jokes about Manny being obviously gay, and to an extent, I agree with her, but maybe it's because we spend more intimate time with him in his element.

"Manny doesn't get to control your love life just because he's an insecure brat." She sucks her teeth. Her words sting because she has no idea who the real insecure brat is.

"It's fine, Christina. I can handle it." I try to assure her and plead with her to drop it at the same time.

"And what are you going to do when Jonah finds out, Bo?" she challenges, crossing her arms across her chest. Her long box braids are falling across her face, but she doesn't toss them back over her shoulder just yet.

"He's not going to find out, Chris. He lives in another town miles away. After it's all over, I'll tell him about everything." I shrug. She's not buying anything I say, and Christina has never been the type of person to hold her tongue for *anybody*, especially me and Manny.

Again, she groans and tosses her head back. "This is why you need to watch those sappy chick flicks you hate so much. He *will* find out Bo; and when he does, it'll be a *disaster*!"

I'm torn between knowing that Christina is right, and staying loyal to Manny and the plan. What's the lesser of two evils? Possibly getting caught and losing Jonah? Or going against Manny's wishes and risking exposing a secret that he's worked so hard to keep?

Chapter Twenty-Four

I'm on the road to Davis before the sun sets on Saturday. I'm both proud and ashamed of myself for how effortlessly I lied and schemed against my loved ones to make sure that this night goes off without a hitch. Geoff thinks I'm going to the Ainsley party with Manny and Christina, then spending the night with the Harris household. Manny thinks I'm home sick with food poisoning. Mark is grounded in Chicago tonight, due to a blizzard, so I didn't have to lie to him.

As I'd predicted, Christina is skipping the Ainsley party. To my surprise, it's because Chris Monte promised to come and sneak in her window later tonight. My guess is he's going to go to the party and meet up with Chantel Grisby, and then finish his night with Christina.

"That way, I can get what I want and still cover for you while you spend the night with your boo." She winked at me after we went over the details just before I left her house this evening.

I wanted to tell her how I felt about Chris Monte and Chantel, but I was too preoccupied with her latter statement. It hadn't occurred to me that I'd possibly end up staying the night at Jonah's house.

What does that mean for us? Kissing is one thing...

But spending the night?

I make it to his house just before 7:30 p.m. When I knock on the door, I hear little girls giggling and music blasting in the living room. It's mid-December but the stiff wind is no match for my heated skin. I'm nervous, anxious, excited, and scared all in one! The anticipation of how this night will pan out is killing me.

Jonah and his gorgeous dimples greet me moments later. He's got a plastic king's crown and a stuffed unicorn horn on his head. There's a red blanket tied around his neck like a cape.

"I can't believe you really came through!" he mimics his words from last weekend.

"I couldn't resist the charm of this one-horse town." I wink at him. He ushers me in, and I'm instantly in awe.

They have transformed their living room into a fortress of blankets and sheets. Pink and white balloons are scattered all around the floor, and streamers and unicorn-themed décor hang from the walls.

"Bowie!" Mia squeals as she climbs out of the giant blanket fort. "You really came to my sleepover!"

"I told you I'd try." I smile at her and run my fingers backward through my bangs.

Mia is wearing long-sleeve thermal pajamas that have little unicorns all over them. On her head is a unicorn horn similar to Jonah's and a tiara. Even her oversized house shoes are shaped like unicorn heads.

I'm sensing a theme here.

"It's pretty magical in here." I look around and nod my approval.

She thanks me and points to the blanket fort. "Jonah made us a unicorn cave." She points to the blanket fort, where several little girls clad in similar unicorn pajamas emerge from the opening. They're all wearing stuffed unicorn horns and smile brightly at me. Even Cooper has a unicorn costume on as he darts around the living room.

"Did you bring your sleeping bag? We're all sleeping in the cave," Mia tells me. Behind me, Jonah laughs.

"I don't think I'll fit in the unicorn cave," I tell her sweetly, resisting the urge to laugh.

"I'm sure you'll fit. You're about the same height as them," Jonah taunts. Mia nods in agreement and I can see the hopefulness in her eyes.

"I'll just sleep on the couch," I tell her cheerfully before throwing a smug look at her brother. His eyes grow wide for a brief second, and I know that like me, he hadn't considered the thought of me spending the night tonight.

"Well, before we get to the sleeping part, we've got to eat and party." Jonah claps his hands and winks at me. There's a stampede of unicorn girls rushing to the dining room table, which is covered with a cotton sheet resembling a bed of clouds, with a buffet of rainbow confections on top.

There's a round, glittery, rainbow-iced cake with a gold twisted horn for a topper sitting in the middle of the table. There are multicolored rice crispy treats piled on a plate, next to a plate of sugar cookies that are iced with unicorn faces. A bowl of frothy pink punch sits at the end of the table, and the plates and cups match the theme as well. Lots of light pink and lavender.

I pick up a purple plastic cup that's filled with a sticky mixture of caramel corn, pink and purple M&M's, marshmallows, and sprinkles.

"Jonah is the best party planner ever," Mia brags proudly.

I nod in agreement and hold the cup out to him with a raised brow. He laughs and shrugs. "That's unicorn poop."

I burst into laughter, along with all of Mia's friends. Mia glares at him as she and her buddies grab plates and begin piling them with sweets.

She corrects him. "It's supposed to be unicorn popcorn, Bowie."

"That's a lot of sugar." I motion toward the table with a smirk. "They'll be up all night."

Jonah wags his finger and shakes his head. "Quite the contrary. They'll crash even harder."

"Is there any actual food at this party?" I laugh. Jonah nods towards the kitchen.

"There's pizza in there. Hungry?"

The girls all retreat to the unicorn cave, and Jonah grabs a slice of pepperoni pizza from the Pizza Hut box for me.

"Cold pizza?" He raises a brow at me. We're sitting on the couch again, with about two feet of space separating us.

"It's not completely cold." I shrug, "But I like cold pizza, yes." Geoff hates it when I grab a leftover pizza slice from the fridge and immediately scarf it down. "And stop staring at me while I eat! It's embarrassing!"

He doesn't look away, and the smile he flashes gives me butterflies. It's simple, with a hint of mischief.

"Sorry I had to cancel on movies."

I shrug and finish chewing the chunk of pizza in my mouth before responding.

"I've got a feeling this is going to be way more fun." I don't mean it to be suggestive. Honestly, the thought of pigging out on unicorn poop and glittery rainbow-frosted cupcakes is fascinating. Geoff rarely keeps confections in the house, and if so, they're usually homemade, with sugar substitutes. Still, the shy smile that creeps across Jonah's face match mine as we both realize that this night will be a huge test of our budding relationship.

I reach up and flick the unicorn horn on his head. "What's with the horn and crown?"

"I'm the Unicorn King." He grins at me and winks.

Mia pops her head out of the unicorn cave and points to the tiara and horn combination on her head. "And I'm the Unicorn Princess!" she announces before disappearing again.

Jonah hops up from his seat on the couch and jogs into the kitchen. He returns a few seconds later with another spiral, gold horn headband and swiftly straps it on my head. I feel shivers as his fingers lightly brush against my face.

"You're really into this, huh?" I tease, adjusting the horn and chuckling softly.

Jonah shrugs and nods his head. "It's probably the last party Mia will want me to help with. Next year it'll be makeup and whispering about their crushes."

"You never know. My eleventh birthday party was a big circus extravaganza. My dads rented out a venue and had an exotic petting zoo come in with all kinds of crazy animals. The most over-the-top party I've ever had. No makeup and definitely no crushes."

"All of that for an eleventh birthday?" He grimaces.

"Geoff said eleven is the year that everyone tries to brush off as no big deal. So he wanted me to feel special on my eleventh birthday."

"I like the way Geoff thinks." He nods in approval.

The little unicorns emerge from their cave, hyped up on sugar and demanding party games. Jonah was so great at planning activities at camp last summer, I'm not surprised by the impressive unicorn-themed party games he's created. A homemade pin-the-horn-on-the-unicorn game is hanging on the wall in the dining room. After a few rounds of the six girls clumsily trying to stick the laminated paper horn cutout to the skillfully drawn paper unicorn, we move on to the next game.

"It's called cloud mouth. Because unicorns fly and they probably eat clouds," Jonah explains.

I scrunch up my face and shake my head at him. "Who told you that unicorns eat clouds?"

"Just use your imagination." He flashes me a grin and explains the game. On each turn, we have to fill our mouths with cotton balls and try to say a sentence, while the others guess what we're trying to say.

It's equal parts funny and disastrous, as no one can guess what anyone else is saying.

"I said, *I have the coolest brother in the world!*" Mia gripes at Jonah after we all fail to translate *"Off-da-ooless-udder-inferal."*

Just before midnight, Jonah's science proves true, and the girls fall into a near-comatose sugar crash in the unicorn cave.

"Well, you certainly get brownie points for being the best big brother ever," I tell him softly so as not to disrupt the slumber of the Unicorn Princess and her friends.

Jonah chuckles lightly as he crawls out of the cave after making sure each girl has a blanket and pillow to sleep with. "I try."

He disappears down the hallway, which I assume is where the bedrooms and bathrooms are. When he returns, he's holding a thick blue comforter and grinning at me. It's more of a nervous grin, which calms me down a little. For someone who's usually cool and sure of themselves, Jonah seems shy right now.

"I figured we'd probably just crash out here on the couch. I can put on a movie," he suggests with a shrug, and I nod and take the blanket from him.

He pulls up a movie on a streaming app and then comes back over to the couch where I'm spreading out the comforter. I'm not sure what girls are supposed to do in this situation. We've cuddled before, we've kissed before, but tonight seems different. Like there's some unspoken air around us.

Again, hormones maybe?

"*Fight Club*, 1999, David Fincher, starring Brad Pitt and Edward Norton." He grins at me as he pulls the covers, and me, towards him. "Ever seen it?"

I shake my head no. "I've read the book, though. Chuck Palahniuk, 1996."

"You did?" he asks me with a cocked eyebrow.

"Yeah, I went through a rebellious phase when I was in ninth grade."

Jonah laughs. "Only you would have a rebellious phase that involves reading."

The movie plays out, and Jonah and I lay on the couch together, our bodies molded together, his chest pressed against my back.

When the credits scroll up the screen, signaling that the movie has ended, neither of us moves, but I know he's still awake behind me.

Eventually, he shifts us, so that he's hovering over me and his bright smile is captivating me.

"You're really beautiful," he mumbles before dropping to kiss my lips. I melt into his kiss and my body reacts without my permission. My arms snake around his neck, and his hands go to grip my hips. It's a normal heated teenage make-out session until he accidentally grinds against my thigh, and I'm brought back to reality by just how excited he really is.

"Jonah." His name comes out a little raspier than I intend for it to, so I try again when he doesn't stop kissing me. "Jonah, we have to stop."

He stops immediately, and I can tell I've scared him. I just need him to realize that things are going to go too far if we don't stop now.

"I'm sorry," I tell him sheepishly. "I'm just not-"

"No, no! It's cool, Bo! I'm the one that should apologize!" He lifts his body off of mine and then helps me into a sitting position as well.

I can feel my face heating and I try to turn away from him and focus my gaze on the Unicorn Cave. "This is all new for me. Sorry, I'm being so difficult."

Jonah gives me a playful snort and shove, so I give him my attention again. "Please don't apologize for being yourself."

I laugh too. "Which part? The shy, inexperienced virgin? or difficult?"

"You're not difficult. You're amazing."

"I'd better head home. I can only keep my phone tracker off for so long before Geoff catches on." I stand and fold up the blanket before grabbing my purse and following Jonah to the door.

"To hell with reading *Fight Club*. I think this is your rebellious streak," Jonah teases before kissing my cheek. He's definitely right about that. I would have never done anything like this a year ago. Not that my friends and I have always had innocent fun, but my parents always knew what was going on. I don't know why I feel the need to hide hanging out with Jonah from my dads. Maybe it's because it's nice to have my own happy secrets for once.

I can still feel Jonah's goodbye kiss as I crawl through Christina's bedroom window and snuggle under the comforter next to her.

"Have fun tonight?" she murmurs, shoving me playfully.

"Did you?" I snort. I shoot up immediately and look around in disgust at the bed sheets.

"Girl, bye. I knew you were coming back, so I swapped out my sheets," she teases and rolls around to face me. "What about you?" She cranes her neck to look at the digital clock on her bookcase. "It's almost four o'clock in the morning!"

"I left before things got too heated." I sigh and flop back down on the pillow.

"Mark would be proud."

"Shut up." I bury my face in the pillow. "I'm going crazy, Chris."

"*Crazy in love*, like my girl Bey!" she sings out.

I laugh at her joke and roll over to fall asleep. Thoughts of Jonah flood my mind and eventually my dreams.

Chapter Twenty-Five

I'm starting to think kissing Jonah is one of the greatest pleasures that life has to offer. There's seafood night when Mark is cooking dinner, laying on freshly laundered sheets that smell like Geoff's *Apple Mango Tango* detergent, and making out with Jonah.

The weeks and months have seemed to blend together with Jonah in my life. We go on dates at least once a week, and we talk and text on the phone daily. On his birthday, he invited me to go overnight camping with him and his friends in the Arbuckle Mountains. I was apprehensive about being the only girl, but after Jonah assured me that another female friend of his would be joining them, as well as a girlfriend of another friend, I gave in and spent the night in a cabin that his mom rented for them; this time with Geoff's permission and my phone tracker on.

I had fake girlfriend duty on Valentine's Day, so we celebrated the weekend after with dinner and a horror movie marathon at my house. Geoff was working late, and Mark was out of town.

Being with Jonah is like finding a new favorite song that you can play on nonstop repeat. I'll never get enough of the feeling of ease he gives me whenever he's around, while still sending me into an internal fit of giddiness.

But much like that favorite song on repeat, I know this won't last long. I won't get burned out on Jonah; I know that for a fact. Christina's words still echo in my mind, though. It's only a matter of time before my double life catches up with me.

"Ready for this little slice of gossip?" Manny cuts his eyes at Christina and me as he flops down at the lunch table. He pauses and frowns at the space where Christina's slice of pizza would normally be.

"You need some cash for lunch, Chris?"

Christina smiles weakly and shakes her head. "Nah, I'm just not feeling well. I'll eat later before work. Thanks though."

"Anyway," Manny turns his glare toward me. Just like that, he can go from being the concerned bestie who would give his last few dollars to ensure Christina ate lunch, to scolding me about something I'm completely oblivious about.

"Kayla McMurray's new beau? AJ Mitchell?"

"What about him?" I shrug.

"I went Facebook-creeping last night because supposedly they're getting pretty serious. I was trying to find out what kind of mental illness this guy had to really be interested in Kayla McMurray." He huffs and gulps his diet coke.

"Manny, that is not nice at all!" I laugh, and Christina chuckles. When I look over at her, I see that she's watching Chris Monte sitting with his arm around Brandi Cross, the newest member of the Chris Monte army.

"Anyway, his account isn't private, so I'm scouring through his pictures—"

"How do you have this much time on your hands?" I cut him off.

"Because my *girlfriend* ditched me *again* Saturday night," he shoots back.

Oh yeah, I was at the movies with Jonah. There was a special screening of *The Godfather* trilogy. I didn't care for the movies much, but it was nice sneaking in a kiss or two (or five) and being snuggled in Jonah's lanky embrace.

Manny doesn't need to know that, though. He thinks I was having a family night with my dads.

"*Anyways.*" He clears his throat dramatically to signal he's ready to reveal the big secret and it would be best if I didn't interrupt him again.

"I'm scrolling through AJ's pictures and I come across this little gem." He pulls out his beat-up cell phone and pulls up Facebook. When he turns the camera towards me, my heart drops.

It's a picture of who I assume is AJ Mitchell standing in front of a blue Camaro next to a tall boy with curly brown hair and a lopsided smile.

"And look at the tag," Manny continues. "I followed that tag to the Facebook page of Jonah Taylor, AJ's cousin."

Kayla McMurray is dating Jonah's cousin. AJ must be the cousin Jonah talks about visiting whenever he's in town.

It's a small freaking world.

"Okay, and..." Christina sucks her teeth, finally bringing her attention back to our table.

"... and if Bowie tells Jonah about our agreement, he might mention it to AJ, and then AJ will tell Kayla, and then Kayla will tell EVERYBODY!" he shoots back in disbelief.

"If I tell Jonah not to mention it, he won't say anything."

"You don't even know him that well, Bo!" Manny sucks his teeth and rolls his eyes. I can feel my face growing hot with irritation. I never lose my cool with my friends, not even Manny. However, the thought of Jonah's character being called out is pushing my buttons.

"I know him well enough," I shoot back smugly, instead of unleashing my built-up wrath on him.

Christina laughs and Manny's jaw drops.

"Are you trying to say that you guys—"

I roll my eyes. "No, Manny, we haven't made it past first base."

"Is first base just kissing?" Christina asks.

"Yes, with tongue," I mumble.

"Chris skipped all the bases and went straight for the home run!" Manny laughs obnoxiously, slapping his knee.

"Well, you'll be too busy catching the ball when you get your first home run," Christina smirks at him.

"Or pitching... you never know," he retorts coolly.

"Baseball is officially dead to me," I groan.

? ? ?

Manny calls me later in the evening while I'm reading chapters for Government class. I hung up with Jonah about an hour ago because I need to have these chapters finished by Friday. I've been neglecting Manny lately, so I closed my textbook and answered the call.

"You're the only nerd I know who reads their homework five days in advance," he teases after I tell him I'm trying to finish our reading assignment on political parties.

"I've already got my final project done," I tell him proudly.

"What the hell, Bo? It's March! That shit isn't due until the end of April!" He's laughing and I can tell he's not surprised. Knowing Manny, he's probably not very far behind me.

Manny will be the first person in his immediate family to go to college. His father runs an auto mechanic shop, and his mother is a stay-at-home mom, caring for his grandparents and three younger siblings, all in one house. Academics are a huge deal to Manny, probably more so than they are for me. He aspires to be an architect. Meanwhile, I have no clue what I want to be in my adult life. I'm too busy trying to figure out who I am *now*.

"Please don't tell Jonah. I've got a bad feeling about it, Bo. It's just two more months, then I'm free. I'll be halfway across the country and I can finally be myself." His voice is soft with desperation, and at that moment I feel sorry for him again because he really is afraid of being ridiculed for being gay.

Manny's fears are the embodiment of the stigmas that society puts on people for differing from the so-called *"norm."* Like the deacon who called my parents out at mass. He lacked the ability to only see my parents as two loving men who had saved a helpless orphan's life. He could not see past their sexual preferences to focus strictly on what amazing people they are.

Manny is a lot of things besides being gay. He's passionate, smart, and loyal (when he's not in fear of being outed). He's a class clown, but very respectful and hardworking. He'll always make it known that his friends' problems are his problems too. No one suffers alone. Manny is amazing. Too bad he feels like he can't just be all of those things *and* openly love who he wants to love. Where

I'm struggling to find myself, Manny *knows* who he is. He's just too afraid to be it.

"I mean, if this whole thing doesn't work out, and he knows about me. He might tell everyone I'm gay just to get back at you."

Did I mention he doesn't hold back what he's thinking for *anybody*?

"Thanks for the vote of confidence," I murmur sarcastically.

"Whatever. You weren't even going to tell me about your new beau. So who's the worse friend?" he shoots back and I can visualize the eye roll.

"I've been a damn good friend, Manny, so don't call me a bad friend." I don't mean to let my irritation slip, but I'm mentally drained already. Remembering that I'm two seconds from an identity crisis will do that to me from time to time.

"You know I was joking Bo. Well, about the bad friend thing. I am still hurt you didn't tell me about you and Jonah. You still haven't said much." He trails off on the last part, and for a second I feel bad again.

I'll never confront him on it, but Manny's been so wrapped up in perfecting this fake relationship that I doubt he wants to hear about my relationship with Jonah. In his eyes, Jonah's just another person who could ruin our plan.

"I'm really tired, Manny. I'm going to go to bed now," I lie. My mind is on full blast, and I doubt I'll sleep much tonight. Reading about Democratic views is probably out of the question too.

I can tell Manny's reluctant to hang up, so I assure him that, like always, his secret is safe with me. I won't tell Jonah about our arrangement.

I spend a few minutes staring at the ceiling. Letting the thoughts that roam my mind flow out from my ears and play out on the tray ceiling above. I want to run into the next room and crawl under the covers with Geoff and cry. Tell him how I really feel about life. But then the guilt takes over. I think about everything they've done for me, and the slap in the face it would be to tell them.

"Hey dads, thanks for saving my life, but I'm pretty upset that I don't have a mom, or know my real dad, or my real birthday, or ethnicity. Your love has been tremendous for the past eighteen years, but nothing can fill the void of knowing that someone wedged you behind a dumpster for reasons you may never know."

Without thinking, I stand up and walk into my closet. I reach up and rummage behind all of my shoe boxes until I feel the small square box hidden between my green Chuck Taylors and Old Skool checkerboard Vans.

I flop down on my bed with the *Ancestry DNA* kit in my hand. I still haven't mustered up the courage to use it. Jonah hasn't pressured me into doing so either. The instructions boast information about a person's ethnicity across over one-hundred-eighty countries. It's a simple swab test with a collection tube that I am to send back to their labs. Results take six to eight weeks to process.

What intrigues me is the part that states that it can match you with relatives who have completed the ancestry kit and are in the database. If my birth parents, or any of their relatives, have completed this process, I might be able to find them.

Then I'd get the answers I'd been searching for.

But then I'd have to tell Geoff and Mark what I'd done, and then I'd have to explain to them how I really feel about my life.

I shake the thoughts out of my head. Jonah spent his hard-earned money on this kit. I finally told someone how I felt, and he wants to help. I *need* these answers.

I'm just about to pull the swab from the sterile tube when I hear a knock on my door. I quickly shove the kit under my pillows and call for Geoff to come in.

"Monday night snack? I made parfait." He holds up two glass dessert cups.

"It's like eleven o'clock at night. Why are you making parfait?"

"It's fruit and yogurt. It's good for the soul." Geoff hands me my glass and kisses my forehead. "Goodnight, Junior. I love you."

I smile and tell him the same. After he leaves, I sit the glass on my nightstand and fish out the swab kit. I grab a pen from the drawer in my nightstand and begin filling out the information card in the box. They'll email me to let me know my results are ready, and then I'll log onto the website and view my results. From there, the database will pair me with any matching DNA.

I pull the cotton swab from the tube and stare at it briefly. I *need* this.

I take the swab and rub it against the inside of my cheek for one minute before placing it back inside the tube. I re-box everything and slide it under my pillow again.

I've waited eighteen years to find out who I really am. What's another eight weeks?

Chapter Twenty-Six

By spring break, all traces of the cold winter have vanished. The trees have all blossomed, the temperature is warm and inviting, and with graduation a little over six weeks away, things are looking very promising.

Our teachers have finally gotten the memo that it's tradition to ditch school the last day before spring break, so there's never any work assigned. I've already read the syllabus enough times to know that we're expected to read *The Kite Runner* over the break.

"I hope your dads have the pool cleaned and uncovered by graduation," Manny states as we walk past the sliding door in the living room.

Christina isn't feeling well, so we decided to just spend our last ditch day together in my room, watching movies and hanging out. Manny didn't seem to mind, since our absence from any group activities like the mall or theme park might *"cause speculation."*

"Why?" I ask him as we ascend the stairs.

"Because the after-party is at your house that Saturday," he responds nonchalantly. He's ahead of me and I gape as I watch him shrug his shoulders.

I stop walking mid-step, causing Christina to bump into me. "Excuse me?"

"What's wrong with that?" He turns around and gives me the dumbest look ever.

"Nobody asked me if they could throw a party at my house. What about my parents?" I frown at him. I shouldn't even have to explain this to him. It's common sense!

"Your dads are leaving for their cruise that day, remember?" He shrugs again, and I want to smack the confusion off his face.

"You didn't think to *ask me* if you could throw a party at *my house* before you invited the entire senior class?" I snap at him. I've never been this upset with Manny before. He's done a lot of selfish things in our friendship, some worse than this even, For some reason, this time I'm finally pissed.

"What's your problem, Bowie?" Manny screws his face up and sucks his teeth.

"Can we continue this conversation off of the staircase, please?" Christina huffs tiredly, but we both ignore her, keeping our stare-down. Neither of us backs down.

"You've been acting so funny ever since you started talking to *Jonah*!"

"This has nothing to do with Jonah. This is about you over-stepping your boundaries, per usual!" I shoot back. "You can't just volunteer my house for a party while my parents are out of town. They'll flip if they find out!"

Behind me, I hear Christina making a gagging sound before pushing past us and bolting up the stairs into my bathroom. Manny and I both stare at the entrance to my bedroom curiously, before shrugging and following her.

"Girl, you know your parents will not care," Manny continues, flopping down on my bed and pulling out his cell phone. "They'll be excited you're breaking the rules if anything."

"It would still be nice if you asked me first before making plans like that, Manny." I sit in my reading nook and hug the stuffed teddy bear Jonah gave me for Valentine's Day.

"Okay, fine." He sucks his teeth and rolls his eyes. "Bowie, can we please have the after-party at your beautiful giant house with the best pool in town?"

"Why aren't the Ainsley twins throwing a party?" I still don't want to give in. What if Jonah comes to my graduation? Maybe he'll want to make plans with me. It'll be the last night I'll have to pretend to be Manny's girlfriend.

"Their parents will be in town that weekend." Manny shrugs and starts texting on his phone.

The toilet in my bathroom flushes and Christina walks out looking tired and pale.

"Got an extra toothbrush? Or some mouthwash?" Her voice is groggy, and she looks miserable.

"Did you just throw up?" I frown and stand up to get an extra toothbrush from the hallway cabinet.

When I come back in, I hear Manny saying, "Eww, if that's the flu, keep it away from me. I do not want to be sick during spring break."

"It's March. Nobody has the flu, Manny." I shake my head. I hand Christina the toothbrush and mouthwash. "It's creamsi-cle-flavored, because... *Geoff*."

Christina sniffs the contents of the mouthwash bottle and gags again. "I'll pass. Thanks."

"So, is that a yes to the party?" Manny asks me as Christina disappears into the bathroom, and I go back to my seat in the reading nook.

"Whatever Manny," I mumble. My phone vibrates, and it's a text message from Jonah.

Jonah: Hey what's up?

Bowie: Ditch Day. Hanging out at my house with friends.

Jonah: Any spring break plans?

Bowie: I've got to read The Kite Runner. There's a movie adaptation *hint hint*

Jonah: I've got to help my aunt and cousin clear out some storage during the break. I bet I can sneak away, though.

Christina finally emerges from the bathroom and groans as she lies across the floor.

I put my phone away, deciding to text Jonah back later. "What's wrong, Chris?"

She sighs and looks between Manny and me. This is serious. Christina is never this dramatic. Even Manny sets his phone on my bed beside him and gives her his undivided attention.

Christina shakes her head, and I can tell by the defeated look on her face that something bad has happened. She looks sad, angry, and scared all at once.

"I'm pregnant."

A gasp erupts in the room, but I'm not sure if it came from me or Manny or both of us at the same time.

"You're kidding," I spit out absently, squeezing my teddy bear to my chest.

"Why would I joke about that, Bo?" she sucks her teeth and frowns at me.

"Sorry," I murmur and stare at her sadly. I'm not sure what else to say, though. This is bad! Christina's only seventeen, and the last time I checked, Chris Monte has moved on to his newest conquest.

"You just got accepted into college, Chris!" Manny gushes in horror. In January, my dads took us all out for dinner, including Ms. Shonda, to celebrate Christina getting her acceptance letter to OU.

"I know," Christina groans and runs her hands over her face.

"Does your mom know?" I ask.

Chris shakes her head and rests her hands on her stomach. My eyes fall onto the still-flat surface solemnly. I can't imagine Christina being big and pregnant in a few months while trying to study for midterms in college.

"What are you going to do, Chris?" Manny asks next, and I eye him incredulously. What does he mean *"What are you going to do, Chris?"* What else can she do?

"Destiny's going to sign the paperwork for me so that I can take care of it," Christina responds with another sigh.

"Take... care of it?" I mimic her in slight disbelief. My brain knows exactly what she's referring to, but my heart doesn't want to comprehend it.

"Yeah, I'm getting an abortion. Des—" Christina says it so blatantly that I don't even think she notices how serious the statement is.

"You can't do that!" I jump up and yell at her, causing both her and Manny to stare at me as if I were crazy.

"What are you talking about?" Christina frowns at me, sitting up slightly.

"You can't kill your baby. Are you being serious right now?" I blurt out. I've never considered myself a pro-lifer. With all the random crap going through my mind daily, I've actually managed to stay away from conforming to any singular belief sets. I figure I have my entire life to picket and rally behind every social and political cause in my adulthood.

Still, the thought of Christina getting an abortion because she was irresponsible and had unprotected sex before she was ready to be a parent infuriates me for some reason.

"Are *you* serious right now, Bo?" Christina counters, deepening her frown. "I can't take care of a baby by myself *and* go to college. My mom is already taking care of Destiny and Isaiah!"

"What about adoption?" I press. I don't even know why I say it. I'm proof that adoption isn't without its flaws in kids, right?

Christina and I have had plenty of minor disagreements, but this feels bigger than any of those.

"I can't do that." She shakes her head. "I'm thinking about my future, Bo. Plus, it's my decision, so I don't even know why I'm arguing with you." She's getting annoyed, and I should probably be more supportive, but I can't see past how wrong this feels!

"You have other options, Christina. You don't have to kill your baby! What if my mom had aborted me when she decided she didn't want me?" There it is. It's out in the open. The real reason I'm so passionate about this. Nothing to do with pro or anti-abortion, it's not about advocating for adoption. It's about me and my abandonment issues.

"Would you rather I leave it behind a dumpster?"

Her words sting, but I don't react. I just stare at her. There's the briefest flash of regret in her eyes before she sighs and looks down at the hardwood floor. Manny gasps and looks between us, unsure of which side to take.

"C'mon guys, you don't mean the stuff you're saying right now," he tries to reason. He looks at me with pleading eyes. "Bowie, we're supposed to be supportive of her."

Oh yeah? Because I know *nothing* about being supportive of my friends' unhealthy behavior?

I don't respond. I cross my arms across my chest and shake my head.

Christina stands up and turns to leave. "I'll talk to you guys later." There are tears in her eyes, and I briefly remember that I've only seen Christina cry twice. She broke her ankle in seventh grade and cried for about five minutes when she found out she would miss my thirteenth birthday party, and again when her grandmother died.

If she's crying now, then she's hurting. Bad.

Manny calls after her, but she continues to storm out of the room and down the stairs. I hear Geoff, who must be home early from work, greet her at the door.

"I'm going to go check on her," Manny says. I hate putting him in the middle of our fight, but I wish he was staying to make sure that *I'm* okay. It's selfish, I know. He'd have no reason to believe that I was drowning on the inside as well.

So, I just nod my head and walk him downstairs.

Chapter Twenty-Seven

My argument with Christina weighs heavily on my mind as the days of spring break fly by. We've never gone this long without speaking, and I miss her. Every time I pick up the tattered borrowed library copy of *The Kite Runner*, I immediately put it down. It's hard to read about friendship when you're in a standoff with your best friend.

I find myself constantly wanting to text her something funny that Geoff did, or gush about Jonah's latest antics. But I don't. Instead, I occupy my time appeasing Manny's fake relationship scheme. When I'm not with Manny and our classmates pretending to be blindly in love with him, I'm taking advantage of the little time I can squeeze out of Jonah whenever he's in town helping his aunt and cousin.

If Mark and Geoff noticed Christina wasn't coming around lately, they never mentioned it, which is odd for them because Geoff has a hard time holding his tongue as it is.

It's the last Saturday of spring break, and Manny and I are hanging out with our usual crowd, minus Christina, in the food court of the mall.

Cole and Bryson are up to their usual stupid banter, and I'm only half listening as they brag about which one of them will take

Arianna Johnson to prom. Arianna is arguably one of the prettiest girls in school. Her parents run a Korean barbecue restaurant. Not traditional Korean barbecue, but a 2-in-1 establishment that serves traditional Korean dishes prepared by her Korean mother and Memphis-style ribs and brisket baskets smoked on the grill by her Black father. Ever since elementary school, I've always been obsessed with her cultural day presentations for class.

I should be home working on my report for *The Kite Runner*, but Manny insisted we hang out as a couple with everyone one last time during spring break. We're all catching a movie soon and then going out to eat, which actually interferes with a movie night with my dads, but I don't mention that.

So I'm here, listening to Cole make crude remarks about Arianna's butt, and bragging about his mom reserving a suite for him at the Hyatt after prom.

"She's probably just trying to get rid of him for the night so she can hook up with Eric Trembley's dad again." Manny leans over and whispers in my ear. We share a laugh at Cole's expense because he's an ass and deserves it sometimes.

"What are you two whispering about?" Cole asks us with a smirk.

"Nothing." Manny's voice goes an octave deeper as he winks at me before dipping in for a kiss.

Scopaesthesia. It's the sensation of feeling like someone is watching you. There's a lot of back-and-forth speculation whether it's a real phenomenon, or if the person is just so anxious that someone might be staring at them, that they accidentally draw attention to themselves so by the time they turn around someone is indeed staring at them.

Whatever the case, as I sit here lip-locked with my best friend, I get the feeling I'm being watched. It's not until I hear Kayla McMurray's energetic voice call out to us that I find out that I'm indeed being stared down.

My eyes don't fall on Kayla's, or even the boy standing with his arm around her. No, my eyes fall on the confused face of Jonah, as he's just watched me stick my tongue down Manny's throat.

This is it. The moment Christina tried to warn me about. The moment my favorite song ends its repeat cycle. That dramatic scene in cheesy romance movies where everything goes to shit.

"Jonah," I choke out hoarsely, and I think he hears me because he shakes his head and turns to walk away. The boy next to him, AJ I assume, looks between me and Jonah's retreating form with the same look of confusion. Next to him, Kayla looks equally shocked.

"Jonah, wait! It's not—It's not like that!" I call out, accidentally knocking my chair to the ground with a loud *clank* when I push it back to stand up. I don't bother picking it up, I just keep on moving across the food court after Jonah.

I grab his wrist just before he boards the escalator and try to tug him back, but he yanks his hand away from me and continues to the escalator. Behind us, Manny and the others have caught up with us. I can hear AJ mumbling, *"What the hell?"* to Kayla, who responds with a hushed, *"I told you guys she had a boyfriend! They've been together for years!"* So Kayla ratted me out. Not her fault, but it still sucks.

I turn to Manny with pleading eyes, "Manny, he's leaving! Tell him!"

When I turn back toward Jonah, he's riding the escalator up, but he's looking between Manny and me curiously. Almost hopefully.

Manny scowls at me. "Tell him what? Who the hell is that, Bo?"

I'm sure my eyes grow to the size of saucers as I throw my hands toward Jonah. "That's Jonah! Manny, he's leaving! He thinks—"

"So, what? You've been cheating on me?" Manny retorts, and I see the look in his eyes for what it really is. It's not anger, like everyone else may think. It's desperation. My words get caught in my throat and my chest caves in. It's almost like an out-of-body experience mixed with déjà vu. I'm Dillion Wilkenson, three years ago. I'm on the other side, and I can see the Manny that I don't like so much. The coward Manny. The person who will do anything to anybody to keep his secret safe.

"Manny..." My voice cracks, and I turn back towards Jonah, who now has his back to me as he rides to the top of the escalator, shaking his head.

"Bowie!" Manny yells at me. "We need to talk!" He grabs my arm, but much like Jonah did to me just a few minutes ago, I push away from him. Chasing after Jonah again.

He's near the entrance this time, and to my surprise, he stops when I call his name.

"It's not what you think, Jonah. I—"

"Funny." He laughs, but I don't think what he's about to say will be very humorous. He's not looking at me, but staring up at the ceiling with a sarcastic smirk on his face. "I meet my cousin's girlfriend for the first time today. She mentions attending high school at North Creek. I say: *"Wow, this girl I'm dating goes there, Bowie Monroe?"* and do you know what she says?" He pauses and looks at me, but again, I don't think he expects an answer. "She says: *"Bowie Monroe has a boyfriend."* And to further prove her point, because of course I didn't believe her, she brings me to the mall where Bowie can be found making out with said boyfriend."

"Jonah, I can explain."

"Be my guest," he scoffs.

"Manny's…" I trail off, catching myself before I can tell Jonah the truth. Manny's pleas are trapped in my head.

"If Bowie tells Jonah, then Jonah will mention it to AJ, and then AJ will tell Kayla, and Kayla will tell EVERYBODY."

"My life will be ruined!"

Jonah snorts again, "Thought so. You know how much I hate liars, Bowie. I thought you were different." And with that, he turns around and walks through the automatic sliding doors, leaving me to stand there looking and feeling like the biggest fool.

Chapter Twenty-Eight

$\mathbf{M}$y dads are snuggling on the couch watching *Here We Stand* when I storm into the house. It's a little after five o'clock, and they're sharing a bowl of popcorn and catching up on Geoff's favorite NBC drama about a dysfunctional family doing dysfunctional things to each other. Tomorrow at church Ms. Shonda and Geoff will probably spend twenty minutes chatting about the latest episode, while Christina and I awkwardly stare at each other because, as it stands right now, I'm not even sure we're friends anymore.

Not that I blame her. I don't blame her or Jonah for hating me. I don't even blame Manny for what happened today. It's all me. Me and my inability to be my own person, because I don't even know who that person is.

"Bo? Is that you?" Geoff calls out, because who else would be walking into our house at the start of the evening?

"Hey Bowie, we weren't expecting you home this early. This episode is almost over. You want to watch a mov—" I've never been snappy or disrespectful to Mark before, but the moment he says my name I feel my blood boil and the Chinese-Cajun chicken and noodles rise in my esophagus.

"*Argh*! Will you stop calling me that?" I scream. My hands turn into fists in my hair, with the cropped strands tangled in between my fingers.

My parents sit up and stare at me, stunned. Like I said, I've never screamed at them before. Even in our back-and-forth banter, Geoff and I have never had a true spat. He's probably jumping with joy that I'm acting like a *normal teenager.*

"Stop calling you what, Bo?" Geoff's eyebrows are furrowed, and he doesn't look the least bit amused.

"That!" I outstretch my arms towards them to emphasize my point. "Bo, or Bowie, or any derivative of that name!"

"Nice choice of words there. *Derivative,*" Geoff muses, and then counters my statement with, "But why can't we call you by your name?"

"Because I'm about 99.9% positive that it's not my name!" I huff.

"Okay, then what should we call you? What's your name?" Geoff shakes his head and looks at me now with a hint of a humorous smile.

This time my hands fly up in the air before flopping back to the side, as I scream, "Who the hell knows! That's the point!" I can feel tears welling in my eyes as I beeline to the glass sliding door and slam it shut behind me.

I'm sitting by the pool having my best ugly cry. I barely hear the door slide open behind me. I'm crying so hard that I'm choking and gasping for air every few seconds. I've never cried this hard in my life. Not even when Geoff made Mark and me take Patches, the stray Labrador mix that I'd been harboring in my Little Tikes

Cottage, to an adoption group. I was eight and kept yelling, *"He needs a home! He's an orphan, just like me!"* and stomping my feet.

"You are not an orphan, Bo." Geoff laughed at me and waved off my comment. *"You have a home here with us. But Patches needs to find a home where the inhabitants aren't deathly allergic."* Geoff isn't even deathly allergic to dogs. He just sneezes a little. Supposedly.

There's still a dark spot in the grass where the Little Tikes Cottage was sitting for the first eight years of my life. Geoff always complains that he needs to have the yard guys lay some new grass there, but Carrie maintains that he secretly likes the dead spot because it reminds him of my childhood years.

Mark sits beside me and doesn't say a word. He lets me cry for another two or three minutes, and when my sobs turn into quiet hiccups and sniffles, he finally speaks.

"I paid twenty thousand dollars for this pool, and I haven't so much as dipped my toes in it the past few years. Don't even get me started on the jacuzzi!" He slips his socks off and slowly drops his feet in the clear blue water. "For twenty grand, I should be swimming in this thing year-round. You should have had a pool party every year on your birthday."

I snort, but it sounds gross because my nose is full of snot from crying like a baby.

"Remember your half-birthday? When Geoff threw you a pool party in June, right before your twelfth birthday?"

This time I give a snort-laugh at the thought of Geoff yelling at Cole because he kept telling everyone that it wasn't my real birthday.

"What's on your mind, Ziggy?" Mark doesn't want to call me Bowie right now, for obvious reasons, so he calls me Ziggy, as in Ziggy Stardust; David Bowie's alter ego.

"Patches," I reply shortly, eyeing the dead spot in the yard.

"Patches, the stray dog?" Mark laughs and kicks his feet back and forth in the water. "Is that what that was all about back there? You want a dog?" His southern drawl is comforting, even with the unneeded humor. I relax a little, unfolding my legs and kicking off my sandals before dipping them in the pool next to his.

"How long have you felt like this?" he asks me next, his tone serious and concerned.

I figure that this is the moment of truth. Everything has built up to this moment. Almost like how all my secrets and lies had paved a path for Jonah to walk into the mall and catch me kissing my gay best friend. That's life, I guess.

I decide to tell Mark the truth because there's not enough ceiling to cover all the thoughts in my head. I need to get this out. It may not make Jonah forgive me, but it will take some of the pressure away from my chest.

"A while." I shrug.

"A while," he repeats, and I can tell he wants me to elaborate.

"Christina's seventh birthday party, when I found out most kids had mommies. Seventh grade when Mrs. Frig gave us a genealogy presentation. Every time someone says, *"What are you mixed with?"*, *"Which one of your dads is your real dad?"* or my personal favorite, *"Have you ever met your real parents?"*."

My words come out so aggressively that I take a moment to pause and catch my breath. Mark sits there silently waiting, allowing me to continue as if he knows there's more.

He's right. There is.

"Everything about me is made up." I feel the tears building and my voice cracks. "My birthday, my ethnicity, my race, my name. I'm an assumption. All because someone decided to stick me behind a dumpster."

Another pause, and more expectant silence from Mark. I can imagine the conversation he and Geoff must have had in the living room after I stormed out. I'm sure Geoff was the first to go after me. It's the nurturer in him. I'm sure Mark stood up and gently pulled Geoff back, assuring him he could handle it.

Mark is the listener.

"I've just got these questions that have no answers to go with them. Sometimes I feel like... Like I'm suffocating." The tears are falling again, so I drop my head.

This time, Mark reaches out and pulls me against him with one arm, stroking my hair and kissing the top of my head. I bury my head in his t-shirt and sob. He smells like the same rich musk that has been a comfort to me my whole life. On stormy nights when I was afraid of the lightning, I'd run across the hall and curl up in Mark's empty spot next to Geoff. His pillow always smelled like him; completely opposite of the fresh scent of Geoff. A clash of abnormalities that was completely normal to me. My entire world.

My parents.

"Why didn't you tell us you were feeling this way, sweetheart?" He kissed the top of my head again, and for a moment I think I hear his voice cracking too.

"I couldn't." That is all I can manage in a single breath.

"Why not?"

I sit up and compose myself. I've come this far, so I might as well come clean about everything. "I felt like... like I was being ungrateful. How could I complain about all the things I don't have to the people who gave me everything? Nice house, nice car, all the love and freedom I could ask for from two hardworking, faithful, supportive parents? What a slap in the face to cry about not knowing what racial slurs should offend me, or why my birth parents didn't bother just dropping me off in the hospital waiting room with a note full of information I may need in my teenage years."

"You don't owe us anything for loving you, Bowie. We are your parents. It's our job," Geoff speaks up and I turn my head to see him standing against the threshold of the sliding door.

"The things you're feeling are completely normal for a girl with your history. It's normal to wonder why certain things happen in your life. It's normal to want to fill in the blanks. But you can't bottle that stuff in."

"But you guys have done so much for me..." I trail off and turn back towards the pool water.

Geoff walks over and slides his ridiculous Harry Potter Raven-claw slippers off of his feet. I call them ridiculous because he didn't handle being sorted into Slytherin House very well when we took the online quiz. He always felt like he had a special connection with Luna Lovegood and the other Ravenclaw members when we read the books together years ago. So now he insists on buying only Ravenclaw items when it comes to Harry Potter memorabilia.

Now we sit, all three of us with our feet in the pool, in silence. Of course, with Geoff, nothing is ever silent for long.

"Instead of thinking about everything we've done for you, why don't you try thinking of everything you've done for us?" he asks, in a tone that is light, but serious as if the thought brings him joy and he wants me to know he means every word. Mark nods in agreement and I look back and forth between them, trying to understand.

"We should be the ones feeling selfish." Mark chuckles. "Before you, everyone doubted us. Especially our families."

"When we adopted you, my mother literally called me and told me I would corrupt a child and ruin her life with my lifestyle," Geoff chimes in with his own laugh.

Mark says, "My father hadn't spoken to me in years, but when a family member caught wind that we'd brought you into our lives, he called me to let me know I was doing you a disservice by being your dad. That I'd just confuse you. His actual words. Said, *If you wanted a damn kid so bad, you should've stayed with Carrie and done it the right way. God's way*"." He says the last part in a low baritone, mimicking his father.

I laugh and kick my foot up, splashing water in the air. "Jokes on him. You guys are the only thing about my life that's not confusing."

"We should send him a family photo on a postcard," Geoff quips and we all laugh. "But seriously, Junior. You proved them all wrong for us. Two gay guys who were destined to fail somehow managed to raise a beautiful, intelligent, respectful, gentle young woman, who will graduate in six weeks and go off to college and become something even greater."

"I think we've had enough emotional talk today," I tell them after nodding my head.

"We've still got a lot to discuss, but do you feel better?"

"Honestly?" I ask, and they nod and wait for my answer. "Not completely better, but I'll be okay for now."

Chapter Twenty-Nine

On Monday, I walk the halls in a complete haze. Geoff and Mark didn't bother me at all after I locked myself in my room for the rest of Saturday and all day Sunday. Geoff and I skipped church with Ms. Shonda and Christina, and I could hear Mark reluctantly leaving for work early this morning.

I make it through my first four classes before I realize people are whispering about me. I catch the tail end of Emma Burke saying, *"got caught cheating"* to Claire Clampton. On my way to the lunchroom, I hear a group of basketball players mumbling something about me *"making it up to Manny."*

Speaking of which, I spot Manny surrounded by Cole and Bryson and some of the other people we hang with. He's standing just across the hall from Chris Monte and those basketball players.

I've ignored his text messages all weekend. I didn't even bother opening them, and I walked out this morning without my phone. After checking every vibrating incoming text until two o'clock in the morning only to find that it wasn't Jonah, I figured I didn't need my phone.

When I walk past them, everyone quiets their voice and nods toward me. Manny looks over and calls out to me just as Kayla's passing me from the opposite direction.

"Hey, Bowie! How'd it feel to sell your virginity for a second chance with Manny?" Kayla's words hit me like a ton of bricks and I stop in my tracks and glare at her. "And they say cheaters never prosper," she adds with a chuckle.

I whip my head back to glower at Manny. He gives me a pleading look, and I feel the urge to strangle him rising.

"Not that I blame you." Kayla's words bring my attention away from my best friend's betrayal, and back to her smug remarks. "I mean, Jonah is really hot."

I don't condone violence at all. The only fight I've ever been in was in kindergarten when I pushed Bryson in the sandbox for pulling my pigtails.

But right now, I want to punch Kayla McMurray in her nose that's a size too big for her slim face. But punching Kayla won't give me answers about the day I was born, and punching Kayla definitely won't bring Jonah back into my life. Right now, that's all I want.

Instead, I walk over to Manny and shake my head at him in disbelief.

"You told people we had sex, Manny?"

"No," he laughs. "I said we made up last night." Everyone around him laughs and slaps him on the back like he's so cool.

"So, you insinuated we had sex." I raise a brow.

"Babe, relax it's—"

"Manny, I can't do this right now," I plead with him, and I feel my emotions rising. In the past forty-eight hours, I've cried more than I've ever cried in my eighteen years of life. I don't know how much more I can take.

"Babe, chill, it's not a big deal—" Again I cut him off.

"It was a big deal to me, Manny, and you know that!" On the outside, people probably think we're talking about my virginity, but the look on Manny's face shows me he knows what I'm really talking about.

"Yeah, well, you weren't going to have it forever," he says through gritted teeth, trying to play along and still send me a message.

"You've got a history of not fessing up when it matters. You know that, Manny?" The challenging statement doesn't come from me. It comes from Christina, who is standing beside me now, having appeared out of nowhere.

Manny rolls his eyes and scoffs at her. "Oh please Chris, handle your own business before you start worrying about others."

I can tell by the look on Christina's face that she wants to air out all of Manny's dirty laundry, and as stupid as it may sound, I pray she has some restraint. No one else understands Manny's jab at Christina but me and Chris Monte, who immediately advances toward Manny, draws back his fist and punches him in the face. Gasps can be heard all around us and a crowd circles the two boys while Bryson and Christina fight to pull Chris away from Manny.

"Serves you right for being an asshole, Manny! Bowie's been your best friend for years! How could you do that to her?" Christina taunts him as he holds his eye, which is already beginning to swell.

My head begins to pound as they go back and forth, insulting each other on my behalf. I feel like my world is crumbling at my feet. My friends are falling apart, I've lost Jonah, and my parents silently have me under suicide watch.

I literally scream and run down the nearest staircase, praying I can make it to the student parking lot before any more drama can befall me today.

I'm crying again by the time I make it to my car, and while I'm giving myself a moment to calm down before I drive, there's a knock on my passenger window. I look over to find Christina smiling at me sadly. I unlock the door and she slides into the passenger seat and doesn't say a word. She doesn't have to, because I know she's here for me. We ride in silence the entire drive to my house.

Manny's beat-up truck is parked on the curb when we pull into the garage. He's sitting outside the entrance to the atrium waiting for us, and I wonder how fast he drove to get here before us. When we enter the house, I don't tell him to leave. I need him here, just like I need Christina. I need my best friends to know the truth.

After we remove our shoes in the mudroom, they follow me outside to the pool. Instead of dipping our feet in the water, we opt to sit poolside in the chaise lounges. They're positioned in a circle so we're all silently facing each other.

Christina glances at Manny and doesn't even attempt to hide her laughter.

"I'm glad you find this shit funny, Christina," Manny huffs, motioning towards his puffy, already swollen eye. There is a dark red and purple bruise already forming around it.

"I thought you two weren't talking anymore? Why the hell would he hit me?" Manny asks. I excuse myself briefly and return with an ice pack from the freezer. I hand it to Manny, and he looks up at me with a sad smile. "Thanks."

"He may have used me for sex and knocked me up, but he's still got my back, I guess. Plus, if you spill the beans that I got pregnant, everyone's going to know it was him. He was protecting his privacy too, I'm sure." We all share a short laugh at Christina's nonchalant attitude, and I'm easily reminded why I love these two. I'm going through one of the toughest weeks in my life, and they're still here, making me laugh.

"I've never seen you so pissed, Bo," Christina comments next, and Manny nods his head in agreement. "And I've never seen you cry like that." She turns and throws an evil eye at Manny. "I knew you liked Jonah, but I guess I didn't realize it was that serious between you guys. Maybe I could send him a message or something? Is he ignoring you?"

I shake my head and wipe a few tears that are threatening to fall. I'm all stuffy and sniffling from crying and trying not to cry, but I have to pull through this. I'm tired of bottling this in.

"It's not Jonah," I tell them hoarsely. "I mean, everything that happened Saturday sucked, and then what happened today..." I pause and stare at my male best friend, trying to form the right words. I can read the fear on his face. Manny may be selfish, but he knows right from wrong. "Today you hurt me, Manny, but it just triggered something that I've been hiding and holding in lately."

Christina and Manny look at each other, and then back at me expectantly.

They don't interrupt me as I spill out my innermost feelings to them. Just like with my parents, I tell them everything through a waterfall of tears and hiccups. In the back of my mind, I think about how easy this conversation was with Jonah, a stranger at the time. I think it's harder to talk to the people closest to me about my issues because I don't want to hurt them. I know they care and I don't want them to think that their love isn't enough. These issues are mine, not theirs.

As I tell them my secrets, my insecurities about my unknown origins, and the shame I felt for being ungrateful for the life my dads have given me, Christina cries with me, and Manny stares at me stoically. There is silence after I stop talking, except for sniffling coming from Christina and me. Manny's head has dropped now and his arms dangle between his legs. He's staring at the flagstone pavement that makes up our patio.

"I'm so sorry, Bo." Christina speaks first. "I shouldn't have made that comment about leaving my baby behind a dumpster. I knew it was a messed-up thing to say, and I've been wanting to apologize to you for a long time."

I shake my head at her statement and wipe my nose with the sleeve of my jacket. "I shouldn't have reacted the way that I did. You're my best friend. I should have been supportive. I've just been so..." I trail off, unable to find the right words, and not wanting to make any excuses for my behavior.

"Girl please." Christina wipes her eyes and waves me off. She moves over to join me on my chaise and wraps her arms around me. "You've got some heavy shit going on. Who cares about all of that?"

"Yeah, well, if you need someone to go with you, I don't mind going," I tell her sincerely.

"I already went." She sighs, and I sit up in her embrace and watch her sadly. "Destiny took me. Me, her, and Chris split the money."

I look over at Manny, who's staring at Christina in equal shock. "We should have been there for you. Are you okay?"

"I'm fine." Christina shrugs. "They just gave me this shot, and then gave me this like, take-home abortion kit, and I was able to do it at home. It hurt like hell, though." She tells us the horrific details of the events of last Monday night. I notice that the whole time she tells the story of the pain and cramping, Manny looks between us solemnly. There's something on his mind, but he's holding it in.

We stay outside, alternating between questions about my confession and Christina's abortion. Manny talks, but he's not as chatty as he usually is. When Geoff comes home shortly after, he insists that Manny and Christina stay for dinner, and I know they only agree because they feel like they have to be here for me. Well, that and Geoff's meatloaf is delicious. Mark comes home just as we're setting the table, and for a few hours I feel normal. Having dinner, surrounded by the most important people in my life, laughing at Geoff's stories.

It's not until I go to bed that night that the emotions and the sadness come flooding back in. I try to project my feeling and thoughts onto the ceiling, but they won't come out.

They just stay in my mind, repeating themselves.

"What are you?"

"Where did you come from?"

"Where is your mother?"

"Why did she leave you?"

"Jonah hates you."

"Your parents have done so much for you."

"How could you be so ungrateful?"

I put my pillow over my head to drown out my own voice in my brain, and I cry myself to sleep.

I'm not alright. But I have to be.

Chapter Thirty

I was supposed to feel better after telling Manny and Christina my secret. At least that's what I tried to tell myself. But now that everyone knows, I just feel embarrassed and even more confused.

On Thursday, as I'm coming home to sulk in my room after school, I hear Geoff in the kitchen talking on the phone. I'm too tired to eavesdrop, so I swiftly and quietly make my way through the mudroom and living room, and up the stairs to my bedroom, but I'm 100% sure it's about me.

When I wake up just before dawn on Saturday morning, I find Carrie's shoes in the mudroom. She's still asleep in the guest room, so I'm sure she flew in last night.

Mark is still home, too.

I go back to my room to shower and dress before returning to the kitchen to find Geoff scrubbing the countertops while simultaneously cooking breakfast. He cooks and cleans constantly, so it's hard to tell if this is normal, or a part of some intervention for me. Given my discovery of Carrie in the guestroom and Mark not going to work, I'll take it as the latter.

He's not facing me, so I softly pad over to him and rest my forehead on his back. He jumps a little before turning to wrap me in his arms.

"You scared me, Junior."

"I don't want you to worry about me," I murmur into the breast of his lounge robe.

"We're not worried as much anymore." He sighs and strokes my hair. "We just love you and want to spend some family time."

"But dad isn't going to work and Carrie's here out of the blue. I don't want you guys putting your lives on hold for me."

Geoff kisses the top of my head as I squeeze him tight. "We're your parents, Bo. That's our job. You are our lives. Not the hospital, the airline, or the art shows. You are."

I can feel someone walking up from behind, and the scent of Mark's aftershave fills the air. My body unconsciously gravitates from Geoff's embrace to Mark's, and I squeeze him just as tight.

"No fancy getaways or presents. Just hugs," I tell him softly, and I know he understands.

He kisses my crown on the exact spot Geoff did and nods.

"I'll even let you guys pick the movie for movie night," Geoff says as he turns back to the stove. "Bowie, go wake up Carrie. She can't just use us for a place to crash and then sleep in during breakfast."

I laugh and do as I'm told.

? ? ?

It doesn't take long for everything to fall back to normal. At least on the outside. I once again put my identity issues to the side and pretend to be the love-struck teenage girl, swooning over Manny Herrera.

Manny is back to his usual self. Cracking jokes at school and constantly the center of attention. But for someone like me, who knows Manny the way I know him, I can tell it's mostly a facade. Not in the *hiding being gay* sense either. Things have been different between us since my poolside confession.

As for Jonah... Well, that's over. I made one attempt to call him, and he sent me straight to voicemail. I was seconds away from driving all the way to Davis and telling him the truth. Then I thought about Kayla McMurray and her possibly spreading Manny's secret, and I changed my mind.

Okay, so that's not entirely true.

Actually, I thought about how confident Jonah is. How sure of himself he's been since we first met. Then, I thought about myself, and how I'm not confident, and I'm not sure of anything, especially not myself. And I realized we aren't that great of a match at all.

"Earth to Bowie!" Manny's annoyed voice breaks my thoughts of Jonah and brings me back to the lunch table. We're at our usual table waiting for the rest of our friends to arrive with their food and usual antics.

"What were you talking about?" I furrow my brow at Manny. Christina's eating again. She has been every day at lunch for the past month. She said the pregnancy was making her nauseous whenever she ate back then. I wondered if my mom was a seventeen-year-old girl sitting at her cafeteria lunch table, unable to eat when she decided she didn't want me anymore.

"Prom?" Manny scoffs at me. The swollen eye lasted about two weeks, and he spent that entire time complaining about it, possibly not healing before prom.

"Yeah, prom. Fake make-outs, ending up in someone's hotel room where people think we finally have sex in some cliché teenage romance type of way," I say with a sarcastic laugh. "Got it."

"Actually, I was hoping we could all go together. The three of us. And since I've recently become a legal adult." He takes a pause and poses regally, causing Christina and I to crack up laughing. "I figured we could get our own room and hang out afterward."

My jaw drops and when I glance at Christina, she's got an eyebrow quirked and an impressed smile.

"You're willing to skip the after-parties?" Christina asks him.

"Yeah, the Ainsley's are getting a suite. That's a prime fake relationship opportunity there." I throw it out there as bait.

Manny shrugs and looks around. "I mean, we are obligated to at least make an appearance, but it's one of the last nights we have to party together. I'll be gone in a couple of months. I want to spend it with my girls."

My heart grows heavy at the thought of Manny cherishing his time with us and with the thought of him being halfway across the country soon.

I nod my head and Christina snaps her fingers and says, "Hell yeah, I'm down. Chris told me he wants to go to the prom alone to avoid the drama." She adds the last part with an eye roll and a death glare at Mr. Monte at the next table over where the basketball players are eating.

"Well, sucks for him." I grab her hand and bring her attention back to us. She faces me with a sincere smile, and I tell her. "Because we're going to have way more fun. I'm bringing Monopoly."

"Dorks." Christina shakes her head and we all laugh at my terrible joke, because we're friends, and that's what friends do.

? ? ?

I have to admit that Manny looks handsome in the navy-blue crushed velvet tuxedo blazer and matching dress shoes that he's been saving up all year to buy for prom. He caught them on sale two weeks ago, so he threw in a matching corsage for me as a surprise.

We started planning this matching look two days after junior prom since Manny felt like our matching red looks were too flashy and that navy would be subtler and more believable.

So, I'm standing in the mirror finger-combing my short curls back and forth on top of my head, clad in a short cocktail-style strapless dark blue dress. The college kid working at the dress shop in Norman kept gushing about the sweetheart bodice and its *"splashes of gold glitter,"* though his eyes were on Manny as he sat on a bench texting while I tried on the custom-made dress.

"It's perfect because you guys still look like a couple, but I look like I belong too!" Christina muses as she emerges from my bathroom in a floor-length gold halter dress. Her baby hair is swooped across her forehead and the rest is pulled into a sleek high ponytail that stops mid-back.

"You *do* belong, Chris." Manny smiles and straightens his bow tie. "We're a package deal."

"Aww, Emmanuel, you're such a sweetheart," she gushes and wraps her arms around his shoulders, kissing his cheek.

"Bowie, get in here for a selfie." I do as I'm told and lean against Manny's chest, resting my head in the crook of his neck opposite of Christina. We all cheese for Manny's front-facing camera, and it's a genuine smile; the kind I'm not used to lately, but can always make an appearance for my best friends and family.

The prom is your typical formal gathering. A DJ playing the top forty, groups of girls dancing together while the guys all huddle around and watch. Some couples dance together. And then there's Christina, Manny, and me. Dancing in a small circle and laughing like idiots at our own insiders.

I only think about Jonah once tonight, which is an accomplishment, considering I spend most of my days refreshing his Facebook and Instagram pages and staring at my cell phone, trying to will him to call or text me. I envision scenarios where he calls me and we finally make up. I get the chance to tell him the truth and then we laugh it off and make out on my bed.

I think about him slow-dancing with me as Manny and I sway back and forth slowly to an Ed Sheeran song.

"I'll miss you the most when I'm gone," Manny breathes out quietly. I look up at him with a raised brow, and he chuckles, flashing me a shy smile. "I'll miss my family, and I'll definitely be happy to be far enough away where I can live... freely, ya' know? But It's going to be hard finally being myself without your support. You've always been there to have my back. Even if you didn't notice it."

My heart warms, and I smile at my best friend proudly. "I'll miss you too, Manny. And I'll always be supporting you, even a thousand miles away." I kiss his cheek, and I hear *Aww* from our peers nearby.

Manny and I look at each other and stifle our laughter, just as the music switches to a more upbeat pop song and everyone begins to jump around and dance again.

Chapter Thirty-One

Mark and Geoff leave early the morning after my graduation dinner. Graduation was the usual drawn-out night of speeches by random speakers we don't care about, and singing songs about transitioning into the future. Afterward, Carrie, the dads, and I went to dinner and ended the night reminiscing and watching movies in the living room. Carrie offered to keep me company for the week while my dads are on their cruise, but for the sake of Manny and the recently graduated senior class, I declined. I doubt a graduation party will be worth anything exciting with an adult hanging around.

It's the last hurrah and the end of our fake relationship. Manny will leave for New York in a month, and my life will no longer revolve around him and the plan.

It's kind of bittersweet.

"I have something to show you," Carrie tells me. We're sitting on the island in the kitchen having breakfast before she has to leave for the airport as well. Geoff and Mark should be in Miami by now, waiting to board their cruise later this afternoon.

Carrie goes to the guestroom and comes back clumsily carrying a large rectangular object. It's obviously a canvas covered by a white sheet, but it's almost taller than Carrie and just as wide as her arm span.

"What is it?" I ask her once she's successfully propped it against the back of the couch and is panting. I leave my last few bites of eggs and walk over to stand in front of the mystery object. Carrie pulls the sheet away. It is indeed a painting. My breath catches in my throat and I instantly feel a pang in my heart.

The painting is of a girl. She is facing forward, but her dull brown eyes look downward stoically. The painting only depicts her bare shoulders and up, but I can tell by the tussled cropped hair, sepia skin, and mask of freckles peppered across her nose and cheeks that she is me. A blend of gold and brown hues creates the textured background.

"I called it *Girl on Mars,*" Carrie says after a minute of me just staring at the beautiful portrait. "It won first prize at the National Showcase."

I'm so over crying. I can't even cry anymore, but this painting is just...

"I have that face committed to memory. I had no idea it was a face made of pain," Carrie continues to speak in my stunned silence. "I struggled to come up with something to paint for this showcase for a year. And then one day. I looked at you and I saw this. It was raw, and it was beautiful. So, I captured it."

"It's amazing," I tell her simply because I do not have the words.

"I don't have the answers to the question you have and none of us knows what will help you feel better about your situation; but know that when I look at you, Bowie." She pauses and walks over to place her hands on my shoulders. "I think back to that little girl. That one who I've watched become a woman, and I think of how she healed my heart." She brushes my bangs back and they drop back into place. I watch her face intently. "I was so bitter, and angry, and lonely. And then the two people I thought I hated the most in life asked me to be a part of something that was so much bigger than our past. You gave me a family and a reason to keep going. You brought me, Mark, and Geoff together and you're the glue that keeps us all in place. When the time comes to search for the answers you're seeking, just remember you don't have to do it alone."

I can't respond with words, so I wrap my arms around Carrie and hug her tight. She hugs me back and I think she may be on the verge of crying too.

"It'll be weird knowing some random person has a picture of me in their house when that sells," I joke when we end our embrace. I help her carry the canvas back into the guest room.

"Oh, it sold that same night. It was quite the bidding war."

I can tell there's more to the story, so I wait for her to tell me the rest once we've safely placed the painting against the wall.

"Mark and Geoff watched the showcase on a live stream. It was supposed to be a surprise for all of you, but that was the night that you revealed your feelings, so we thought it was best to let you rest. As soon as the auction started and the bids were live, Geoff was on it." She laughs. "So, I'm sure this will hang up in the living room somewhere."

I feel a pang of guilt about missing the showcase. Carrie has always been there when I needed her. Instead of beating myself up anymore, I just laugh with her and then hug her tightly.

"Thanks, Carrie. I love you so much."

"I love you too, Bo."

? ? ?

After dropping Carrie off at the airport, I pick up Manny and we stroll through Walmart buying pool toys and party supplies for the night. Actually, Manny is buying everything. The house is my contribution, and much to my displeasure, Cole is supplying the liquor.

"Promise me things won't get too crazy. My neighbors aren't cool like the Ainsleys' neighbors. They *will* call the cops, and they *will* tell Geoff and Mark."

"Everything will be fine, Bo!" Manny waves me off as he grabs a bunch of pool noodles and a couple of inflatable beach balls. I'm having the worst anxiety about tonight. If there was ever a time to take a stand against Manny and his plans, it would be now.

"So, have you tried calling Jonah?" Manny's question catches me off guard. He's never asked me about Jonah, and honestly, I've been fighting to forget about him and move on lately. I saw AJ at graduation last night, most likely there to support Kayla. Two months ago, I would have imagined Jonah there. Not anymore.

"No." I shrug and follow him down the *Summer Fun!* aisle. I'm not sure how I'm going to explain the extra pool toys to my parents. Not that it matters. Mr. Franklin next door will rat me out before Mark gets the garage door open next Saturday.

"Why not?" Manny asks me, "I'll be gone soon. Maybe you can hash things out. We could tell him we broke up! That you left me because you'd rather be with him—"

"It's fine, Manny," I cut him off. "It wasn't going to last, anyway. You were right."

Manny doesn't respond. He just stops walking and looks at me.

I sigh and shrug again. "Jonah and I had nothing in common. He was cool and confident, and I'm just a ball of angst and self-loathing. I'm not sure of anything, really. Especially not myself. He deserved someone more like him."

"That's not what I meant when I said that, Bo!" Manny drops his jaw.

Again, I shrug. "It's true though."

"No, it's not, Bo!" he yells at me. We're on an aisle with a mother and her two toddlers, and at the sound of Manny's outburst, she ushers them around the corner to the next aisle.

"Calm down, Manny. It's not that big of a deal." I look between him and the spot where the woman was once standing and laugh slightly.

He looks like he wants to argue, but to my surprise, he stays quiet. I pick up an inflatable drink holder that is shaped like a flamingo and wave it in his face whimsically before tossing it into the basket.

? ? ?

Trusting Manny that *"everything would be fine"* was a stupid idea. By 11:00 p.m. everyone from our graduating class has piled into my backyard and music is blaring from speakers that Bryson brought,

Luckily, I did some detective work after Manny and I returned home from Walmart and discovered that Mr. Franklin's daughter, who lives an hour and a half away in Tulsa, went into labor. He was rushing out of the house to meet her at the hospital and even asked me to keep an eye on his house while he was gone. The Ponces on the other side of our house are out of town for the weekend, and the couple across the street is attending a wedding all evening and won't be home until early tomorrow morning. This means all the houses surrounding me will be vacant for the night. Perfect.

There are about thirty teenagers in my pool with plastic cups, and I pray nobody drunkenly drowns as I make my way through each crowd inspecting everything. The inside of the house is off limits; the one thing I put my foot down on.

Tyler Ainsley made a snide remark about how every party that they've thrown allowed for people to hang out all over their house. I told him I refused to disrespect the sanctity of the home my dads worked so hard to build. He just mumbled something under his breath and walked over to the pool.

"You really need to relax, Bo." I hear Bryson say from behind me. "Here." He extends his arm out and attempts to hand me a red Solo cup. I eye it suspiciously.

"I need to watch over the party. Plus, you know I don't drink."

"There's like, this much vodka in there." He pinches his thumb and index finger together. "You'll be fine. I'll help you watch over the party. I won't let anyone go inside the house and I won't let things get out of hand," he tries to assure me. "But you should be celebrating too."

Just then, Cody Walsh picks up one of Geoff's garden gnomes and cannonballs into the pool with it cradled in his arms. I grab the cup from Bryson's hand and chug it fast.

Bryson lied. There's more than *"this much"* vodka in this cup. My head instantly feels fuzzy.

"Want another one?" Bryson laughs, and I nod and hold up one finger.

After I down the second drink, he gives me a third, and then we join Manny and Christina by the fire pit where they're talking to Cole and some of the other guys. Manny has been quiet all night, despite this party being his pride and joy.

I flop down on the pool chaise next to Manny and rest my head on his shoulder. "Why are you sulking?"

"I'm not sulking. Why are you drunk?" He leans back slightly and smirks at me.

"I'm not drunk, I'm buzzed. Bryson gave me a spiked drink."

Manny glares at Bryson, who puts his hands up defensively.

"Girl, you are drunk!" Christina laughs and then sips from her red cup. "But you deserve it," she adds with a wink, and I smile in response.

"That's exactly what I said!" Bryson announces proudly.

About fifteen minutes later, while Cole and the guys are goofing off and bragging about their summer plans, Bryson asks me if he can go inside to use the bathroom. I escort him inside to the downstairs guest powder room and stand watch outside the door.

"I can't believe we have to take off our shoes just to walk to the bathroom," he calls out from behind the door. There's an echo of his pee falling into the toilet in the background of his words that makes me shudder.

"Please refrain from talking to me while you pee, Bryson." I have to lean against the wall to control my spinning head. This is why I don't drink; three cups of pineapple juice mixed with cheap vodka, and I'm barely standing. College should be a blast!

Thinking of college brings me melancholy.

After Facebook stalking Jonah, I learned he got his acceptance letter to OSU a few weeks after the mall incident. We'll be at the same college just like we'd hoped for and now... he hates me.

"So, what's up between you and Manny now?" Bryson's taller figure hovers way too close to my body.

"Are you close enough?" I ask, pushing him back slightly as he attempts to press me against the wall with his body. "And you already know *what's up* with me and Manny."

"Yeah, but after that whole *you cheating on him* thing, no one has said anything else about it."

"I didn't know that it was any of your business." I raise a brow at him curiously. I'm getting annoyed, but I don't want to be mean to him.

"I don't get it!" he snaps in a desperate tone, causing me to jump in place slightly.

"Get what?" I frown. We've been friends since elementary school, so I'm not afraid of him, just confused. We've both been drinking, so I'm sure that doesn't help.

"I can tell you don't really like him, Bo. It's been that way all year. I've been wanting to tell you how I felt about you, and then you cheated on Manny and I thought—"

"You thought what?" I cut him off in a harsh tone and side-step away from him. "You thought you had a chance? Because I was easy?"

"No!" he yells and throws his arms out defensively. "I mean, no. Everyone... else thinks you're... But I... I know you're not like that, Bo."

"Everyone thinks I'm what?" My eyes grow big and my heart drops. Bryson just drops his head and stops advancing toward me.

"Get out of my house, Bryson," I tell him while simultaneously fighting off an oncoming panic attack. He looks up at me in shock, but then reluctantly walks towards the glass sliding door, grabbing his Nikes on the way out. I want so badly to run upstairs to my room, but the small sober, rational part of my subconscious reminds me I shouldn't leave intoxicated and hormonal teenagers in my parents' backyard.

Instead, I'm sitting on the sectional, replaying the memory of the day Jonah and I had the Kubrick marathon, when Christina and Manny come inside looking for me.

"Bo, what's wrong?" Christina asks immediately. She flops down on the couch next to me, and Manny sits across from us.

"Everything," I mumble. "But to start, I think Bryson just confessed his love for me while also telling me that everyone has been calling me a hoe behind my back."

"What?" Christina screeches. "What are you talking about?"

I shrug. "After the mall fiasco. I bet Kayla McMurray told everyone." I pause and turn to Manny. "I guess you were right not to trust her." Manny's frown deepens. If I didn't know any better, I'd think he was about to cry.

Christina sucks her teeth and rolls her eyes. "Who cares what they think? High school is over. We know the truth, so to hell with them."

I shrug and sigh again. I miss the old Bowie who bottled everything inside, because crying, shrugging, and sighing all the time sucks.

"Honestly, I'm just disappointed in myself. For not standing up for myself and not doing what I wanted to do. For not being confident enough to do what I knew was the right thing to do." I pause and glance over at Manny. "No offense."

He just shakes his head and diverts his eyes from mine.

"Girl, fuck all of that. Let's go back out here and either A.) Tell these two-faced hypocrites to get the hell out of your pool and go home; or B.) Fake it and enjoy our last high school party together."

I decide to go with option B, and we all stand up together and go outside as if nothing happened.

The party is in full swing, so I'm not surprised to see Manny branch out and disappear as soon as we exit the house. I spend the next hour running around, trying to prevent people from breaking things and hooking up in the pool, with Christina laughing behind me.

I bump into a solid body as I'm power walking around the pool trying to make sure no one conceives any post-grad babies in Mark's twenty-thousand dollar pool. I look up and find Bryson staring at me, sheepishly.

He scratches the nape of his neck and tells me, "I told you I'd help keep the party under control." I frown at him. He sighs and says, "Look, Bo, I—I'm sorry about earlier. I didn't mean to offend you. I guess I just—"

"It's fine Bryson." I cut him off to spare him the humiliation of reliving our scandalous living room drama. "We were both pretty intoxicated. We can just forget it ever happened and remain *friends.*" I put a hard emphasis on the word friends so that there is no confusion about where we stand.

Again, Bryson looks like he wants to say more, but he doesn't. Instead, he just smiles, content with the fact that we're back on good terms again. He's telling me about his acceptance to the same college as me when we hear Cole calling out to Manny to make *"One last speech."*

Manny's speeches are legendary. After he and Arianna were crowned prom king and queen, Manny just had to give an over-the-top, non-customary speech that was both hilarious and borderline inappropriate. His graduation speech earned him a standing ovation and applause from the staff and parents, even though none of them realized he was simply quoting rap lyrics.

Manny seems reluctant as Cole and some football players push him towards the makeshift podium, which is actually one of Geoff's Greek columns that he has lined around the firepit.

The firepit that Manny *knows* he shouldn't be standing on!

I bolt towards him and yank him down, but as I'm turning to make my way around the pool, Manny's words stop me in my tracks. Manny normally already has these speeches prepared and ready to send any crowd into a fit of laughter with crude humor that matches his facade well.

So, when he starts this speech with, *"I'm not going to miss high school at all,"* my interest instantly piques.

"High school sucks, and even though I've had fun and made great memories with all of you these past four years, I'm so glad it's over."

"Umm, what's going on?" Bryson mumbles and nudges me.

"I have no clue," I murmur back.

"We'll all look back and want to remember the first wild party the Ainsley twins threw or the time Chris Monte and Rochelle Smith went joyriding in Principal Thompson's car and then parked it around the corner from the school."

Behind me, I hear Chris and the basketball team slapping hands and chuckling proudly.

"We'll look back on being prom king and queen, and homecoming court, and class president. Best dressed and class clown, and all of these other stupid titles that we're given that only hold weight in the yearbook."

I look around the crowd of faces, watching Manny intently, waiting for the punchline. I'm looking for Christina because maybe she knows what's going on with Manny and this weird speech when my eyes land on something that causes my heart to drop.

Ringlets of dark curly hair atop a head that towers over most of my classmates.

Jonah.

Chapter Thirty-Two

He's staring at me.

While everyone else is watching Manny, Jonah is staring straight at me. I move toward him instinctively, and I notice a shift in his demeanor when he sees I'm heading his way. If he wasn't staring straight into my soul with Christina standing right next to him looking up at Manny, I'd think he was just a tipsy illusion. I'm prepared to say anything just to get him to speak to me again. I mean, he is at *my* house! What else would he be here for?

That answer will have to wait because my attention is instantly drawn back to Manny when I hear him say, "All of these bullshit social titles don't mean a thing if you're just living a lie."

I stop walking and turn my attention back toward my best friend.

"I've been lying to you all for so long, but most importantly, I've been lying to myself. I've hurt the people who care about me the most with all of these lies, a—and I'm tired of pretending that I'm not the bad guy."

Is he about to...

"Especially you, Bo."

I'm suddenly hyper-aware and self-conscious. I hate being the center of attention, and if the patio lights on my parents' house could move, I'd swear there was a spotlight on me now. I'm suddenly aware that my yellow floral print romper may be a tad bit too short, and maybe a smidge too tight around my boobs and butt. I'm tipsy—no, maybe I'm full-blown drunk, and Jonah is less than twenty feet away from me. And Manny...

Manny is about to...

"The truth... is." To my slight relief, Manny's words draw everyone's attention back to him. He takes a deep breath and exhales slowly. It's then that I know for sure what he's about to do.

"The truth is, I'm...gay." He almost seems to force the words out of his mouth.

There is a silence that follows, not even a gasp. I feel my heart drop again, and now everyone is looking at me again. I'm not sure what to do or how to react, because this is definitely not a part of the plan.

"And my best friend has been helping me hide it," Manny continues, and once again, the crowd is back on him.

"She sacrificed her entire high school life pretending to be my girlfriend because I was too afraid to be who I really am. So that I could hide from all of you."

"I was selfish, and I did so many things to hurt my best friend. I sabotaged her happiness because I was too afraid of what you all would think of me if you knew the truth."

I notice he refuses to say the words *"I'm gay"* again.

"And now that I've realized that I don't give a damn what you guys think of me anymore. I hope it's not too late." He pauses and looks at me with pleading eyes. I smile weakly at him, still in shock at what is transpiring.

"Bowie Monroe is easily the greatest person in this crowd, and we don't need to put that in the yearbook for it to mean anything. She's been loyal to me even when it hurts her. She wanted nothing but the best for me."

"I'm sorry I lied to you guys, and I'm sorry I didn't trust you enough as my classmates and friends to show you who I really was, but... well, here it is."

He falls short and then drops his head, allowing silence to engulf my backyard. Everyone is kind of just looking around at each other at this point. Some of them are mumbling to themselves, but there is no outburst or slow clap like in the movies.

Finally, after several more seconds of quiet, Chris Monte speaks up.

"Man, that ain't nobody's business but yours, Manny. You don't have to explain shit to us."

"Yeah, Manny," Bryson chimes in from behind me. "We're just pissed you've been hogging all the Bowie for the past four years." Bryson's words cause the backyard to erupt into laughter, and I give Chris an appreciative nod before playfully punching Bryson's arm.

"I mean, it's kinda—" Cole gears up to make his usual tasteless comments, but Christina snaps at him from across the yard.

"Don't even try it, Cole!"

He shuts his mouth and pats Manny on the back.

Manny looks stunned, staring at the crowd of our classmates in disbelief. I can see the wetness in his eyes and the staggered breathing against his chest. He's about to cry.

"Can we finish the party? I need some fun since Manny brought the mood down by being all... *dramatic*." Cole finally slips in a joke. I'm relieved when the music plays again and the attention is away from me and Manny.

Manny hops down from the fire pit and pushes through the crowd in a rush, heading towards the side gate that leads to the front of my house.

I take off after him, only to slam into Jonah's chest instead.

I'd almost forgotten about him!

"Hey." He smiles at me sheepishly.

"Jonah," I breathe out with an equally shy smile. "What are you doing h—" I stop because I hear the wooden gate slam closed, and I remember a crying Manny running out a few seconds ago.

"I'm sorry, Jonah, but I've got to go check on Manny."

His sheepish smile turns into his signature grin as he nods, "Yeah."

"How'd you know to come here? Nevermind, let me guess, Christina."

He shakes his head. "Actually, Manny sent me a DM. Told me I should come talk to you tonight."

I'm stunned, but I know I need to find Manny before he leaves the party. "I'm sorry I lied to you. There's so much I need to explain. Just... just stay here," I tell him and then turn to follow Manny's tracks out of the wooden gate.

I find him walking near the Franklins' yard.

"Manny!" He ignores me and keeps walking through Mr. Franklin's manicured lawn.

"Emmanuel Herrera!" I shout at him before drunkenly stumbling over one of Mr. Franklin's stupid yard gnomes. He bought them after spying over our fence and seeing the ones Geoff had set out in the backyard garden. I guess he figured he'd one-up us for the *Yard of the Month* by putting them up in his front yard. Too bad they're freaky and hideous no matter where you put them.

Manny finally stops and turns to face me, shaking his head in what appears to be a mixture of disappointment and amusement.

"You are a complete mess, Bo."

I pull myself off of the ground and snort at him.

"Ha! You're one to talk to. You—" I halt my rebuttal in favor of turning my head and hurling all of my dinner and vodka into the Franklins' bushes.

"Shit!" I curse and stand up straight to examine my work.

Manny is laughing now. "How are you going to survive college if you can't even handle a few cups of mixed liquor?"

"Some of us are actually going to college to learn, not to party," I shoot back. "Now what the hell was that back there, Manny?"

He just shrugs and I glare at him.

"I don't know, Bo." He sighs and throws his hands out. "I felt like shit. It's like I finally noticed what Chris and Geoff were always trying to tell me about this whole thing and how it affects you, too. I was so heartless when it came to Jonah, and then everyone started thinking you were a slut. I just finally saw what I was doing to you and I hated it!"

"You're the most important person in the world to me, Bo. I couldn't live with myself if I hurt you again, and I needed to show you I cared. I couldn't handle you hating me. You're my best friend, Bo."

"Manny," I breathe out as I look into his pleading eyes. He's wearing this look of despair as if he honestly believes that I could ever hate him.

"I'm so sorry, Bo." His voice is almost a whisper.

I take the last few steps toward him and close the gap between us with a tight hug. He's only a few inches taller than me, so once he gets over the brief shock of me hugging him, his chin rests perfectly on top of my head.

"I could never hate you, dummy." My face buried in his chest muffles the words.

"But I ruined things between you and Jonah. He was perfect for you!" Manny wines.

I shake my head, "There will be a million Jonahs that may come into my life. But only one Manny."

"Bullshit. That guy really likes you. I told him to come tonight, and he actually showed up. He's probably here to kick my ass."

I laugh at the thought of goofy Jonah beating up anybody. "Yeah, I saw him, but that can wait. This is more important. Manny, when we told you to be yourself, we didn't mean for you to declare your sexuality to the masses. You didn't have to do that."

"When you told us about your feelings, did you feel better?" he asks me.

I shake my head against his shirt. "No, but it gets better, I think. As long as we've got each other."

"I know y'all ain't out here being mushy without me?" Christina calls out as she exits the backyard and approaches us.

"And Chris," Manny replies, hugging me tighter. I can hear the smile in his voice.

"Definitely need Chris." I nod just as she walks over and wedges herself into our embrace.

It's a perfect moment. One that makes me forget all the things that make me sad or anxious. It makes me forget about being abandoned at birth, or even the fact that Manny just came out to all our friends who, for a few numbing weeks, spread rumors about me.

I forget about Christina having an abortion without my support, or that despite what I tell them, my parents are always going to worry about me now that they know how I feel. I forget that somewhere there is a woman who, for whatever reason, one that I may never know, left me behind a hospital dumpster during a blizzard. I can lie to myself and pretend to know for a fact that she did it to give me a better life, which I've definitely had; but I'll never know the truth.

And for now, that's okay.

Because I remember that I'll always have moments like this. Hugging Christina and Manny. Geoff and Mark's unconditional love, and possibly going off to college with Jonah.

And then I know I'll be just fine.

Epilogue

"**D**ad, c'mon! Jonah's outside!" I call out from downstairs. Geoff is upstairs taking his time, prolonging the inevitable. Last night, we helped Christina move into her dorm half an hour away in Norman. Manny's been in New York for almost two weeks now.

Today it's finally my turn.

I never imagined that Geoff would be this sad to see me move. He won't let me take any of my belongings from my bedroom, instead opting to buy everything I need for the dorm brand new. He says he wants everything to stay the same, so it *"feels like I'm still with them."*

I'm going to college an hour and forty-five minutes away, not dying.

The doorbell rings and I open the door to greet Jonah.

"Don't worry about the shoes," I tell him as he walks in and stops at the mudroom to take his sneakers off.

"You sure?" He eyes me skeptically, looking around for Geoff.

"Positive. Geoff is already in full drama mode, and we need to go now! Mark already left with most of my things."

After the graduation party, Jonah and I were finally able to talk about everything. Making up was effortless, and he wasted no time in asking me to be his real girlfriend. He only asked that there be no more secrets between us. An easy promise to keep, because I want Jonah to know everything about me.

"I just need to grab my dad and my laptop and we'll be ready to go," I tell him, turning to head toward the living room before stopping again. "Oh, and he's kind of sensitive today, so I might need to drive down with him. Sorry."

Jonah shrugs, "It's fine. My mom just didn't want me to drive down alone. If I'm following you guys, then I'm technically not alone."

"Loophole." I wink at him before jogging through the living room and up the stairs.

My laptop is sitting open on my bed and just as I'm about to close it an email notification pings. The short preview of the message on the pop-up notification reads: *ANCESTRY DNA—*. The rest of the message is cut off in the small notification box.

My heart drops, but curiosity gets the best of me and I open the email.

"Ms. Bowie Monroe, we're excited to inform you that your DNA has matched you with 3 direct ethnic groups and several lower percentages too! We have matched you with 0 immediate relatives! Please click the link below to see your results in detail!"

I drag my index across the mouse pad, hovering the cursor over the link. It sucks that the test didn't find any relatives, especially a parent; but at least I can finally see my ethnic background.

That's a start.

Then why am I hesitating? Isn't this what I've wanted to know?

"C'mon, Junior. You rushed me all morning, and now you're up here playing on your computer?" Geoff's voice startles me, and I slam the MacBook shut.

"Sorry, I just needed to grab this. Are you ready?" I shake the nervous thoughts out of my head. The DNA test results can wait. For now.

"That's a loaded question." He smiles at me. I can tell by the slight redness in his eyes that he's been crying this morning.

"Jonah's downstairs." I smile and walk over to kiss his cheek.

We hit the highway, with Jonah following behind us in his Camaro packed with all of his clothes. He and AJ moved his other belongings to his dorm last week.

"Do us a favor and try not to come home pregnant by Thanksgiving." Geoff side-eyes me when he catches me checking the side mirror for Jonah's car.

"I'll wait until Christmas break. Make it a little more festive for you." I give him my best smile.

"Cute." He sneers at me playfully.

We fall silent and I pull out my phone and open up the ancestry email. Again, I hesitate on clicking the magical link that could answer most of my questions. It feels weird, like I'm not ready to know the truth, or maybe I'm just selfish and upset that they found no familial match.

"One more favor, Junior?" Geoff breaks the silence, and I take my attention from the phone to give it to him.

"What's that?"

"When those feelings come back. Call us." He looks away from the road briefly to stare at me. His expression is almost pleading.

I nod. "Please don't worry about me. I'll be fine."

"It's in my nature to worry about you. I'm your father. Supposedly, parents have this innate intuition, believe it or not."

"I believe it."

I return my attention to my phone and move the email to the trash folder. Finding out what's behind that link means a lot to me, but it's not the most important thing at the moment.

Right now I'm sitting beside Geoff, headed to my future home for the next four years, where Mark is waiting and Jonah is following. Carrie is out there in the world, ready to be the fairy godmother I'll always need. Christina will have a chance at a successful future and will beat the statistics.

I think of Manny, fifteen-hundred miles away, happy and himself. Living his truth.

Having those few solid figures in my life is worth more than any biological mother or father.

And that is enough, for now.

Acknowledgements

This has been such an amazing journey. Maybe not always fun, but the years of rewrites, self-doubt, and writer's block make the journey truly incredible. This story was born in my heart, and the love I have for my characters is pure and unwavering. This novel is my dream come true and, much like Bowie, I could not have done it without my amazing support system.

To Sharlah — My very first beta reader. Thank you for the weeks you spent at a time reading every version of this story. Your honest feedback was everything I needed to continue to mold this story into what it is today. You'll never know what those tea time sessions bouncing my ideas and doubts off of you meant to me. You know that as a writer, sharing your work for the first time can be the most terrifying part. Thank you for being my comfort zone and the most trusted member of this process.

To Stephanie R — The first person to ever meet Bowie and her friends and family before they'd even made it to the keyboard. I introduced this story to you during our closing shifts at the grooming salon. You'd listen for hours as I allowed this story and its character to live outside of my heart and play out for you. Your enthusiasm for this book before it had even been written is what encouraged me to keep going and finally start the journey of becoming an author. Thank you for those storytelling sessions, and expect to see your name in the acknowledgments of many more. Because as you know, there are so many more.

To Mikyla — My sister. My Brother-Lady. My biggest supporter. Your love and enthusiasm are unmatched. Thank you for beta reading and even line editing this story. For laughing with me over Geoff's antics, and building the hype that brought us to this moment. The only person who might love this book as much as me. Thank you for being a cheerleader, a confidant, and the best big sister an aspiring author could ask for. I love you!

To Nae — My best friend and beta reader. My book club sister. I trusted you the most to provide feedback because this genre means so much to both of us. Thank you for your feedback and for taking the time to dive into this story with me. Thank you for always checking on me and my progress. For pushing me to stay positive. For your support in helping to find bookstores and spreading the word. Your dedication to our friendship and this journey will never go unnoticed!

To Richie — My heart. My fact-checker, my comic book king. Thank you for listening to me rant and whine for years during this journey. Thank you for knowing when to crack the right joke to make everything better on those stressful days when I doubted myself. Thank you for providing Jonah's voice and some of his interests. This journey and most definitely my life wouldn't be the same without you. I love you more than words can express.

To Cookie and Andrew — For creating and sharing promotional materials to help get the word out there, I thank you both. But more than anything, thank you for maintaining a space where I felt free from the stress of this journey. Our nightly gaming sessions, our endless group chat, and the nonstop laughter. There is no other friendship like the one we have. An unbreakable bond of support and love.

To Mom — Thank you for passing along your love of literature. For being the first person to put a book in my hand. My Geoff, who encouraged me to read and love characters. *Wuthering Heights*, *To Kill a Mockingbird*, VC Andrews, and most importantly, *A Clockwork Orange*. You pushed me to enjoy reading. Enjoying reading pushed me to love writing. I love you!

And to Granny — This book will be released on your birthday. It will be released on the fourth birthday I will spend without you, and it is dedicated to you and everything that you were to me and our family. You taught me the kindness that I poured into Bowie's character. I wish I could call you and finally tell you I am an author. That I did it. I wish I could hear the grin in your voice as you say "Alright! Big Girl!" I love you so much.

To the readers, my friends, my family. To every person who liked, commented, and shared a post promoting the release of *Please Excuse Our Confusion*. To anyone who prayed, sent good vibes, good juju, or simply thought to themselves, "Good job, Jasmine."

I thank you all. See you next time.

About the Author

Jasmine Cartwright was born in Oklahoma City. Her family moved to Sacramento, California after she was born, and stayed there during her early adolescent years before moving back to OKC. She is an advocate for mental health, prison reform, and marginalized voices. Combining her dedication to these social issues with her passion for fictional storytelling, Jasmine strives to create a safe space for the voiceless. An avid reader, she always found herself chasing *"that one story."* When she couldn't find that story, she decided she'd write it herself, and that passion turned into an ambition to become an author. Jasmine writes stories about young people who find happiness at the most inconvenient of times. She finds inspiration for her stories through traveling, reading, and personal experiences. She graduated from Southern New Hampshire University with a Bachelor of Arts in Creative Writing and English, specializing in Fiction Writing.

www.ingramcontent.com/pod-product-compliance
Lightning Source LLC
Chambersburg PA
CBHW061221310726
48971CB00007B/1898